Samuel Evans was a man in his element, she decided.

He was comfortable not only with the isolation of his remote mountain retreat, but also in the company of strangers, one of which was a newborn infant. It was a dichotomy that a man who clearly cherished his privacy would relinquish it without any trace of resentment. Most people, at least the people that Ellie had known, would not have been so gracious.

Then again, she instinctively realized that Samuel was not like most people.

Ellie watched in fascination as Samuel stepped into view carrying what appeared to be a large woven basket with legs.

'I thought he'd be more comfortable with a bed of his own,' Samuel explained.

'It's a cradle,' Ellie whispered, marvelling at the exquisitely woven basket. 'I've never seen anything so intricate.'

The gesture touched her heart. Samuel Evans was indeed an extraordinary man.

Dear Reader,

Welcome to this months fantastic Special Edition™ line-up. In Victoria Pade's *Cowboy's Love*, Savannah Heller is passionately reunited with her one true love Clint Culhane. The latest in the A RANCHING FAMILY series, this is a wonderfully warm story.

Has eccentric uncle Max finally met his match? Find out in Cathy Gillen Thacker's final HASTY WEDDINGS title *Spur-Of-The-Moment Marriage*, when lawyer Cisco Kidd weds Gillian Taylor, a woman with a mysterious past! Also this month a new story from Diana Whitney on the theme of babies and parents—Samuel Evans isn't sure he's prepared when he has to deliver a *Baby in His Cradle* after a *heavily* pregnant woman turns up at his door.

It's a case of opposites attract, when a sparring couple come together in Tracy Sinclair's *Lucky in Love*. And a beautiful young widow marries her boss when her custody of her unborn child is threatened in Trisha Alexander's *With This Wedding Ring*.

Finally, things are hotting up at the *Honeymoon Ranch*, Celeste Hamilton's endearing tale about two lifelong friends who unexpectedly find they're sexually attracted *after* they're married.

Happy reading!

The Editors.

Baby in His Cradle

DIANA WHITNEY

*Silhouette, Silhouette Special Edition and Colophon are
registered trademarks of Harlequin Books S.A., used under licence.*

*First published in Great Britain 1998
Silhouette Books, Eton House, 18-24 Paradise Road,
Richmond, Surrey TW9 1SR*

© Diana Hinz 1998

ISBN 0 373 24176 3

23-9811

*Printed and bound in Spain
by Litografia Rosés S.A., Barcelona*

To Barbara and Mandy Wilson, who have been thoughtful, supportive and great for a writer's fragile ego. Your friendship is deeply appreciated. Oh, and thanks for all the wonderful snow stories!

DIANA WHITNEY

says she loves 'fat babies and warm puppies, mountain streams and California sunshine, camping, hiking and gold prospecting. Not to mention strong romantic heroes!' She married her own real-life hero over twenty years ago. With his encouragement, she left her long career as a local government finance director and pursued the dream that had haunted her since childhood—writing. To Diana, writing is a joy, the ultimate satisfaction. Reading, too, is her passion—from spine-chilling thrillers to sweeping sagas, but nothing can compare to the magic and wonder of romance. She loves to hear from readers. Write to her c/o Silhouette® Books, 300 East 42nd Street, 6th Floor, New York, NY 10017, USA.

Other novels by Diana Whitney

Silhouette Special Edition®	*Silhouette Sensation*®
Cast a Tall Shadow	Still Married
Yesterday's Child	Midnight Stranger
One Lost Winter	Scarlet Whispers
Child of the Storm	
The Secret	*The Blackthorn
*The Adventurer	Brotherhood*
*The Avenger	†*Parenthood*
*The Reformer	
†Daddy of the House	
†Barefoot Bride	
†A Hero's Child	
†Baby on His Doorstep	
†Baby in His Cradle	

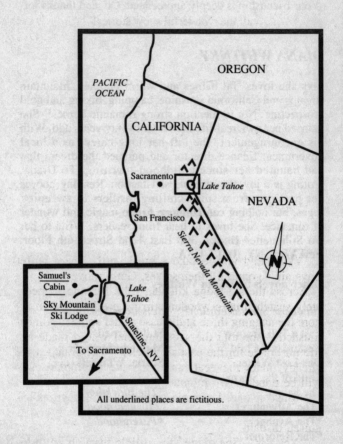

OREGON

PACIFIC
OCEAN

CALIFORNIA

Sacramento

Lake Tahoe

NEVADA

San Francisco

Sierra Nevada Mountains

N

Samuel's
Cabin

Lake
Tahoe

Sky Mountain
Ski Lodge

Stateline, NV

To Sacramento

All underlined places are fictitious.

you clean that, girl," mumbled Sylvia. "Look when
you're going."

Chapter One

"Who told you to take a break, girl? Them buffet trays ain't gonna fill themselves. Get a move on."

Across the ski-lodge kitchen, Ellie Malone immediately snatched up a wooden stirring paddle, tried to ignore the nagging throb at the base of her spine. "Almost finished," she told the scowling chef who'd made her life miserable for the past six weeks. "The potatoes are already under the heat lamp, and the scrambled eggs will be done in two minutes."

"Make it one. I got me a schedule." He grumbled under his breath, eyed her distended belly with undisguised disdain.

"Yes, sir." She zigged the paddle through hot eggs to judge moisture content, then grabbed a towel, using both hands to hoist the heavy iron skillet and transfer its contents into a gleaming stainless-steel buffet tray.

A muscle spasm struck like a fist. Ellie gasped, twisted. The skillet clanged to the floor.

"You clumsy fool!" the chef yelped. "Look what you've done."

Steadying herself on the counter, she bit her lip until the pain eased. When she finally caught her breath, wet yellow lumps were strewn over the polished pine planking. "I'm sorry...I'll clean it up."

The furious man was not consoled. "I told 'em you wouldn't be no help," he ranted. "If it ain't morning sickness, it's backaches or sore legs or just plain feeling poorly. In my mama's day, pregnant folks didn't force private problems on everybody else. They stayed home where they belonged."

"I know. I'm sorry." Squatting awkwardly, she retrieved the skillet, wishing she had the strength to fling it at her obnoxious boss. At the moment a job was more valuable than dignity. "I'll take care of everything, I promise. It won't take more than five minutes to scramble a fresh batch—"

Chef yanked off his floppy white hat, flung it on the cutting board. "I ain't got five minutes, missy! Look outside."

He wiggled a hairy finger toward the mullioned window that faced the lodge parking area. "The tour bus just pulled up, and all them hungry Christmas skiers are gonna hit the brunch buffet like starving vultures. What am I supposed to tell 'em, that they can't eat 'cause my pregnant cook needs a back rub?"

Frantic, Ellie retrieved the skillet, pulled herself into a standing position and lumbered toward a sink already filled with hot soapy water. She tuned out the chef's ranting, plunged the pan into the water and glanced out the window to gage the size of the morning's crowd. Her heart sank. The parking lot was indeed packed with parka-clad tourists, their faces flushed by the icy air, eyes mirroring disappointment that the ski lifts had been shut down in deference to the coming storm.

Thwarted skiers were renowned for their appetites. Since the bar wouldn't open until after noon, they had nowhere to go except the already crowded dining room.

Behind her, the chef continued to rail against the injustice of being saddled with useless help while harried busboys hustled to carry out fresh buffet trays of steaming sausage, crisp bacon, eggs, Belgian waffles and tempting fruit trays to waiting guests.

Ellie swallowed a surge of panic. Much as she disliked her foul-tempered boss, she had to admit he was right. She hadn't been able to keep up with the other cooks. If not for an empathetic personnel director with four kids and a soft heart, the employment application of a woman in her seventh month of pregnancy would have been summarily dismissed without a second glance.

But luck had been with Ellie, who'd arrived at the Sky Mountain Ski Lodge over a month ago in desperate need of work. Now that she had the job, she was determined to keep it despite problems created by fatigue, backaches and a burgeoning belly. For the past couple of weeks Ellie found herself standing so far away from the stove she could barely reach the upper portion of the grill. She'd planned to work right up until her due date, which was less than a month away, but on bad days—days when her legs throbbed and her back muscles screamed and constant heartburn turned her chest into a lava pit of pure pain—Ellie wondered if she'd be able to survive even another hour, let alone another month.

Not that she had a choice. She had to work, had to save enough money to move from a sparse room shared with one of the lodge housekeepers to a place of her own, a place where she could create a warm and loving home for the child growing inside her.

A son. The doctor had said that she would have a son, a beautiful boy-child. Ellie's heart fluttered with anticipation. She was so anxious to hold her baby son, to count his tiny fingers, to gaze into curious little eyes blinking up at the mother who would adore him forever.

A booming voice shattered her thoughts. ''Where'n hell are them eggs?''

''Coming right up.'' Refocusing on the task at hand, Ellie rinsed the skillet, wiped it dry and angled another quick glance out the window just as a gleaming luxury sedan pulled up in front of the lodge's main entrance.

A tiny spasm of fear tickled her throat.

The passenger door opened, and a lithe blond woman emerged sniffing the air with predatory intent. The man exited from the driver's side. Eyes narrowed, he scanned the area, lips thin with grim determination.

Panic surged like bitter bile. Ellie pushed away from the sink, ripped off her apron and dashed to the employee lounge oblivious to the chef's vile oaths. He was screaming that she was fired, but that didn't matter anymore.

Snagging her jacket from a coatrack, Ellie snatched a backpack out of her locker, dashed out the rear exit toward the woods and the safety of a nearby cabin that had been vacant since summer. Adrenaline pumped like fire through her veins, dulling the throb at the base of her spine, easing the sting of wind-driven snow in her face.

She ran blindly, oblivious to the boiling gray clouds, the surrounding forest blurred by blowing snow and wind-whipped pine boughs. Escape was all that mattered now. They had found her. She had to get away.

* * *

The axe blade sliced air, split the log cleanly. Samuel quartered the halves and tossed the firewood atop a huge pile stacked against the east side of the cabin, where it would be partially protected from drifting snow. He buried the axe in the cutting stump, tugged his sheepskin collar up to block the howling wind. A few sharp ice crystals stung his skin, signal of the storm. Black clouds boiled at the forest's edge. The snow would be thick tonight. Several feet would fall by week's end.

Samuel Evans didn't mind. Sierra Nevada could be treacherous in winter, but it could also be beautiful—a mysterious wonderland of wilderness blanketed in white, draped in tranquillity, shrouded in silence. In the belly of the mountain only nature dared raise its voice, howling with the wind or whispering through the trees or simply revealing itself in the comforting scrunch as tiny feet scurried over crusted snow.

Samuel loved it all, the magnificence, the power, the absolute silence after a storm. Most of all he cherished the isolation. This was God's country, where a man could be alone with his thoughts, consider the past with quiet reflection, contemplate what might have been.

A rustling from the cabin porch caught Samuel's attention, and was followed by the hollow click of doggy toenails on rough-hewn planks. A moment later, his aging, flop-eared hound lumbered around the corner, dropped a pinecone at his master's booted feet. Old Baloo sat gingerly on the icy crust, his liquid fudge eyes peering bright and hopeful from beneath saggy lids.

"What's the matter, 'Loo? Don't you think I've had enough exercise today?"

Baloo rolled his head toward the patchy dirt road cutting a crusted swath through the trees, then lopped a glance up at his master with a dare-you gleam in his eyes.

Smiling, Samuel scooped up the pinecone, bounced it on his gloved palm. "One hundred yards." The old hound yawned, shifted his forepaws in the canine equivalent of a shrug. "Hey, cut me some slack, will you? I just chopped half a cord of firewood."

Heaving a lazy sigh, Baloo pleated a graying muzzle, and focused an intent gaze on the pinecone his master held.

Samuel widened his stance, squinted down the road to gage distance. Using both hands, he grasped the cone like a baseball, raised it over his head, lowered it slowly to midchest.

Anticipating the game, Baloo swished a happy tail, pranced in place. Samuel took a deep breath, held it, angled a covert glance at the gray-muzzled mutt. "Double or nothing," he told the excited animal. "I feel lucky." With that, Samuel wound up, kicked forward, uncoiled his arm and threw.

The pinecone arched into the wind, hovered a moment, then sailed sideways and landed barely fifty yards away. Muttering, Samuel rubbed the back of his head. "Misjudged the wind," he told the disappointed animal, who was much too lethargic to chase pinecones, but enjoyed watching his master throw them anyway.

Flipping a reproachful look over his shoulder, Baloo lumbered back toward the cabin's covered porch. Samuel trudged the same path, found the dog at the base of the porch steps, staring down the forest road with unique intensity. "What is it, boy?"

The hound whined and to Samuel's surprise suddenly shot across the clearing toward the road. "'Loo!" Samuel cupped his mouth, emitted a sharp whistle to which the dog had been trained to respond. This time, however, the old hound simply disappeared into the trees without a backward glance. "Damn."

It wasn't the first time the normally lazy old hound had initiated a game of tag with a lurking deer or meandering rabbit. Samuel was annoyed by the abrupt departure, but not particularly concerned. Old Baloo knew these woods like the back of his paw, and had even been called upon to sniff out disoriented skiers who'd lost their way.

Knowing the stubborn animal would be back when he was ready, Samuel knocked the ice off his boots on the porch steps and headed into the cabin to start supper.

An hour later, the woodstove was glowing, stew was simmering on the propane cooktop and the tempting aroma of freshly brewed coffee permeated the interior of the primitive but cozy cabin that Samuel's father had built nearly three decades ago. The open design was simple but efficient.

In the front of the cabin, a central woodstove divided the living area from the sleeping area, over which was the cramped loft where Samuel and his older brother had once slept. There was a serviceable kitchen area large enough for a round pine table and four chairs. The compact bathroom had been walled off between the sleeping area and the kitchen, extending beneath the loft.

Now Samuel glanced out the kitchen window, saw the snow settling wetly on the mullioned frame. It was still in the twenties outside, although the temperature would dip well below zero by morning.

Frowning, he studied a wall clock shaped like a leaping trout, worried because Baloo hadn't returned. He shivered at the thought of venturing out into the frigid storm, but knew perfectly well he would. That lazy old hound dog meant the world to him. He'd do anything, even freeze himself solid, to protect his loyal companion.

Heaving a resigned sigh, Samuel had just reached for the trusty sheepskin-lined jacket that was warmer than a down sleeping bag when a familiar whine was followed by a thin scratch at the cabin door. His heart leapt in relief. "Thank God." Crossing the narrow room in three strides, he yanked open the door. "Where in hell have you—"

The question died in the howling wind as he rocked back on his heels. Baloo whined again, shifted to support the weight of the woman leaning against him with her frigid fingers locked in a death grip on his collar. Her face was white as a blizzard, lips blue as bruises. Beneath the neon blue parka hood, a tangle of sable hair twisted wetly at her trembling jaw. A smattering of snowflakes clung to her frozen lashes, and the only sound she uttered came from the convulsive chatter of her teeth.

"Good Lord." Samuel swayed in surprise, then leapt forward to grasp the rigid woman around the waist. A lumpy backpack dangled over one of her shaking shoulders. Firming his grasp on the shivering woman, he slipped the pack off, tossed it into the cabin. "You're going to be all right," he whispered, urging her forward. "It's warm inside."

Her glazed eyes stared straight ahead, gave no indication that she'd heard, but she dragged one foot forward a few inches, flinching at the effort.

Realizing that her feet must be numb from the cold, Samuel wrapped her free arm around his neck, supporting her weight on his own shoulders. "Just a few more steps," he murmured, reaching down to unfurl her frozen fingers from Baloo's collar. "We'll have you thawed out in no time."

Assuming, he thought grimly, that her extremities weren't completely frostbitten. When released, Baloo trundled into the cabin, his saggy eyes bright with concern while Samuel scooped the exhausted woman up in his arms, and was staggered by her weight. Grunting, he kicked the door shut behind him, struggled to the sleeping area where he deposited her on the bed, grateful that the effort hadn't snapped his spine. The frail-faced woman was heftier than she looked. "Just relax," he told her. "You're going to be fine, just fine."

She blinked up in confusion as Baloo hoisted his paws to the mattress. Whining, the animal licked the woman's face while Samuel checked her pupils, took her pulse, then pulled off her leather shoes and soaked cotton socks, scrutinized her skin for discoloration associated with frostbite. Relieved to find none, he carefully wrapped her icy feet in a towel that he'd retrieved and warmed on the woodstove, then turned his attention to the jacket she was wearing.

It was one of those colorful rayon things, with quilted padding designed more for fashion than function. He unzipped the garment, stumbled back a step and nearly fainted on the spot.

The woman was pregnant.

Not just kind of, sort of pregnant. She was *very* pregnant, fully-ripe-and-ready-to-burst pregnant.

Her eyelids fluttered. As she focused on Samuel, a perplexed frown creased her brow. Samuel swallowed hard, slipped an arm beneath her, lifting her slightly so he could remove the wet jacket. When he'd done so, he tossed it aside, lowered her back onto the pillows and covered her with a warm blanket.

She blinked up at him.

"Do you know where you are?" he asked.

Her lips parted but no sound emerged. She shivered

violently, laid trembling hands protectively over her swollen belly. All at once her eyes widened in sheer terror. ''Ah-h-h...'' Gasping, she clutched at her abdomen, curled her head forward until her chin brushed the white cotton collar protruding from her bulky knit sweater. Her lips formed a frantic *O,* then stretched thin as her teeth clicked together.

Stunned, Samuel squatted beside the bed, sat on his haunches and prayed that he wasn't seeing what he thought he was seeing.

A moment later, the woman fell back against the pillow, panting. She licked her lips, emitted a soft groan of relief. Her eyes fluttered open, focused on Samuel. ''A cramp,'' she murmured weakly. ''Don't...worry.''

Samuel fervently hoped that was true. ''When is the baby due?''

She shifted, brushed a shaky hand through her tangled hair. ''In three weeks.''

''False labor contractions are common during the final month of pregnancy.'' He stood, retrieved his medical kit from a curtained corner of the sleeping area that served as a closet. ''They're frequently associated with extreme stress or strenuous physical activity. You picked a lousy time for a nature hike.''

''Yes,'' she said, and fell silent.

Samuel draped the stethoscope around his neck, turned toward the bed and saw that she'd levered up on one elbow to study his movements. Her gaze settled on the thermometer he held. ''I'd like to check your temperature,'' he explained.

She considered that a moment. ''Are you a doctor?''

''No.'' Samuel sat on the edge of the narrow mattress. ''But I've had some medical training. Lean back, please.'' When she settled back against the pillows, he extended the thermometer. He noticed the caution in her eyes before she finally parted her lips and allowed him to tuck it beneath her tongue. Her eyes were well focused now, dark and wary, exotically shaped. Quite lovely, although Samuel was more interested in her vital signs than her vital statistics. He checked her pulse again, found it stronger, but still thready. "What's your name?"

She shifted the thermometer with her tongue, mumbled out of the corner of her mouth. "Ellie."

"That's a nice name," he murmured, reverting to the calm voice and efficient professionalism that was protocol for soothing frightened patients. "I went to school with a girl named Ellie. Her full name was Eleanor, but she preferred Ellie. Is your name Eleanor?" The question was posed as he retrieved a small penlight from his pocket.

She reared back.

"I'm not going to hurt you, I'm simply gauging the reaction of your pupils to the light."

The thermometer vibrated. "Why?"

"To make sure you haven't suffered any head trauma." He flashed the beam at each eye, was satisfied when the pupils contracted normally. "What were you doing out in the storm?" He retrieved the thermometer so she could answer.

The woman shifted against the pillows, her gaze skittering around the room. "I guess I got lost. I was heading for a friend's cabin."

After noting that her body temperature was below normal but not dangerously so, Samuel recased the thermometer. "Another hour out there and you'd have probably died," he said bluntly.

She flinched, said nothing. On cue, Baloo hoisted his forepaws on the bed with a worried whine, and received a thin smile for his trouble. "My hero," she told the animal, who wagged his tail at the praise. She managed to stroke the dog's sleek head once before her hand dropped away, as if the exertion had been too much. Her eyelids fluttered closed, her breath shallowed.

She was pale, Samuel thought, too pale. White as death. He hooked the stethoscope around his neck, laid a questioning hand on the woman's shoulder. "Ma'am, ah, Ellie, I'd like to examine you, if you'd permit it."

She opened one eye. "Examine?" she repeated as if she'd never heard the word before.

"I'd like to listen to your baby's heartbeat, just make sure everything is okay in there. Is that all right with you?"

A cautious frown creased her brows. She studied him for a moment, as if trying to determine if he was worthy of trust. Air slid from her slack lips a moment before she issued a feeble nod.

Samuel lowered the blanket, raised the hem of her bulky sweater, and pressed the stethoscope against the cotton shirt stretched tightly over her bulging abdomen. He shifted the device several times, searching for the soft, rhythmic swish of a fetal heartbeat.

Beneath Samuel's probing fingers, the woman's abdomen tightened like steel. She reared up, emitted a choked cry. Her eyes were huge with terror and disbelief. She didn't seem to know what was happening. But Samuel knew. A bad situation had just become interminably worse. And there wasn't a damned thing he could do about it.

Ellie thrashed in her mind, crawled through memories of bitter cold, numbing terror. Around her snow swirled with white death. Pain sawed her spine, gripped her belly like a barbed garrote. She stumbled forward, grasping branches that whipped in the wind. Every tree

looked the same, every rock looked like another. Her
ears rang from the howling wind, ached from the freezing cold. She couldn't feel her feet.

It was over. She knew it. She felt it. Her life, her
hopes, her dreams of happiness for the child nested in
her womb, it was all over now.

She couldn't go on.

The angel appeared out of nowhere, a living angel
radiating warmth, nudging her forward with amazing
strength. She grasped the apparition, allowed it to pull
her onward, guide her through the terrifying maze of
forest, weeping trees with storm-gnashed boughs, grasping branches that slapped and scratched.

In the distance a curl of smoke coiled above the trees.
The angel led her toward the smoke, a sanctuary of
warmth, of safety. Almost there.

She could see the glow of windows, feel the radiating
heat. Almost there.

She stumbled against the steps, rough planks scraping
her soles. Almost...

The door creaked. A sliver of golden light sprayed
through the swirling snow.

...there.

The door opened slowly, slowly. Slowly. She trembled.

A face appeared, shadowed in backlight. Fear gnawed
the base of her spine, an encircling throb gripping her
slowly, slowly. Slowly.

Squinting into the brightness, she focused on the face
of her rescuer. He smiled in welcome. The smile broad-
ened into a grin, teeth flashing white as ice. A laugh.
Familiar. Evil.

Terror twisted her belly, sliced like a blade. He had
found her. This time there was no place to run.

* * *

"Here, drink this." Samuel slipped his arm beneath Ellie's shoulders, touched the rim of the soup mug to her colorless lips. "Careful, it's hot."

She sipped delicately, curled her trembling hands around the warm mug, and sipped again. After a moment, she turned her face to signal that she'd had enough.

Samuel set the steaming soup aside, lowered her to the pillows, and smoothed a dark tangle of hair from her face. "You need nourishment."

"Not hungry," she whispered, forcing a thin smile. "But it was very nice. Thank you."

A puff of breath escaped her slack lips as her eyes closed. Her breathing deepened. She was drifting off to sleep again. That was good. The ordeal in the woods had exhausted her. She'd need strength for what was to come.

Samuel continued to stroke her soft skin, her dark hair, separating the disheveled snarls with his fingers. It was thick hair, rich and slightly waved. He imagined how a hairbrush could polish it into a glossy, glowing mane, with alluring tentacles caressing sculpted cheekbones a model would envy. Her skin was pale as creamed buttermilk, flawless except for the bruiselike crescents beneath her eyes.

Under normal circumstances she would have been beautiful, Samuel thought. Her bone structure was perfect, her lips so full and lush that he half wondered if they'd been surgically enhanced. But her eyes were her most exotic feature. When open, they were coffee brown, almost black, with an alluring tilt that made her look surprised, amused and seductive all at the same time. There was something unique about her, something innately fascinating.

Even as Samuel was drawn to her vulnerability, a

peculiar sense of foreboding prickled his nape. He was not a fool, and didn't for a moment believe that a woman in her delicate condition would have chosen to walk in the woods during the onset of what was predicted to be one of the worst storms on record.

Something had driven her into those woods, perhaps the same terror that made her whimper in slumber, thrash through dreams. Or nightmares.

Samuel knew all about nightmares.

The muted click of doggy toenails on polished pine heralded Baloo's arrival from the kitchen, where he'd just washed a kibble dinner down with half a bowl of fresh water. The animal yawned, laid a soggy chin on Samuel's knee and focused worried eyes on the sleeping woman.

Samuel scratched a floppy ear. "What do you think, 'Loo?"

Baloo whined, shifted, curled one forepaw over his muzzle.

"You're right, it is strange that she's never asked me to call anyone." Not that he could, since the cabin had no phone, but it was nonetheless peculiar that she hadn't made the request. "There must be someone out there who's crazed with worry about her. Friends, family—" His gaze settled on her swollen stomach. "—a husband."

Baloo swung his head around, issued a soft yip.

"Yeah, I know. I was thinking the same thing. Maybe that's who she was running from in the first place." Irrationally angered by the thought, Samuel stood, raked his hair, and gazed down at the sleeping woman. She didn't seem the type to tolerate a bully, let alone make a baby with one.

Granted, he didn't know much about his unexpected house guest, but Samuel's profession demanded the ability to judge character quickly, with a high degree of accuracy. When he'd looked into Ellie's eyes, he'd seen fear, yes, but he'd also seen extraordinary strength of will.

That was good. Samuel knew that she'd need all the strength she could muster. And she'd need it soon.

The pain started slowly, crept along her spine so gently she barely noticed. Like pulsing fingers, it massaged its way around her belly, pressing harder, deeper, until her breath caught and her lungs felt as if they would explode.

"Breathe, Ellie. Breathe." From a great distance, the voice settled around her like loving arms. "That's right. Take short breaths, quickly, quickly, just for another few seconds. There, that's good, easy now, easy."

The pain dissipated as quickly as it had arrived, replaced by a relaxed tingle of supreme well-being. Sleep rolled over her, swaying gently, whispering in her ear until she gave herself to the warm, sweet darkness. And for a few precious moments she felt safe again.

Samuel alternately paced and warmed his hands by the woodstove. Ellie's contractions came faster now, every eight minutes at last count, and they were strengthening. Outside, the storm raged with chilling intensity, with wind so fierce that the cabin shuddered under the assault and snow thick enough to bury the blackness of night in a blanket of solid white. There was no way in, no way out. Not for Ellie; not for him.

The baby was coming and there wasn't a damn thing Samuel could do to stop it.

Samuel huffed out a breath, tried to calm his trembling hands by reminding himself that he'd delivered dozens of healthy babies. Of course, the conditions had never been this primitive, but birth itself was a primitive process evolving eons before the advent of modern medical technology. This baby would be born not because of Samuel's past experience, but in spite of it.

He closed his eyes, crossed his arms to tuck his hands into the warmth of his armpits. Rocking back on his heels, he fought the terror burgeoning inside his chest. Familiar terror. Too familiar.

Something butted his thigh. He glanced down to see Baloo gazing up helpfully. "Yeah, make it a double," he told the dog. "Straight up, no ice."

Baloo yawned, padded over to the living area of the cabin and began sniffing something beside the maple-armed sofa that Samuel's mother had purchased during her Early American furniture phase nearly three decades ago. The dog whined, scuffed at the object with his paw.

"What have you got, 'Loo?"

Lumbering back a step, Baloo swung a look backward, then returned his attention to the object that Samuel now recognized as the woman's backpack. He'd forgotten all about it, and now realized with some anticipation that the pack could contain helpful clues about his mysterious guest.

A prickle of guilt had him sneaking a covert glance toward the bed, where the woman dozed fitfully. Rooting through her things was an overt invasion of privacy, but circumstance dictated a certain entitlement, so Samuel pushed his conscience aside and went to investigate.

The first thing he found was a sweatsuit, plain gray fleece rolled into a compact cylinder. He set it aside, and pulled out a few personal items, including a hairbrush, a tube of lipstick and a small grooming kit, which he didn't open. He also found some items of clothing, including a couple of adult-size T-shirts and several tiny infant gowns along with a partially knitted nursery cap still attached with knitting needles to a ball of yarn. He put the knitting aside, held up one of the miniature garments, relieved that the child could be clothed in something besides a clean flannel shirt. There were also two small receiving blankets.

Clearly Ellie had been preparing for this baby with love and great anticipation. It was just as clear that this lumpy nylon duffel contained just about all of the woman's worldly goods.

From a wallet located in a zipped side pocket, Samuel discovered a California driver's license with a Sacramento address issued to one Eleanor Elizabeth Malone. The photo showed a smiling Ellie just as he'd imagined, with a glossy mane of sable hair swished around her lovely face, liquid eyes as soft and dark as a mountain lake at midnight.

He studied the picture for a moment before tucking it back into the wallet. There was also a social security card and a few dollars in cash, but no credit cards and nothing to personalize its owner except a photograph of a smiling older couple and a pay stub from Sky Mountain Ski Lodge.

Tapping the stub on his palm, he wondered if a woman in her condition could have possibly made the eleven-mile journey from the lodge. Of course, cutting across the woods would have shortened the trek by several miles, but the terrain was treacherous, difficult for even a seasoned hiker.

Where she'd started her journey was beside the point, he supposed. She was here now, and with the worst blizzard in a decade raging through the mountains, there was nothing Samuel could do about that either.

The scream awakened Samuel, who started upright in the chair, too groggy to realize that the horrific sound hadn't come from his own nightmare. A second shriek raised him to his feet, wiped the sleep from his eyes and pumped adrenalin through his veins with jackhammer force.

Across the cabin Baloo was barking, running frantic circles beside the bed where the woman continued to howl as if she was dying.

Samuel lurched forward, dodged the woodstove and dashed toward the bed, snatching the stethoscope from a wooden nightstand while the woman writhed in agony. "It's all right," he murmured, more out of habit than conviction. "Everything is going to be fine, just fine."

"My baby," she shrieked, then curled forward like a shrimp, her face contorted in purple pain.

"Your baby's fine, he just wants out, that's all." Samuel scurried to grab the clean towels he'd laid out, rearranged the privacy drape, and prayed harder than he'd ever prayed before. "Short breaths, Ellie, puff your cheeks and pant like a dog."

The woman complied, then sucked in a wheezing gulp of air. As she collapsed exhausted against the pillows, a whining Baloo leapt onto the mattress and frantically licked her face. Samuel dropped the towels, grabbed the animal's collar. "Get down, leave her alone."

Seeming undisturbed by the damp remnants of canine concern glimmering on her cheek, Ellie managed a smile. "Maybe he thinks I need panting lessons."

"Yeah, well, you don't need to be drooled on," Samuel muttered. He yanked the dog away from the bed, pointed toward the living area. "Go lie down or I'll tie you to the kitchen table."

As Baloo slunk off, the woman's eyes fluttered shut. "You're a hard man," she murmured. "Remind me never to tick you off." Her hands flew back beside her head. She gasped, clutched the sides of her pillow. "Ooh..."

Samuel checked his watch. His heart sank to his toes. "How long have the contractions been this close?"

"Ah-h-h-h!" She gritted her teeth, thrashed like a hooked trout for nearly a minute before the agonized wail burst forth like the death wail of captured prey.

Outside, the storm raged with demonic fury. Across the room Baloo threw back his head and howled while Samuel rushed around with practised efficiency, checking the woman's pulse, monitoring the fetal heartbeat, gauging dilation and cervical effacement. He slipped easily into the past, detaching himself from the woman's pain with objective professionalism. Emotions interfered with the job. Empathy bred fear, fear created chaos, chaos was failure, and failure was death.

So Samuel blocked out the woman's terror and her agonized screams. He blocked out the rumble of the raging storm, the howl of the worried hound. He blocked out everything except the whisper of his own mind.

"Help me. Please, help me."

Images erupted from the past, swallowing him whole. Dark eyes, wide with terror. An outstretched hand. A plea for help.

Fear crawled into his belly.

"Help...me."

The desperate voice filled his head, reverberated through his skull, fed his darkest nightmare. He froze, unable to move, unable to breathe, unable to control the paralyzing flood of memories even as chaos exploded around him. The storm raged. The woman screamed. The dog howled.

Samuel heard only the whisper of his mind. And he was terrified.

Chapter Two

Pain pummeled her, unrelenting, unmerciful, twisting, crushing, clenching her ravaged body in a convulsive fist that left her shaken, terrified. Alone.

For the first time in her life, Ellie Malone couldn't run away from her fear, couldn't escape the torturous grasp of something larger than herself, something utterly beyond her control. The pain was an inconvenience but the loss of control was terrifying. She was helpless. *Helpless*.

And she was alone.

The woman needed him. Samuel saw it, felt it, tasted it along with the metallic fear that flooded his mouth. He couldn't move. Need. Desperation. Life and Death. He held these things in the palm of his hand. Again.

He didn't want any of it. He didn't want to be needed. He didn't want to be responsible. He didn't want to fail. Again.

Her eyes opened, dark and pleading. She reached out. Her lips moved. No sound emerged, but Samuel recognized the words she was too weak to utter. He'd heard them countless times before. *Help me*.

His eyes watered as if stung by a cold wind.

Help me.

His ears roared with remembered sound, the boiling rush, the choppy thrum. And a whisper.

Help me.

It rose above the cacophony of noise, the pandemonious din, a simple plea that had always touched his heart, committed his body, controlled his mind. He'd always heard, always responded, always done his best.

Now Samuel had no choice but to respond again, do his best again. He prayed that this time it would be good enough.

She felt the warm palm at her brow, heard the soothing murmur of encouragement. "You're doing good, Ellie, very good. Everything is fine."

Something cold and wet touched her lips. She turned greedily toward the ice he held, emitted a thin moan of pleasure as the sweet moisture dripped into her parched mouth. The joy lasted only a moment before her lungs spasmed and her body coiled into convulsion.

But it was different now. Samuel was with her, whispering softly, telling her not to be afraid. "Don't fight the contractions," he was saying. "Imagine that each one is a friend, a companion to embrace your baby in loving arms, hugging him, nurturing him, protecting him on his journey into a brand-new world."

Ellie clenched her teeth, concentrated on the gentle touch, the soothing voice. She floated above the pain, recaptured her coveted control. The man beside her was the key. Without him, she'd be lost in an abyss of agony and fear. He kept her safe. She needed him.

She needed him.

"Push, Ellie. Push!"

"I...can't."

"You have to. Your baby's coming. He needs your help." The voice was strong now, determined. "You can do this, Ellie. I know you can."

She could do this. She had to do this.

"Push now!"

A low moan evolved into a strangled wail. Ellie knew the sound was coming from her, but ignored it, ignored everything but the insistent male voice and determination of her own will. Her baby was almost here. Her baby needed her.

Her fingers flexed into the mattress, her chin dug into her chest. Red and yellow stars collided in her mind. Her belly exploded.

She fell back, panting, deafened by the frantic gush of blood roaring past her ears. In the distance a choked mewing sound captured her attention. She struggled to lift one eyelid, absorbed the spray of gray dawn light, a blur of movement at the foot of the bed. A dog whined, barked. The tiny mew rose into an indignant wail.

Ellie squinted, too weak to lever herself up. A moment later, Samuel was leaning over her, his blue eyes gentle and proud. "You have a son," he whispered, cradling the wrapped infant in her arms. "A beautiful son."

Ellie stroked a trembling fingertip across the baby's soft red cheek. "His name is Daniel," she said softly. Then she smiled, closed her eyes and drifted off to sleep.

* * *

Time slipped away in a blur of floating weariness. Small snatches of awareness wakened Ellie gently, captured her senses for a few fleeting moments as her baby suckled at her breast, or while her gentle protector held liquid nourishment to her lips. Then reality undulated back into the blessed warmth of a deep and healing slumber.

Her surroundings met her there, in the distance of her dreamlike state. It was there she could study the moments, savor their meaning and intensity. In the clarity of her mind, she remembered the gentle man with clear blue eyes tearing sheets into diapers, then tending her child with such tender reverence that it brought tears to her eyes. She recalled everything, from the savory smells wafting from the kitchen as he'd stirred a pot on the stove, to the shiver of icy air as he'd ducked out into the storm, then returned ladened with firewood and whiplike branches of fragrant cedar.

In the filmstrip of her mind, Ellie remembered everything about the rugged stranger who had saved her beloved child. Roughened fingertips tingling her brow with tenderness; eyes the color of a spring sky, crinkling at the corners with his smile; a voice like raw honey, sweetly coarse and satisfying.

The scrape of his boots across the planked pine floor. The scent of his damp leather jacket, a flash of its woolly lining as he shook off the snow. And through it all, the wonderful scent of cedar permeated each jog of consciousness.

To Ellie it was all a dream. A wonderful dream. It would be days before she realized that it had been real.

Samuel studied the sweep hand of his watch, counting the thready cadence of Ellie's weakened pulse. He did so every hour, and was concerned by her dwindling strength.

He was also concerned about the infant. Little Daniel was understandably tiny but surprisingly well developed for a preemie, and was probably closer to full term than his mother had believed. Still the baby was frail, and the stethoscope had revealed a worrisome gurgle in the boy's tiny lungs.

Outside, snow piled in drifts halfway to the windows, and the wind continued to howl like a rabid wolf. He wondered when the weather would clear enough for him to hike to the fire tower and contact help. Days, perhaps even weeks. All Samuel could do was pray that he could keep both mother and child alive that long.

He tucked Ellie's hand beneath the bedclothes, smoothed an errant strand of hair from her face. She looked so peaceful, almost angelic. She smiled in her sleep. Samuel found that startling. For him, sleep was an enemy. For Ellie, it was clearly a cherished friend. Her dreams must be sweet, he decided, and was cheered by the thought. After all she'd endured, she deserved sweet dreams.

And she deserved to live.

A feeble cry filtered from the makeshift crib Samuel had constructed in the living area. At the sound, Baloo instantly awakened, lumbered over to peer through the slatted rails of the chair that his master had propped beside the sofa. The animal regarded the fussing infant for a moment, then swung his head around, fixed Samuel with an anxious gaze. The dog barked once, then trundled into the kitchen. A moment later he reappeared dragging the ratty, threadbare sports blanket his master had rescued from a garage sale and used to pad his doggy bed.

Samuel smiled. "A generous gesture, 'Loo, but I think the baby is warm enough."

Baloo spit out the blanket and whined.

"I'm coming." Samuel cast a final glance at the wan woman asleep in his bed before crossing the cabin to tend her tiny son. He gazed down at the wriggling infant, brushed his fingertip along the tiny, grasping hand. Minuscule fingers opened, quivered, closed into a small red fist. Samuel's heart leapt in wonder. "Did you see that, 'Loo? He tried to grab my finger."

Baloo stood with a snort.

"You don't think so? Just watch." Samuel repeated the process, and Daniel again flexed his baby fingers. "See?"

The hound huffed, sat stoically with a so-what expression that made Samuel smile. "Just can't stand to be wrong, can you?"

Heaving a bored yawn, Baloo deliberately avoided his master's gaze, so Samuel turned his attention back to the fussy infant. "What's going on, little guy. Are you hungry again?" He unwrapped the wriggling child, chuckled softly. "Aha. Damp in the drawers, hmm? Nothing we can't fix."

At the sound of his voice, the baby stopped fussing, blinked up with huge blue eyes struggling for focus. Samuel's heart twisted as if squeezed by a giant hand. He'd seen babies before, lots of them, but he'd never felt this sense of attachment, this sense of protectiveness and wonder. Of course, he'd never had the responsibility of caring for such fragile life, either. There had always been someone else around to take over. Now there was only Samuel. That frightened him, but it challenged him, too.

Determined, he set about the routine of tending his tiny charge, treating the healing umbilical with antiseptic salve, protecting the infant's sensitive skin with cornstarch and talc that he'd mixed himself then poured into a sterilized saltshaker for convenience, and completed the changing chore using a fresh diaper fashioned from a clean, white bedsheet.

The infant blinked, grimaced, heaved a burp loud enough to make Baloo perk his ears.

"Whoa, that's got to make a fellow feel better." Samuel dragged the stethoscope from his shirt pocket, warmed it with his palm. "Let's take another listen, buddy. You know the drill." He positioned the instrument on Daniel's little chest, heard the mild wheeze with each shallow intake of air, and was relieved to note that the sound hadn't gotten any worse. In fact, the baby's lungs actually sounded a bit clearer. Not a lot, but at this point, even a small improvement seemed like a miracle.

Pleased, Samuel replaced the scope in his pocket, glanced at the pot of cedar bark simmering atop the wood stove, its fragrant steam permeating the cabin with the nostalgic aroma from his childhood. The remedy was one that his mother had sworn by for the relief of bronchitis and other respiratory infections. As a child, Samuel had been comforted by the warm tingle in his chest as he inhaled the scented steam. To this day, the smell of cedar brought back those carefree days of childhood, made him feel nurtured all over again, and made him feel loved.

Perhaps someday Daniel would hike a mountain forest with the same sense of well-being, and a faint reminiscence of his first days of life when he, too, had been cherished and nurtured. And loved.

"I won't let you down, buddy." Samuel brushed a gentle knuckle across the dark fuzz scattered across the baby's velvety scalp. "You and your mama are going to be just fine," he said, and was surprised to realize that he truly believed that.

After covering the dozing child with a receiving blanket, Samuel returned to a kitchen table heaped with peeled twigs of smooth, pliable cedar and continued to weave a gift for the child with whom he'd already established a deep abiding bond.

As he worked, his mind cleared, his heart warmed, and he quietly smiled to himself. For the first time since Ellie Malone had stumbled into his remote cabin retreat, Samuel was at peace.

Samuel shifted in the hard-backed chair, started awake by the peculiar voice crooning clear and sweet, a gentle whisper floating through slumberous clouds. "Sweet baby boy with the sleepy eyes, Mama's going to sing you a lullaby."

Blinking, he struggled to focus on the vision seated at the edge of the bed softly serenading the infant cradled in her arms. The melody was familiar, although she appeared to be creating lyrics as she went along.

"A lullaby of hope and love," she sang, carefully unwrapping the baby's cocooning blanket to examine each tiny red foot. "Bright as a sunrise, soft as a dove." She paused to kiss each tiny foot before continuing. "And when sweet Daniel wakes for lunch," she crooned softly, rewrapping the blanket back around her sleeping son. "Mama's going to hug him a whole big bunch."

Samuel stared at her. "A whole big bunch?"

Now it was Ellie's turn to be startled. She looked around quickly, flushed and emitted a melodic laugh that made Samuel's chest flutter. "At least it rhymes." Averting her gaze, she brushed a fingertip along the infant's cheek, smiling when his tiny lips quivered. "Isn't he beautiful?"

"Yes." But not nearly as beautiful as the exquisite woman who held him. Awake now, with sparkling eyes and pinkened cheeks, she was without a doubt the most beautiful creature Samuel had ever laid eyes on.

"I'm sorry about last night."

"Last night?"

She skimmed a glance up as Samuel stood and flinched as a painful kink twisted the base of his spine. "You had to sleep in that chair because a strange woman had commandeered your bed. It was pretty rude of me to drop in unannounced, turn your home into a delivery room and promptly fall asleep in your bed. You must be rather put out at me."

"Not at all."

Her smile flashed brighter than a Christmas star. "You're a very kind man. If I knew your name, I could thank you properly."

"Samuel Evans," he replied.

"Pleased to meet you, Samuel. I'm Ellie and this is Daniel." She caught herself, chuckled softly. "But then you two have already met, haven't you?" Her smile faded, and Samuel saw a white flash as her teeth scraped her lower lip. "I remember you bringing him to me last night so I could feed him. I wanted to thank you, but the words wouldn't come." She glanced toward the window, studied the gray daylight misting above the snow-packed sills. "It's Christmas Day, isn't it?"

Samuel hesitated. "Christmas was last week." When her eyes clouded in puzzlement, he touched her wrist, found her pulse to be stronger, more rhythmic. "You've been very ill," he explained. "Daniel was born six days ago."

"Six days?"

Samuel released her wrist, steadied her shoulders when she swayed. "It's not unusual for patients to lose track of time during a serious illness. How are you feeling now? Any dizziness, nausea, pain?"

Ellie shook her head, shifted the infant in her lap, looked so crestfallen that Samuel's heart ached. "Six days," she murmured. "You took care of me for six days." Her eyes widened. "And you took care of Daniel, too. You changed him, you brought him to me, you walked him at night when he fussed. You gave me soup and warm tea and sponge baths and…and—" A crimson flush stained the hollows below her magnificent cheek bones. "It wasn't a dream at all, was it? Those things really happened."

"Yes."

The color drained from her face as quickly as it had appeared. She sucked a quick breath, held it. "Does anyone know I'm here?"

"No, I'm sorry. I had no way to contact anyone." When her lungs deflated all at once, Samuel assumed she was upset by that news, and laid a comforting hand on her shoulder. "The weather is expected to clear sometime next week. Now that you're feeling better, I'll be able to leave you long enough to hike to the radio tower and—"

"No!" The vehemence of her response was startling. "I mean, there's no need for you to do that."

Samuel noted her evasive gaze, the dart of her tongue to moisten her lips. "Your family must be worried sick."

"Daniel and I have no family," Ellie murmured, suddenly fascinated by a loose thread on the receiving blanket.

"Surely the baby's father—"

She interrupted angrily. "He's not a part of my life."

"That's too bad," Samuel replied, pinching off a twitch of anger that the child would have no father. It was none of his business, of course. Still, it annoyed him. A boy needed his father.

"Your friends then." When she shook her head, Samuel narrowed his gaze. "You mentioned that you were trying to reach a friend's cabin when you lost your way."

Ellie moistened her lips again, was clearly unnerved by the questions. "They weren't expecting me. That is, the cabin is vacant. The owners are wintering in Palm Springs. They gave me a key, and asked me to keep an eye on things."

"I see." He didn't, of course, but was perplexed by her sudden nervousness. "What about your employer?"

A subtle vibration jostled her shoulder. "My employer?"

"Yes, the ski lodge." A prick of guilt had him glancing away. "I found a pay stub in your backpack."

"Oh." The intensity of her gaze made him squirm, but she thankfully issued no comment about the blatant invasion of her privacy. "I don't work there anymore."

That made sense, Samuel supposed. Most women took maternity leave during the last few weeks of pregnancy. Still, the stub was dated just a few days before her arrival at the cabin. Before he could question that, Ellie suddenly lifted her head and drew a deep breath.

"That smell," she whispered, catching sight of the steaming pot on the woodstove. "That wonderful woodsy smell. I thought I'd dreamed it." She turned toward Samuel, her eyes wide with wonder. "What is it?"

"Boiled cedar bark. It helps dilate the bronchi, makes breathing easier."

"You're a doctor, aren't you?"

Samuel felt the furrow tighten across his brow, made an effort to loosen it. "No. I used to be a paramedic."

She cocked her head, regarded him with peculiar empathy. "Used to be?"

This wasn't a discussion Samuel wanted to encourage. "You must be hungry."

She hesitated a moment, then offered a sad smile, as if she'd recognized his pain but respected his right to keep it private. "I'm famished."

"Good." He stood, moved the chair back with a flick of his wrist, and stepped around Baloo, who lumbered over to lay his chin on the bed.

Ellie smiled, used a free hand to stroke the animal. "My hero," she murmured. "I owe you a huge steak." The hound rolled his rheumy eyes, huffed an ecstatic sigh and moved his head until her fingers massaged the back of his ear.

Ellie skimmed a glance upward, was struck by a reverent glow in Samuel's eyes as he gazed upon the infant sleeping on her lap.

Even in his disheveled state he was a handsome man, with a ruggedly sculpted face jutting sharply from plane to corrugated plane as if carved by a kitchen fork. Creases crinkled around his eyes, fluted furrows bracketed a surprisingly generous mouth and his stubbled jaw squared sharply into a strong, determined chin.

But it was his eyes that captured her, large wide-set eyes beneath thickly curved brows, and so blue that they seemed to bore into her very soul. She remembered those eyes. In her dreams, they had studied her with apprehension, comforted her with gentle warmth, supported her with cool determination. She had trusted those eyes in her dreams. She trusted them now.

"You're my hero, too, Samuel." The whisper eased

around the lump forming in her throat. "I don't know what I...we would have done if you hadn't been here."

The heartfelt praise startled him. Clearly he wasn't used to or comfortable with the touting of his accomplishments. With a nervous shift, he managed a thin smile. "For starters, you'd have to make your own oatmeal, but since that cranky old cookstove and I have an understanding, I guess I'd better handle that for now."

"You don't have to wait on me anymore. I'm feeling much better."

A sly gleam lit his gaze. "In that case, there's a half-dozen diapers that need scrubbing, we're nearly out of firewood, the cabin floor needs mopping and when you get around to fixing supper, keep in mind that I'm partial to pot roast but meat loaf will do in a pinch."

Ellie stared at him for a moment before she burst out laughing. "Are you sure you don't want me to give the dog a bath, too?"

Baloo widened his eyes.

"Only if you have time," Samuel replied as the dog bolted from the room. "Meanwhile I'll just put your son down for a nap so you can enjoy your breakfast. With the day you've got planned, you're going to need the nourishment."

After expertly scooping the sleeping child up in one arm, Samuel used his free hand to assist Ellie as she pivoted back into bed and settled against the plumped pillows.

She smiled her thanks, studied him as he sauntered comfortably into the homey living area with her tiny son nested in the crook of one arm. He was, she decided, a man in his element, comfortable not only with the isolation of his remote mountain retreat, but also in the company of strangers, one of which was a newborn infant. It was a dichotomy, a peculiar enigma that a man who clearly cherished his privacy would relinquish it without any trace of resentment or rancor. Most people, at least the people that Ellie had known, would not have been so gracious.

Then again, she instinctively realized that Samuel Evans was not like most people. He was undoubtedly a very special man.

Ellie watched in fascination as Samuel bent behind the woodstove, out of sight. A moment later, he stepped into view carrying what appeared to be a large woven basket with legs.

"I thought he'd be more comfortable with a bed of his own," Samuel said in response to her stunned expression. "It was either this or the silverware drawer." He set the basket beside Ellie's bed, close enough that she could touch it, but not quite see inside.

"It's a cradle," Ellie whispered, marveling at an exquisitely woven basket shaped like a hollow egg and tied atop X-shaped legs fashioned by inch-thick branches that had been trimmed, peeled and lashed into cross members with thin leather strips. "I've never seen anything so intricate. How did you do it?"

He shrugged. "Just wove a few peeled cedar twigs into shape is all. My mama taught me how."

Her ears perked at the tidbit of personal information being offered. "Your mother?"

"Our family spent summers here." Samuel smiled as if reliving fond memories, slid his hand along the cradle's neatly formed edge. "Mama didn't like fishing, so she was alone in the cabin most of the day. She taught herself basket weaving because there was a whole forest full of free materials. Pretty soon we had baskets and mats coming out our ears, but I have to admit she was pretty darn good. One year she made a trout creel for my dad's birthday. He still uses it."

"Does your family still spend summers here?"

Samuel's expression grew thoughtful, then veiled. "No, they moved to Florida a few years ago, and my brother lives in New York."

"That's sad," she murmured. "It sounds like you were a close family. You must miss them."

"They're happy where they are. I fly out to see them when I can."

She hesitated, then took a chance. "It must be difficult to get the time off. From your job, that is. Paramedics work long hours." When he said nothing, she forged ahead. "Of course, you mentioned that you weren't a paramedic anymore, so perhaps your new profession allows a more flexible schedule."

Instead of responding, Samuel squatted beside the cradle's cross members. "There are rockers on the bottom. All you have to do is reach out and give a light push." He demonstrated, the cradle swayed gently. "Daniel likes that. The motion seems to soothe him."

Ellie cocked her head. "I take it that you'd rather not discuss your job."

Samuel stood, rubbed his palms together, angled a glance toward the kitchen. "I'd better get that oatmeal on."

Before Ellie could reply, he was halfway across the cabin. A moment later, she heard the clunk of a metal pot and the gush of water from a faucet. She leaned into the pillows, suddenly overcome by exhaustion. A floating sensation lulled her into a light sleep, and when she opened her eyes again, Samuel was standing beside the bed with a tray of steaming food.

"Goodness," she murmured groggily, and pushed herself into a sitting position. "That was fast."

He settled the tray in her lap. "There's more if you want it."

Her eyes widened in awe at the largest bowl of oatmeal she'd ever seen, along with buttered toast and a massive glass of milk. "How on earth did you get real milk?"

"Define 'real.'" His sheepish smile was endearing. "Wintering in the mountains requires certain, er, adjustments. I happen to like milk, but since it's months between trips to the grocery store, I stock up on the dried stuff and just add water as I need it. It's not too bad, actually." He brushed his palms together, was clearly anxious to start another task. "The wind's picking up again. I've got to get that firewood in before the next storm hits. Will you be all right for a few minutes?"

"Of course," she murmured, feeling guilty for taking up so much of his time. "Please, do whatever you need to do. I'll be fine."

He gave a curt nod, pivoted on his boot heel and headed toward the cabin door, pausing to yank his tan leather jacket off a nearby wall peg. As he shrugged the garment on, Ellie noticed that it looked different than the jacket she recalled in her garbled memory. The leather hung loosely, seemed thinner than she remembered.

As he opened the cabin door, he ducked into the wind, flipping up the protective collar, just as she'd remembered seeing him do in her dreams. But this time, there was no flash of white wool from the sheepskin lining, and the listless leather flopped uselessly against the back of his neck.

Ellie bolted upright. "Samuel—?"

The cabin door closed, and he was gone.

Stunned, she moved the breakfast tray to the mattress and eased out of bed, pulled herself up beside the beautiful woven cradle. She took a deep breath, peered inside, and saw exactly what she'd expected—her precious baby nested in a soft cloud of sheepskin. Samuel had sacrificed his own warmth and protection to provide an extra measure of comfort for a stranger's child.

The gesture touched her heart, and brought grateful tears to her eyes. Samuel Evans was indeed an extraordinary man.

"Looks like our luck is changing," she whispered to her dozing son. "They can't find us here, my darling. We're safe now." Tears leaked down one cheek. "We're safe."

Chapter Three

For the next two days, Samuel continued to wait on Ellie hand and foot while yet another blizzard slammed Sierra Nevada. On the third day, gray gloom was shattered by glittering sunlight. Samuel's mood changed from one of solicitous solemnity to anxious anticipation. He hurried through breakfast preparations, sneaked yearning peeks from every window as if fearing the blue sky would disappear if he tarried too long. Even Baloo pranced in anticipation of an extended snow romp.

"Why don't you leave those?" she said as he prepared to wash breakfast dishes. "This lovely break in the weather probably won't last long."

Samuel swung a hopeful glance over his shoulder, steadied a twitchy grin. "You could be right," he intoned with forced gravity. "I'd hate a new storm sneaking up on us before I have a chance to shovel the woodpile path. Snow's getting thick on the roof, too, heavy enough to stress the support beams."

"Well, there you go. The roof over our heads certainly has priority over breakfast dishes."

Spinning away from the sink, he dried his hands on his jeans. The same hands, Ellie recalled, that had tended her with tenderness, glided over her skin with such sensual warmth. "Will you and Daniel be all right?" he asked suddenly.

She jerked her gaze up, felt a tingling heat at the notion he could perceive her thoughts. "Of course." Adding the reinforcement of a confident smile, Ellie set her knitting aside, leaned back against the bed pillows with her hands primly folded in her lap.

Samuel edged toward the cabin door. "I'll be close by. You just holler if you need me."

"Daniel and I will be fine, Samuel, just fine. Please go do whatever it is that you would be doing if we weren't here."

"Well, if you're sure."

"I'm sure."

Flashing a smile to die for, Samuel crossed the cabin like a bear on a food trail, shrugged on a heavy pullover sweater, then snatched his thin, unlined jacket from a coat peg. A blast of cold, fresh air burst into the cabin as Samuel opened the door. Baloo shot forward. Man and dog tripped over each other trying to squeeze through the narrow opening at the same time.

Baloo won. Samuel cursed under his breath, tossed an apologetic look over his shoulder as he stumbled outside. The moment the latch spring creaked and the cabin door swung shut, Ellie flipped off the bedclothes, her feet itching for the feel of the floor. "Ahhh." She stood, indulged in a luxurious stretch. Heaven, pure heaven.

Other than trips to the bathroom that Samuel supervised as if escorting a frail octogenarian on a nature hike, Ellie had been confined to bed so long her bottom was numb. It felt wonderful to stretch, bend and move under her own power.

Freedom. How sweet it was.

Humming to herself, she scurried to the window, blinked at the glare of sunshine off freshly fallen snow. When her eyes accustomed themselves to the brightness, she was stunned by the sheer magnitude of what she saw. Eight-foot snow drifts crawled up tree trunks, burying everything else in their path. During other brief storm breaks Samuel had kept the porch shoveled, along with a narrow walkway winding toward east side of the cabin where Ellie presumed the woodpile was located.

He had done so much for her and for Daniel. A grateful throb rolled around her heart. Samuel. The name suited him. Rugged, yet gentle, with a sensitive strength that made her shiver. He made her feel safe. Almost as safe as did the magnificent isolation of the cabin.

"Oh, Daniel," she whispered, although the infant was dozing peacefully in his intricately woven cradle. "I've never seen so much snow in my life. Even a snowmobile couldn't get through those drifts."

She inhaled all at once, couldn't contain a giddy smile. It was perfect, absolutely perfect. No one could get out.

No one could get in.

"Mountain roads," she sang softly, "white with snow, keep us safe, and all alone—" She fell silent, cocked an ear. Baloo's distant barking served as a reminder that Samuel wasn't the only one who had work to do.

After hurriedly slipping on her shoes, she headed to the kitchen to wash dishes, clean the laminate counter until it shone like a new penny, then inspect the two enameled green doors leading from the kitchen. One, she discovered to her delight, opened into a huge, well-stocked pantry, with a small basement root cellar and enough food to last for months. The other led to a six-foot-by-ten-foot screened back porch with a 1930s style wringer washtub and a propane food freezer filled to the brim with butcher-wrapped meat. Clearly Samuel had not planned on a trip to the grocery store until spring.

"Perfect," Ellie murmured again. Things couldn't have worked out better if she'd planned them. Peering through the screen, she saw what appeared to be the roof of a small building peeking from beneath a massive mound of snow. It looked like a shed of some kind, positioned perhaps a hundred feet from the cabin. Whatever it was, it would take hours of shoveling to trench a path to it, so Ellie promptly put the shed and potential contents out of her mind.

Shivering, she returned to the warm cabin with its lacquered, knotty pine walls and blazing, black-iron woodstove. Her curious gaze promptly fell upon the ladder leading up to the loft. Every night Samuel climbed up that ladder; every morning he climbed down. Sometime she heard him moving up there, and could imagine his powerful body flexing in the darkness. The image made her pulse race. He was a gorgeous man.

Of course, the last thing Ellie needed in her life was a man, gorgeous or otherwise.

Still she was dying for a peek at Samuel's private sanctum. She sauntered over, fingered the rough-hewn steps and cast a guilty glance around the cabin, as if expecting Samuel to pop in the front door and yell, "Aha!"

The comforting rasp of a snow shovel on the roof indicated that wasn't likely. Unless, of course, Baloo was the most dexterous and clever canine snow shoveler on earth, which Ellie seriously doubted. He was a sweet old hound, though, and he was her doggy champion. She'd have to fix him something special for supper.

At the moment, however, Ellie had some serious snooping in mind, and ascended the loft ladder for a quick peek at Samuel's sleeping quarters.

The first thing she saw was a crudely hung clothesline on which a half-dozen hand-cut diapers had been draped. Ellie clung to the ladder, stunned, grateful and feeling supremely foolish.

During the two days in which she'd been awake and aware she'd blithely used fresh diapers from the folded pile without thought of replenishment. Even now with the proof dangling a few feet in front of her startled face she could barely believe what she was seeing. Few men would tame testosterone surges long enough to wash diapers. Even fewer would do so without expecting at least a modicum of appreciation for their efforts. Not only had Samuel had never said a word, he'd apparently timed laundry activities to coincide with Ellie's sleep schedule because she had never once seen him scouring out Daniel's things or carrying the wet laundry up to be hung.

An odd flutter vibrated deep inside her chest. It made her feel uncomfortable. The last time a man had gone out of his way to show kindness, she'd felt that same flutter of gratitude. But there had been a method to that man's madness, a hidden agenda that had nearly destroyed her life.

The experience had changed Ellie. She wasn't gullible anymore, nor did she take things at face value. Of course she was grateful for kindness, but she was also wary of it. Kindness could be blinding, addictive. In the blink of an eye, one could end up hooked and needy, utterly immobilized by an ever-tightening noose of dependence. Samuel Evans's motives might be different, of course.

Then again, they might not.

Ellie had to be cautious. She had no choice.

Before descending the ladder, she cast a quick glance around the loft, noted several cardboard boxes in the corner beside a tackle box, a fishnet and a couple of fishing rods. Two cots were pushed against the far wall, one of which was heaped with books, folded clothes, a duffel bag and a tangled heap of unidentifiable junk.

The other cot contained a neatly rolled-out sleeping bag and a single pillow. Adequate, she supposed, but hardly as comfortable as the lovely bed she'd usurped as her own. The creaky loft was cluttered, dusty. And it was cold.

Sobered, Ellie returned to the kitchen to peruse the huge pantry. Of course she planned to take on her share of the household chores. That was an expected courtesy. But Ellie's plan required more than merely fulfilling Samuel's expectations. She'd draw upon her own life lessons and turn them around.

Ellie planned to tend Samuel's every need, kill him with kindness, make him so dependent upon the comforts she provided that she'd become much more than a cheery convenience. If the grief she'd endured had taught her anything, it was how to become indispensable to a man. And that was the only way she could think of to keep Samuel from sending her away.

Leaning on the snow shovel, Samuel pulled one glove off with his teeth, stuffed it in his jacket pocket. He flexed his stiff fingers and warmed his bare hand with his breath. Clouds were gathering again, and only half the roof had been shoveled. He was tired, out of shape. Hungry.

A glance at his watch confirmed it was past noon. Ellie would be hungry, too. He was wondering if he could get a few more square feet of roof cleared before fixing her lunch when a melodic call from below caught his attention.

"Yoo-hoo...hello up there."

Samuel laid down the shovel, picked his way along the slippery shingles until he could see the porch steps below. Sure enough, Ellie was standing there, squinting up, with her cheeks flushed and rosy, her hair tousled like a woman fresh from a lover's bed. She looked different. Beautiful. Sexy. Alluring. Samuel stared at her, as stunned by the change in her appearance as by the startling tightness in his groin.

She grinned when she saw him. "Hey there, snowman, ready for lunch?"

He shifted, shook off the sudden sexual image invading his mind and tried for a bland expression. Judging by a knowing sparkle in her eyes, the attempt didn't succeed. She recognized his attraction and was amused by it. A slow heat crawled up his throat. "I was hoping to get more work done, but if you're hungry, I'll fix you something."

"Oh, I'm hungry, all right but you don't— Yikes!" She fell back a step, laughing as Baloo skidded around the woodpile path and leapt up to plant a pair of snowy paws on her shoulders. "Whoa, enough," she sputtered as the dog slapped her face with sloppy kisses. "Yes, big fellow, I've got something special for you, too."

Baloo instantly sat, sniffed air, then shot onto the porch out of view. A moment later, Samuel heard the spring-loaded front door creak open, slam shut.

Still chuckling, Ellie wiped her face with the back of her hand. "Exuberant, isn't he?"

Lord, she was beautiful. Samuel wondered why on

earth he'd never noticed that before. Oh, he'd realized she was attractive, and had even gone so far as to admire her when she wasn't looking. But he'd never noticed how her eyes flashed with electric energy when she laughed, or the way her cheeks curved into dimpled apples with her smile.

Ellie cocked her head, shaded her eyes with her hand as the sun peeked from behind a passing cloud. "As I was saying, you don't have to fix lunch today because it's already on the table. All you have to do is come and get it."

Samuel blinked, more to erase the erotic image from his mind than to clear his eyes. The content of her message finally sank in. "You fixed lunch?"

"Yep, and I did a good job, if I do say so myself. You'd better hurry up before it gets cold."

"Gets cold," he repeated stupidly, remembering the creak of the front door as Baloo had pushed his way inside. "Ah, when you said lunch was on the table, you didn't mean that literally, did you?"

A baffled frown puckered her forehead. "Sure, why?"

"Uh-oh." Samuel yanked off the second glove, headed for the ladder. Halfway down he heard Ellie's footsteps on the porch. Another creak of the door spring was followed by a distressed wail. His heart sank as he leapt from the ladder, rushed into the cabin and saw exactly what he'd feared.

Politely seated at the table, Baloo had pawed the serving bowl within reach, stuck his face into the spaghetti and was sucking it up so fast that strands of pasta whipped into his busy mouth like fishing line on a greased reel.

Ellie stood beside the woodstove, her back rigid, elbows cocked, hands pressed to her mouth. Suddenly she curled forward, her shoulders vibrating as if bursting into silent tears.

"Dammit, 'Loo," Samuel growled, shrugging off his jacket and flinging it at the coat peg. "Look what you've gone and done."

Baloo glanced up, licked his saucy whiskers.

"Bad dog!" Samuel wiggled a finger at the dog's bed in the corner. "Go lie down. Now!"

Dutifully hopping down from the chair, Baloo lumbered over to his bed where he curled up on his tacky blanket, laid a sticky red chin on his paws, and looked exceptionally pleased with himself.

Samuel shifted, reached out to lay a comforting hand on Ellie's trembling shoulders, urging her to turn around. She did, but her face was still buried in her hands, and she was making soft gasping sounds that nearly broke his heart.

"Oh, gee. Please, don't cry. It's no big thing, really. I'll just whip up another batch and—"

Ellie lifted her head, took a wheezing breath before collapsing again. Samuel stepped back, stunned. She wasn't crying at all. She was laughing, laughing so hard that she could barely breathe, let alone speak. All she could do was clutch her abdomen, point at the sticky-faced dog with spaghetti stuck to his ear and howl until tears ran down her cheeks.

Samuel wanted to kiss her.

After a lunch of cold tuna sandwiches Samuel finished clearing the roof while Baloo snored in his bed and Ellie flitted around the cabin to implement phase one of her plan. She'd figured out how to use the old wringer washtub, and by the time Samuel dragged himself back inside just before sunset, fresh laundry flapped on the loft clothesline and a garlic-studded pot roast simmered on the stove.

Ellie smoothed the clean plaid shirt Samuel had loaned her, absently flipped her fingers through her freshly brushed hair, and flashed him a cheery, welcoming smile. "I hope you're hungry. I've cooked a roast the size of Wyoming, and made enough gravy to flood a small river."

Samuel stood there, stone-faced. His shuttered gaze slipped from Ellie to the steaming pot on the stove, then down to Baloo, yawning and stretching in his bed. "You didn't have to do that."

"I wanted to."

"You were supposed to rest this afternoon."

Ellie swallowed a pinch of annoyance, managed to keep her sunny smile from wavering. "I feel fine. Besides, you've been working hard all day. You deserve a hot meal." She cocked her head, adding, "I'm a very good cook."

Without another word, Samuel shrugged off his jacket, shook snow off his head and marched into the bathroom. A moment later, the shower blasted on.

Ellie wasn't sure what reaction she'd been expecting, but that certainly wasn't it. She frowned as Baloo trundled over to lean against her thigh. "Is he always this grumpy before supper?"

Baloo whined, lifted her hand with his head and was rewarded by a satisfying neck scratch. "Well, at least someone around here appreciates a home-cooked meal." Ellie chewed her lip, gazed apprehensively at the closed bathroom door and worried that she'd already overstayed her welcome. She swallowed hard, hugged Baloo's big head. "Oh, well," she told the animal in a voice that shook only a little. "We were looking for a place when we found this one. I just hoped we'd have a little more time…"

The words dissipated as a cranky mew from the cradle captured her attention. She hurried over, smiled down at her fussy son. "Don't you worry, precious boy. Mommy isn't going to let anything bad happen to you."

Scooping Daniel up in her arms, she hummed softly and nuzzled his silky scalp. Samuel said that the baby's lungs had cleared almost miraculously, and according to a cleverly converted trout scale, the baby had gained nearly two pounds since birth. Daniel was thriving. Ellie could have wept with relief.

This was the perfect place for her son, the perfect place for her to gather her thoughts, plan their escape. She'd hoped for more time, but if that didn't happen, she'd manage just as she always had.

Ellie was good at escaping.

As a child, she'd escaped into the fantasy of her mind, a happy place where people were kind to each other because they wanted to be rather than out of sickness or greed. Not that Ellie's childhood had been dreary. Far from it. She'd been loved and well cared for, the only flaw being that her unhappy mother had martyred herself with a life of selfless servitude Ellie had no intention of emulating. Life was short, after all, meant to be savored and enjoyed, not merely endured.

Ellie had always enjoyed life, had craved fun and laughter, avoided conflict like the plague and changed jobs at the first hint of confrontation. She understood that about herself, admitted to being an escapist who turned her back on unpleasantness and ran from trouble as a matter of emotional survival.

Now it was a matter of life and death. She couldn't tell Samuel why she'd sprinted into the woods that fateful day. She couldn't trust him, couldn't trust anybody.

Yet how could she *not* trust him? For the first time in her life, Ellie had nowhere to run. That scared her to death.

"Would you like another slice? There's plenty." Ellie lowered the serving platter when Samuel shook his head and pushed away from the table. "How about some more coffee?"

He regarded her for a moment. "That would be nice."

She hopped up, snatched the pot off the old cookstove. "You know," she murmured, filling his outstretched mug. "I was thinking that if it's nice tomorrow, maybe we could make a snowman. It would be fun, and Daniel has never seen one before."

Samuel sipped his coffee, peering over the rim. He set the mug down, stared into the steaming black brew. "It's a bit chilly out there for a newborn."

"Oh, I wouldn't take him outside." Ellie replaced the coffeepot on the stove, and returned to her chair across from the somber man who'd spoken less than a half-dozen words throughout the entire meal. "We'd have to place it so he could see from the window."

Samuel didn't look up, although his brow quirked a bit and Ellie thought she saw a half smile twitch the corner of his mouth. "Daniel's eyes haven't developed enough to focus on anything beyond shades of light and a few bright colors."

"Fiddlesticks, he follows my every move."

"He perceives motion," Samuel agreed. "And instinctively follows the sound of your voice. At this age hearing is considerably more acute than vision."

"How do you know all that?"

"It's been scientifically proven."

"Ah, now you're a scientist?"

"Not really."

"First you're not really a doctor, although you play one in real life; now you're not really a scientist, although you clearly keep abreast of scientific theory." She chuckled, thrilled to have finally engaged him in conversation, despite the banality of banter. "You also have an undeniable knack for child care. So tell me, Mr. Not Really, how many babies have you raised lately?"

He blinked, looked stung. "I don't have children, if that's what you're asking."

"I'm sorry," she whispered, mortified to have inadvertently wounded him. "Your personal life is none of my business. I was just being my normal smart-aleck self. I have a talent for hopping on one foot because the other one spends so much time in my mouth."

"If I did have children," Samuel continued quietly, "I'd be with them, which is exactly where any father worth his salt would be."

Ellie felt her face heat, and realized she'd opened the door into a discussion that she really did not want to have. "I'll take care of the dishes," she muttered, snagging a plate in each hand. "You just relax and drink your coffee."

He leaned back, watched her with reflective intensity as she bustled around filling the sink with soapy water. "Where's Daniel's father?" he asked.

A plate clunked against the sink. Ellie flinched, laid the stoneware carefully into the dishwater. "I told you, he's not a part of my life."

"That's your choice," he replied amiably. "It's not necessarily Daniel's choice. A boy needs his father."

Ellie bit her lip, clutched a soapy bowl so tightly it was a wonder it didn't crack under the strain. "There's a big difference between a father and a sperm donor."

Behind her, a chair leg scraped the floor. "You were artificially inseminated?"

Startled, Ellie tossed a quick look over her shoulder and saw that Samuel's question was absolutely earnest. She turned away again, focused on washing dishes. She hated lying and wasn't particularly good at it. Still the unpleasant subject of Daniel's father was clearly destined to be visited and revisited unless she could lay it to rest once and for all. Samuel had just provided the perfect means to do that.

She cleared her throat, swallowed the lie and offered a reticent response designed to imply more than it confirmed. "That's a very personal subject," she murmured demurely, setting a rinsed glass in the drainer. "I'm sure you understand why I'd prefer not to discuss it."

She held her breath, waiting.

Finally Samuel spoke. "You have a fine, healthy son. That's all that matters."

The chair leg scraped again. Ellie glanced up just as Samuel strode toward the living area, pausing at the cradle. He bent over, smiling. "Hey, buddy, you're awake." A responsive coo emanated from the cradle, which tickled Samuel immensely. "Smart for your age, aren't you? Here, little man, let's test your grip. Whoa, not too shabby. We'll have you splitting firewood in no time."

Ellie watched quietly, and was touched by the fatherly pride Samuel took in little Daniel. He was a good man, she decided, and an honest one. She hated deceiving him. She was just so damned desperate—

"I think he's hungry."

"Hmm?" Ellie blinked up, saw Samuel standing beside cradle regarding her with unnerving acuity. "Oh, of course. I'm almost done here."

She rinsed the last of the silverware, wrapped meat scraps in newspaper and took them out to the screen porch, then wiped her hands on a tea towel and hurried over to ease her bright-eyed infant out of the cradle just as Samuel settled on the sofa to select a book from a stack beside the coffee table.

Balancing her son in her arms, Ellie glanced at the volume Samuel was perusing. "Real-estate law?"

He flipped a page, said nothing.

"I noticed that you also have books on investment management and public finance. Thinking of a career change?"

Samuel shifted, never took his eyes off the page he was reading. "I heard a helicopter this afternoon."

Ellie froze, swallowed hard, couldn't have responded if she'd wanted to.

"A sheriff's rescue copter. I saw it over the trees." He leaned back against the cushions, propped his ankle on his bent knee. "It was performing a search pattern over Miner's Ravine."

Licking her lips, Ellie laid Daniel on the bed and tried to change his diaper. Her hands were shaking. "Probably looking for some daredevil who got lost skiing a closed run. That happens all the time."

"Does it?"

A furtive glance confirmed that Samuel had lowered the book and was staring right at her. She quickly looked away, tucked the damp diaper in a plastic bag and snatched a clean one from the stack. "While I was working at the lodge, they had to send out rescue parties two or three times a week. Dangerous areas are clearly posted, but I guess some folks don't believe in signs."

The sofa squeaked. "Some people are like that, I suppose."

"Yes, some are," she whispered. Despite trembling

fingers, she only stuck herself once while fastening the safety pin. Finished, she scooped Daniel into her arms, settled onto the bed. "This, ah, helicopter. Just out of curiosity, how close did it come to the cabin? I mean, I didn't hear anything, so it must have been fairly far away."

"Miner's Ravine is about ten miles across the valley."

"Oh. Well." She cleared her throat, scooted back against the pillows and loosened her clothing, preparing to nurse. "I hope they find whoever they're looking for."

"They always do."

The warning in his soft reply sent chills down Ellie's spine. The helicopter sighting unnerved her. Fair enough, the aircraft had been too far away to be a threat, but where would it be tomorrow or the day after? She wondered if Samuel had recognized her anxiety, but when she looked up she saw that he'd hoisted the open book in front of his face—too high to be comfortable, but high enough to block Ellie from view as she breast-fed her baby son.

It was a chivalrous offer of privacy, although rather unnecessary considering the intimacy of their initial hours together. All she remembered about Daniel's birth was the soothing sound of Samuel's voice, the kind glow of his blue eyes. If not for him, she would have died that night. So would have Daniel.

Guilt settled like sour bile in the pit of her stomach, guilt at having rewarded his selfless heroism with deception and deceit. Ellie knew she should tell Samuel the truth, but trust was such a frightening thing. Those with whom it was shared possessed incredible power—power that if abused became evil and destructive. Deep down, she couldn't believe that Samuel would ever abuse that power, betray her trust.

But she hadn't believed that Stanton would betray her, either. She'd been proven wrong in the cruelest way imaginable.

It was after midnight when Ellie awakened with a start. She held her breath, listened to the darkness. Then she heard it, a groan of agony, a raspy gasp of fear.

Above her, the loft floor vibrated as if the cot were being thrashed by demons. A guttural cry from above propelled her out of bed. Samuel was having another nightmare, and judging by the intensity of his utterances, this one was the worst yet.

She tiptoed to the base of the ladder, hesitated, then began the ascent, planning only to wake him, assure him that the tormentors of his mind weren't real, that they existed only in a dream.

But halfway up the ladder, a bloodcurdling scream froze her in place. It was the screech of a dying animal, the snarl of a demon from hell. It was the most hideous sound she'd ever heard.

And it wasn't human.

Chapter Four

The scream rose into a shriek, rumbled into a snarl, was joined by a bloodcurdling pandemonium of yelping howls. Ellie sucked a panicked breath, her white-knuckled fingers frozen around the ladder stiles.

Only when the usually mellow hound dog yelped in fear and dived under the bed did Ellie snap into action, retreating down the ladder at the same time as Samuel's bulk loomed above her.

He swung down from the loft, leapt pantherlike onto the floor. Clad only in snug print boxer shorts, he dashed across the cabin, bare torso glittering with reflected glow from the woodstove window. His shoulders rippled; his lean thighs flexed as if tempered steel. He was beyond doubt the most glorious male creature Ellie had ever laid eyes on.

After yanking a rifle out from under the sofa, Samuel spun around, finally noticed Ellie standing at the base of the ladder clutching her chest. Their eyes met, held. His widened in surprise, hers rounded in utter shock while her heart pounded so hard she barely noticed the animalistic snarls and shrieks emanating from behind the cabin. Intellectually she understood that something terrible was happening on the screened porch, but all she could see, all she could think about was Samuel's bare chest gleaming in the firelight.

He was magnificent, lithe, lean hipped and broad shouldered like the heart-stopping hero of a romance novel. He was also half-naked.

"You'll freeze," she stammered like a fool.

Rifle clutched at the ready, he swung around, crouched like a commando, hissed, "Stay here."

A howl louder than the rest jarred her to the marrow. "My God, what *is* that?"

Samuel didn't answer. He was already slinking toward the dark kitchen.

Exhaling all at once, Ellie tiptoed cautiously behind him while he warily knelt beside the back door. As he reached for the knob, she leaned close, whispered, "Be careful."

Startled, he whirled around, fell back against the wall. His gaze narrowed. "You don't take orders well, do you?"

"No, actually." She flinched, scrambled backward when a thudding crash reverberated the porch wall. The frenetic yelping seemed more distant now, but was still too close for comfort. "There's something out there," she announced, wiggling a frantic finger. "An animal or...or something."

Samuel gave her a withering look. "Gee, really?" Clearly perturbed, he flipped a switch beside the jamb. A thin string of light spilled beneath the door, against which he braced his knee before easing it open an inch to peer out through the crack.

Behind him Ellie wrung her hands. "What is it? What's going on out there?"

Samuel shifted without comment, cocked his head, presumably to get a better view of the area.

"It's not a bear, is it? I mean, aren't bears supposed to be hibernating now?" When he still didn't reply, Ellie's fear gave way to curiosity. She bent to peek under his outstretched arm, saw ripped hunks of greasy newspaper strewn across the porch floor with remnants of the wrapped roast scraps. "Uh-oh."

Samuel turned his head slowly, skewered her with a look. She shrugged helplessly, offered an apologetic smile.

Muttering under his breath, he refocused his gaze through the crack in the doorway. Ellie did the same.

Shredded screening caught her eye, along with several hulking shadows beyond the porch perimeter. One of the shadows ventured toward the torn screen. The animal hoisted its forepaws onto the lower deck wall, turned a pointy-snouted face toward the doorway where two curious humans were watching.

"A coyote," Ellie whispered. Before the words were out of her mouth, the doglike creature emitted a startled howl as a snarling hunk of fur churned out from behind the porch freezer. The coyote leapt away with a yelp, while a half-dozen shadowy silhouettes scattered in the moonlight, and melted into the night.

The snarling hunk of fur swished around, focused beady black eyes at the porch door behind which Samuel and Ellie were crouched. "Why, it's nothing but a fat little ferret," she murmured.

"That's no damned ferret," Samuel snapped as the hissing beast bared its teeth, and made a beeline straight for them. He slammed the door, whipped the slide-latch lock into position, and yanked Ellie away mere moments before the snarling creature hit the door shrieking, and tried to claw its way through the wood.

Astounded that an animal the size of a small footstool could be so vicious, Ellie stumbled backward, clinging to Samuel's arm like a terrified tick. "Do something!" she implored as the kitchen door shuddered violently. "Make it stop."

"If it gets inside, I'll shoot it," Samuel replied with maddening calm.

"If it gets *inside?*" Ellie swayed at the thought. "Dear God, you mean that creature is actually capable of chewing through a door?"

Samuel shrugged, shifted the rifle. "There isn't much a perturbed badger can't do if he sets his mind to it."

"A badger?" Staring at the vibrating door, Ellie tried to compare her vision of badgers as placid, lumbering creatures with this ferocious wood-eating beast. "I thought badgers were harmless."

"Badgers are a lot of things, none of them harmless. One that size can stand up to a grizzly, gut a mountain lion without breaking a sweat and hold its own against a pack of hungry wolves. Or coyotes," he added grimly.

Trembling, Ellie sagged against Samuel's arm, pressed her cheek to his shoulder. "Will it go away?"

"Eventually." His muscles rippled warm against her skin. "When it realizes we're not a threat to its meal, it'll stop clawing the door and go finish the supper that you so kindly left out." He swung his head around, gave her a look that could freeze meat. "Perhaps I should have mentioned that the scent of food draws wild animals. Around here, that's considered a really bad idea."

Feeling foolish, Ellie flashed a bright smile. "On the

other hand, how else would we have this unprecedented opportunity to view nature up close and personal?" Then to her horror, she giggled.

Clasping her hand over her mouth, she struggled to stifle her amusement but the entire situation was just too ludicrous for words. The look on Samuel's face when that badger had charged them had been utterly priceless. As for Ellie, well, she'd been so terrified that she'd nearly wet herself. Now *that* would have been funny.

"I'm, ah—" Clamping her lips together, she wrestled the stubborn grin, contritely cleared her throat. "I'm truly sorry, Samuel. I should have put the scraps in the trash under the sink, but I was afraid they would, well, smell bad."

"Smell bad," he repeated dully. He stared at her for a moment, then rubbed his forehead, which had puckered into an adorable frown. "Let me get this straight. Garbage offends you, so you place it on the porch, thereby inviting every nocturnal carnivore in the woods to slime the place with personal calling cards that stink a hell of a lot more than rotting meat scraps. Hey, it works for me."

"I'm so very sorry, truly I am." She tried to muster an apologetic expression, but Samuel just looked so adorably piqued that she couldn't fight back a smile. "I'll be more careful from now on. I promise."

Samuel scraped her with a look. "Oh, goody."

Ellie's heart sank. The last thing on earth she wanted was for Samuel to be angry with her but she couldn't seem to do or say anything right.

The sound of splintering wood was suddenly replaced by the scuffle of scurrying paws across the porch's planked floor and the telltale crinkle of ruffled newspaper. Ellie angled a glance upward, reluctantly released her grip on the glowering man beside her. "I guess you were right. He seems to have gone back to, er, whatever.''

''Uh-huh.'' Samuel snagged a chair from the kitchen table and propped it under the doorknob.

''That's a good idea,'' she offered lamely. ''Just in case he gets feisty again.''

Samuel heaved a long-suffering sigh, pulled out a second chair, seated himself and laid the rifle across his lap. ''I'll keep watch. You go back to bed.''

Puffing her cheeks, Ellie blew out a breath, rubbed her upper arms through the floppy gray fleece of a sweat suit that doubled as pajamas. The torn neck opening slipped over her shoulder, making her feel even more frumpy and foolish. ''I, ah—'' An irritable wail emanated from the sleeping area. Ellie sighed. ''Daniel's awake.''

Samuel didn't respond. His gaze was riveted to her bare shoulder with a smoldering expression so explicit, so sexually charged that her own body responded in kind. Electric energy tingled from her chest to her groin, exploding into white-hot shards that shocked her motionless. Their eyes met, her breath backed up in her lungs. She couldn't move, couldn't breathe.

Then Daniel emitted another cranky cry, breaking the fragile link between them. Samuel jerked his head, stared at the porch door with forced intensity. His jaw twitched, tightened. ''Better see to your son,'' he said.

Ellie replied with a taut nod, then hurried away.

Samuel stared straight ahead, flexing his fingers around the stock and barrel of the rifle in his lap, and calling himself six kinds of a fool. The woman had given birth less than two weeks ago, and he was practically salivating over an innocuous peek of bare skin. It was unseemly, boorish and completely beyond the pale of the gentlemanly behavior on which Samuel had prided himself. Clearly he'd been celibate far too long.

There was no doubt about it. It was going to be one hell of a long winter.

Daniel was having a bad night.

Reclining on the loft cot where he'd finally retreated after two hours of sentry duty, Samuel was wide-awake and throbbing, his senses acutely attuned to the sounds of movement and whispered words from the sleeping area below. Ellie was murmuring to Daniel, her voice lilting and melodic, so soft he couldn't quite make out the words over the dog's raucous snores.

Samuel was used to Baloo's nightly nasal noise fest, but tonight the sleeping hound's raspy snorts grated like a chainsaw on concrete. Samuel's nerves were chafed raw.

He sat up, swung his feet quietly to the floor and leaned forward, not understanding the compulsion to actually view the crooning woman below him, but indulging it nonetheless. He was amply rewarded.

With Daniel cradled in her arms, Ellie walked to and fro at the foot of her bed, close enough to the woodstove for warmth. She was humming softly, a melody Samuel vaguely recalled from his days at Scout camp.

Then she started to sing very quietly, but her sweet voice wafted up to the loft. "Does your hound dog snore," she crooned. "Do his nostrils buzz and roar, does it keep you up all night, does it shake the cabin floor?"

A private smile tugged Samuel's lips. As always, Ellie created her own lyrics as she went along.

"Does it rattle like a buzz saw, and make your eardrums sore?" Her voice softened. "Does your hound—" she bent to lay her son in the cradle

"—dog—" she lovingly covered him with a blanket "—snore?" The final note was a whisper as she gently stroked the sleeping infant.

Samuel's heart melted on the spot. He watched greedily as Ellie gazed at her slumbering child with the serene smile of maternal perfection. Samuel was drawn to her on a visceral level, fascinated to the point of being mesmerized. Ellie Malone was unique, one of a kind, a woman of intelligence and humor and compassion all rolled up in a package so breathtaking and sexy that he couldn't take his eyes off her, or erase her smoldering image from his mind. She was without doubt a very special woman.

She was also a woman with a secret.

Samuel hadn't forgotten Ellie's frightened pallor when he'd mentioned the helicopter, nor had he been fooled by her lackadaisical reply. Despite her insistence to the contrary, Samuel suspected there was considerably more to Ellie's sudden appearance on his porch than he'd been led to believe. Part of him didn't care; the rational part, however, did care. He didn't like being deceived. He didn't like being played for a fool.

But most of all, he didn't like complications. Ellie evoked feelings in him. Deep feelings. That was a complication. It was also the last thing on earth that he needed right now.

Samuel had his own secrets, secrets that had pursued him to this mountain retreat, secrets that haunted his heart and stalked his slumber. Secrets that would reveal his failures to the world, reveal them to Ellie.

Samuel couldn't risk that. He laid back on the cot, tucked his hands beneath his head, and stared into the blackness. He'd come here to be alone, to lick his wounds and scrape up the ragged tatters of a life in ruins. Ellie Malone was a distraction he couldn't afford. It was time, he decided, for her to leave.

The next morning Ellie awakened at dawn to feed Daniel, then crept toward the screened porch to examine the damage before Samuel woke up. She removed the chair wedged beneath the knob, cracked the door open for a cautious peek.

The porch looked as if it had been bombed. Spilled laundry detergent was scattered from one end of the porch to the other, a segment of screening was in tatters, the floor was littered by tufts of fur and shredded newspaper and smeared with a greasy, foul-smelling substance more noxious than anything she'd ever found in Daniel's diapers.

It reeked.

Closing the door, Ellie blew out a breath, then squared her shoulders, grabbed a bucket and mop from the broom closet and went to work.

By the time Samuel stumbled to the kitchen in a blurry-eyed stupor, the porch had been swept tidy, all badger remnants had been meticulously scoured into oblivion, and an aromatic batch of bacon sizzled on the old cookstove.

She flashed him a cheery smile, and set a mug of strong black coffee on the table. "Good morning. How do you like your eggs?"

Unshaven and clearly exhausted, Samuel collapsed onto a chair, propped his elbow on the table, and laid his chin on a fisted hand. "Sunny-side up," he mumbled, using his free hand to rub his eyelids. "But since all we've got left is powdered eggs, that might be a problem."

Ellie grinned. "Which is why I was hoping you'd say scrambled."

"You don't have to wait on me."

"You've waited on me for days." She felt a pinch of guilt as he rolled his head, flinching, and rotated his shoulders as if working out kinks. "If it wasn't for me, you wouldn't be sleeping on that miserable old army cot. Breakfast is the least I can do. So, what'll it be?"

He blinked up in surprise. "Scrambled is fine."

"That's kind of boring. How about an omelette?"

"Whatever." He took a sip of coffee, widened his eyes. "Wow."

"Good coffee, huh?"

"Very good."

"Temperature is the key. These old stove-top percolators can be tricky. If the heat is too high, the coffee will be bitter."

He took another healthy sip, smacked his lips. "I'll remember that—" His gaze fell on the porch door. "Where's the chair?"

"I, ah, moved it." Turning away, Ellie poured a dollop of water into a bowl of egg powder and mixed madly. Behind her the silence was deafening.

"Tell me you didn't go out there," Samuel said finally.

She sneaked a peek over her shoulder, flinched at the reproach in his eyes. "I was very careful to make sure our visitor had left first."

Samuel heaved a sigh, set the coffee mug on the table and shook his head. "Did you at least have enough sense to take the rifle in case the danged thing had holed itself up behind the washtub?"

The thought hadn't crossed her mind. "Would you prefer the bacon mixed in the omelette or on the side?"

"That's what I thought. Dammit, Ellie—"

"Say, I saw some canned mushrooms in the pantry." She set the bowl down, hustled across the kitchen to investigate. "You do like mushrooms, right? Oh, of course you do, or you wouldn't have a pantry full of them." She grabbed a can from the well-stocked shelves, returned to her cooking station.

From the corner of her eye she saw Samuel glaring at her with his arms crossed firmly across his chest. "Do you enjoy living dangerously?" he asked as she fiddled with the antiquated can opener. "Or are you just a fool?"

She sighed, finished draining the mushrooms, mixed them with the eggs and poured the omelette mixture into a frying pan before turning to face him. "Probably a bit of both," she admitted. "But the truth is that I created the problem, and I didn't want you to get stuck fixing it."

"You should have waited for me to check things out first."

"And if I had, would you have let me clean the place up on my own?"

He shrugged, almost smiled.

"See how you are?" Chuckling, Ellie returned to her cooking duties, expertly rolling the pan to spread the egg mixture into a thin pancake. "By the way, I repaired the screen with some duct tape that I found in a cabinet but the, er—" she cleared her throat "—the doorjamb is a little, well…"

"Scratched up?" Samuel offered helpfully. "Splintered?"

She angled an apprehensive glance over her shoulder. "Umm, it's kind of gone."

He sat forward. "Gone?"

"Only partially gone. The doorjamb now starts about two feet up from the floor. I think he ate the rest of it."

"Good Lord."

"I'll pay for the damage."

"Don't be silly." He wearily rubbed his eyes, softened his gruff tone. "It's nothing, Ellie. Don't worry about it."

"Please, I want to. I feel so bad about, about…" She spun around, lifted a pleading hand, then let it fall to her side. "About everything," she finished lamely.

Samuel regarded her, and for a moment his eyes filled with the most exquisite sadness. Then he blinked and it was gone, replaced by a noncommittal stare that Ellie found even more unnerving. "There's a padlocked storage bin by the woodpile," he said quietly. "The garbage cans are inside it. Be sure you use them from now on."

She issued a nervous nod, slid the finished omelette onto a plate with a half-dozen bacon strips and set it on the table. Samuel murmured his thanks, snatched up a fork and attacked the food with gusto. Ellie watched, smiling. Samuel was clearly enjoying his meal, and she was enjoying his enjoyment.

After pouring herself a cup of coffee, she joined him at the table. "Would you happen to have a pair of gloves I could borrow?"

"Sure, I guess so. Why?" He forked a bite of egg, cast a wary gaze across the table. "No, let me guess. Because you can't build a snowman with bare hands, right?"

"Why, Mr. Evans," Ellie purred with a grin. "I do believe there's hope for you after all."

Samuel's back felt like a rusty spring. Two hours of digging, and he'd cleared a path less than halfway to the shed. Sixty feet to go. God, he felt old. Useless. Set adrift in a world he'd once thought he controlled until reality had clubbed him upside the head. That's when Samuel had realized he wasn't invulnerable or invincible, that *failure* was more than a nondescript word wedged between *faille* and *fain* in the dictionary.

Failure was the enemy, the conqueror, the vanquisher of dreams. Failure was Samuel's reality now.

Or at least it had been until Ellie Malone stumbled into his life with her silly tunes and eternal cheer to brighten even the grayest winter day. Ellie didn't understand the truth about Samuel. She regarded him with reverence, with gratitude. She thought him a god.

That's why she had to leave before she learned what he really was, before a pool of bitter disappointment clouded those sparkling eyes.

Of course Samuel understood that he'd saved Ellie's life, saved her baby's life, and was humbly thankful for the training that had allowed him to do so. But he certainly wasn't a god. Sometimes he wondered if he was even a man.

"I need a mouth."

Startled, Samuel swung around, saw Ellie by the outside corner of the screen porch, peering down into the four-foot-deep snow chasm he was shoveling. He wiped his forehead with a sleeve, tried not to grin. Lord, she was a sight. The front of her jacket was coated with snow, her mink-colored hair was appealingly tousled, with damp tendrils frozen against cheeks so rosy that they seemed to glow from within.

As Baloo lumbered over panting, Ellie dropped to her knees atop the snowy embankment, rubbed her nose with the floppy finger of an oversize glove, and repeated her odd statement. "I need a mouth."

Samuel leaned on the shovel, kept his face passive. "Did you finally wear out the old one?"

"Are you implying that I talk too much?" she asked with a cheery chuckle.

"Nope, I'm saying it outright. You've been outside

the kitchen window yabbering to yourself for nearly an hour. If any mouth on earth has a right to be worn-out by now, it's yours.''

''I'll have you know that I was not talking to my-self.''

''No?''

''No.'' She sniffed, tried to look insulted but couldn't quite manage it through the silly grin she was fighting. ''Daniel is watching me from the kitchen. I was talking to him. And Jasper, of course.''

''Of course.'' Samuel decided that he wasn't going to ask. He didn't want to know and he wasn't going to ask. Wasn't going to— He heaved a sigh, stuffed a hand in his pocket. ''Okay, I'll bite. Who's Jasper?''

Her grin broke free. ''Our snowman.''

Samuel shook his head. ''I knew I shouldn't have asked.''

''He's the one who needs the mouth,'' she explained, absently stroking Baloo's head. ''Mine is working just fine, thank you.''

''Pity.''

''Since sleep deprivation tends to make a person grumpy, I'll let that comment slide. Now, what about Jasper's mouth?''

He shrugged, scooped a palm-size rock from a cleared portion of the path. ''How about this?''

She flicked the suggestion away with a derisive snort. ''I don't want poor Jasper looking like he's in a per-manent state of shock. He'll frighten Daniel.''

Flipping the rock away, Samuel decided against men-tioning that Daniel was a bit young to interpret facial expression. As far as Ellie was concerned, the infant possessed cognitive powers bordering on superhuman. ''So now we need a happy mouth.''

''Happy would be good.''

"Draw one."

She frowned. "You're not taking this seriously."

Unable to dispute that, Samuel simply cocked a brow and said nothing.

"I saw some dried apple rings in the pantry," she muttered. "If I cut one in half and—" Thrilled, she stood suddenly. "Do you have a red felt marker somewhere?"

"Uh, I think so. In the kitchen drawer where I keep my wallet and keys."

She spun quickly, shoes spitting snow. As she dashed off to complete her mission, Baloo tossed Samuel a distressed look then trundled after her.

"Traitor," Samuel muttered, and would have said more had he not heard clunking noises in the kitchen, followed by a string of nonstop chatter as Ellie described to Daniel exactly what she was doing and why it was a good thing. Samuel's ears might have been playing tricks on him, but he could have sworn the infant issued gurgling replies in all the right places.

He shook his head, swatted his ears to clear them. The cold must be muddling his mind. It wouldn't be the first time.

Meanwhile footsteps continued to vibrate the cabin's raised floor as Ellie rushed from one room to the next, chattering happily. When the front door finally squeaked and slammed, Samuel stopped shoveling and waited.

Ellie's voice now emanated from the west side of the house, where she'd been building her snowman in front of the kitchen window. "Hold still, Jasper, don't wiggle… Voilà! Perfect, absolutely perfect. Oh, you are just the handsomest thing. Daniel, look, isn't he the handsomest thing?" There was a minuscule pause, as if she was awaiting a reply. "You see, Daniel agrees, and babies never lie— Oh, Baloo, no! Don't you *dare* do that on poor Jasper. Go find a tree." A contrite canine whine was drowned out by more of Ellie's cheery chatter. "Now where were we... Ah, yes, let's see how the hat looks."

Samuel's head swung around. Hat?

"Ooh, smashing. Now the shirt."

Dropping the shovel, Samuel scrambled up the snow wall, rounded the screen porch and jerked to a stop with his jaw agape. Perched atop a four-foot blob of fat, packed snow was his favorite Sacramento Kings cap— the one that had cost him thirty bucks at the team's one and only playoff game in Arco Arena. Even worse, Ellie was happily tying the arms of a matching, fifty-dollar sweatshirt around the snow blob's nonexistent neck.

"The preppy look is 'in,'" Ellie muttered as she fussed with folding the sweatshirt arms just so across the icy barrel representing the snowman's chest. She didn't notice Samuel, but Baloo, who'd been placidly watching the snow-dressing process, certainly did. The animal took one look at his master's thunderous expression, and slunk toward the front porch, sniveling.

"What the hell are you doing?" Samuel growled.

Ellie spared him a glance. "You don't expect my child to be traumatized by the sight of a naked snowman, do you?" She patted the blob's shoulder, and stood back looking enormously pleased with herself. "There. *Très chic*."

"That's my King's hat," Samuel sputtered. "And my favorite sweatshirt. It's never even been worn."

"How can it be your favorite if you haven't worn it?"

"I haven't worn it," he gritted through tightly clamped teeth, "because I don't want to get it dirty."

She frowned prettily. "That's silly. Everyone knows

that fleece isn't even comfortable until it's been washed a few times. The way I see it, Jasper and I did you a favor.'' Grinning madly, she whirled toward Samuel and gleefully hugged herself. "Look at him! Isn't he just the most perfect snowman you've ever seen in your life?''

Stuffing his hands in his pocket, Samuel angled a grumpy stare at the snowbeast with two triangular dog treats for eyes, a traditional carrot nose and the inked apple mouth. ''What, no freckles?''

Without so much as a blink, Ellie snapped her fingers. ''Ohmigosh, freckles. I almost forgot.''

Before Samuel could open his mouth to say that he was kidding, Ellie rushed toward the front porch and disappeared around the corner.

Puffing his cheeks, he blew out a breath, watched it condense into steam and waft toward the kitchen window, the lower sill of which was even with the four-foot snow base. He squatted, peered down into the kitchen and smiled. There in the middle of the kitchen floor, Daniel peered up from his cradle with huge, curious eyes. Samuel waved at the infant, who seemed excited by the movement.

Maybe Ellie was right, he mused. Maybe Daniel was an exceptional child. The baby certainly seemed to be interested in things that according to every book Samuel had ever read on the subject were well beyond the realm of the physiological and emotional development of a two-week-old infant. Certainly, the child was growing, thriving, gaining weight at a rate that seemed nothing less than miraculous considering how small and sickly he'd been at birth.

Samuel remembered the dark days immediately following the delivery, and how he'd carefully peeled and woven cedar boughs simply to keep his hands busy and his mind from dwelling on the gravity of the infant's condition.

For the first few days after Daniel's birth, Samuel hadn't expected the infant to live, had feared the cedar cradle he'd fashioned would become the baby's coffin. Instead it had become a second womb. Within hours of being nested on soft sheepskin, the tiny boy's breathing had eased and his color had improved. Samuel couldn't explain it. The change had been, well, magical.

A kink in his calf muscle forced him to stand. He stretched his leg, rotated his foot, was vaguely aware of a soft swishing sound behind him.

The snowball splattered against the back of his head. He gasped in surprise, spun around and saw Ellie about twenty feet away, grinning madly as she shaped another snow wad in her floppy gloved hands. "Prepare to defend yourself, infidel!"

Samuel stared foolishly as the next snowball exploded against his chest. He looked down at the icy globules clinging to his jacket, then focused on the woman who was doubled over with laughter. "You must have a death wish," he informed her.

She threw back her head and hooted. "The look on your face!"

"I'm pleased you're amused."

Still chortling, she scooped up more snow. "Arm yourself or perish," she taunted. "I don't fight fair."

"What a coincidence. Neither do I." Samuel pulled off one glove, extracted a lighter from his pants pocket. Ellie wound up her arm, preparing to heave another ball of packed snow. Samuel responded by flicking the flint with his thumb. A menacing flame whooshed up in front of Jasper's perennially grinning face. "Drop your weapon," he said lightly. "Or the snowman dies."

Ellie's arm froze in midair. "You wouldn't."

With an evil smile, Samuel brushed the flame close enough that a sweaty puddle oozed beneath the icy chin.

Her eyes widened in horror. "Murderer!"

Samuel shrugged, melted off a snow glob that might have been an ear.

With a horrified shriek, Ellie dropped her snowball, flung her hands in the air. "Stop, you win! Don't hurt him anymore."

Gloating, Samuel blew out the flame, spun the smoking lighter in his hand then stuffed it back into his pocket as if holstering a revolver. "I thought you might see it my way," he murmured as Ellie scurried over to repair the damage.

"You are evil," she muttered, slamming a fresh wad of snow against the wounded snowman's head. "And to think that I actually wanted my son to grow up just like you."

For some odd reason, Samuel's chest felt as though it was filled with warm pudding. "You did?"

She cast a perturbed glance over her shoulder. "I'm rethinking that now. You tortured my snowman." Her reproachful expression actually made him feel guilty. "And in front of Daniel, too."

Samuel's gaze skittered down through the window, where the bright-eyed infant lay cooing in his cradle. "I, ah, guess I wasn't thinking."

Ellie issued a haughty sniff as she patted the newly formed snow ear into place. "No, you certainly weren't."

"I'm sorry."

"Don't tell me, tell Jasper."

This was too ridiculous for words. "I am not going to apologize to a stupid pile of snow."

She shrugged. "Very well, but don't blame me for the consequence. Jasper is quite unhappy with you."

"I'm not too thrilled with him either," Samuel heard himself growl. "He stole my damned hat."

"He did not steal it, he borrowed it."

"Well, I want it back."

Heaving the long-suffering sigh that parents use with recalcitrant children, Ellie spun to face him, juggling her hands behind her back. "You'll get your hat back and your shirt, too."

"When?"

"When Jasper is through with them."

"And when will *that* be?"

"In the spring, of course." She flashed a flirty smile, yanked out Samuel's collar to dump a handful of snow down his sweater, then took off running while Samuel bellowed and stomped and flapped his arms like a drunken pelican.

"That was a present from Jasper," Ellie called from the safety of the front porch. "Just a friendly reminder that snowmen don't get mad, they get even."

With that she ducked out of view. The front door creaked open, slammed shut while Samuel hurriedly yanked out his shirttail to shake out the snow. He straightened, glared at the grinning snowman. "I want my hat back."

The snowman said nothing.

It suddenly occurred to him that he was not only talking to a snowman, he was actually waiting for a reply.

Feeling like the world's biggest fool, Samuel trudged back to the shed path muttering to himself. It wasn't his fault that he'd completely lost his mind. Two weeks with Ellie Malone would drive anyone nuts.

Chapter Five

"Look, Daniel, it's snowing." Shifting the infant against her shoulder, Ellie urged him to gaze out the living area window. "Ooh, big fat snowflakes. See how they swirl and sway, as if dancing with happiness." Head bobbling, Daniel blinked huge blue-gray eyes at the lazy white whirls while his mother crooned softly. "Snowflakes in the dark of night, bright as silver in their flight—" A loud baby burp abruptly ended the song. "Oh, fine," Ellie murmured, rubbing the infant's tiny back. "A music critic."

Samuel glanced up from the book he was reading. "It's a tough job but someone's got to do it."

"*Et tu,* Brutus? And here I thought you liked my singing."

"Whatever gave you that idea?" he asked wryly, although his eyes sparked with good humor.

"You never asked me to stop."

"Would it have done any good?"

"Of course not." She chuckled lightly, kissed Daniel's silky cheek. "Time for beddie-bye, snookums."

The couch creaked as Samuel shifted, absently brushed from a cushion the hairy remnants of Baloo's nap. "He doesn't look particularly sleepy."

"Maybe not, but I read somewhere that a predictable routine is very important for children. It comforts them."

Ellie gazed lovingly at her son's wide-eyed and curious little face. Although acknowledging a slight maternal bias, she was nonetheless convinced that Daniel was the most precious, most beautiful and certainly the most brilliant newborn on the entire planet. The redness of birthing had faded from a tiny face that had plumped nicely, with squirrely cheeks and fat folds demurely tucked beneath a dimpled baby chin. A few feathers of golden brown hair shadowed a dewy soft scalp, gathering in profusion around the delicate indentation at the apex of an otherwise perfectly round little skull.

He was perfect. He was gorgeous. He was hers.

And hers alone.

"Ellie?"

It took a moment for the sound of her name to sink in. When it did, she blinked up, saw Samuel's perplexed expression and realized that Daniel was fussing and squirming in arms that suddenly held him much too tightly.

Instantly she loosened her grip, pressed her cheek to his. "Was Mama squeezing you, sweet pea? Poor little precious."

"Are you all right?" Samuel asked her quietly.

"Sure." She managed a bright smile. "It's just that he's so darned huggable."

Samuel regarded her skeptically, but said nothing as

she hustled Daniel toward the kitchen. "Let's say nightie-night to Jasper, sweetie. Look, there he is!" She shifted the baby, gently waved his fragile little fist at the window, beyond which stood the stoic snowman with its maniacal apple grin. "Can you say nightie-night— Oh!"

The ceiling light flickered and brightened as a peculiar vibration crawled the cabin floor.

"Ohmigosh!" Clutching Daniel to her shoulder, Ellie spun around. It felt as if a helicopter had landed on the cabin roof. There's was no *chucka-chucka* sound, but the engine noise, the vibration—

Dear God, they had found her.

The metallic tang of terror flooded her mouth. "What is it? What's happening?"

Samuel flipped a page, replied without looking up. "The generator kicked on."

"The generator?" Clutching her son, Ellie rushed into the living room, eyes darting wildly. "What generator? I don't see a generator."

"It's outside, under the screen porch floor." He glanced up, startled by her distress. "There's nothing to worry about," he assured her. "Electricity for the lights and well pump comes from industrial-size batteries in a compartment under the cabin. There's a master control that monitors power levels, and automatically turns on the generator when the batteries need to be charged."

"How come I haven't heard it before?"

He shrugged. "It only comes on once or twice a week at most. Half the time I don't notice it myself."

"Oh." Relieved but still unnerved by her initial fright, Ellie tucked Daniel into the cradle, took a moment to gather her thoughts. Behind her, Samuel was watching, wondering. She could feel his suspicious gaze on the back of her neck. Fear could give her away. She had to control herself, control her terror. "Nightie-night, precious," she murmured. "Sweet dreams."

Ellie took a calming breath, licked her lips, then straightened to face Samuel with the brightest smile she could muster. "So, we run on batteries around here. Clever."

A wary glitter sharpened his gaze. "My father was an inventor of sorts. The cookstove, fridge and porch freezer all use propane, but we needed electricity for the well pump and a few lights. When the power company refused to string lines this far into the wilderness, Pop engineered his own solution."

"He sounds like a brilliant man," Ellie chirped in a voice that was much too cheery for the circumstance. "That must be where you inherited your own cleverness. I mean, weaving cradles, creating baby powder from pantry supplies, turning sheets into diapers. Wow, I am really impressed, really, really, impressed." Her frantic gaze settled on the book in his hands. "Still reading about real-estate law, hmm? That's impressive, too. Tough job. All that showing and selling, then thousand-page contracts with print so tiny you need the Hubble Telescope to read it. Why do you want to be a Realtor, anyway? And what about all those other books on mechanical drafting and financial management and—"

Thankfully, the need for breath cut off her uncontrollable ramble. She filled her lungs desperately, noisily, while her head swam and her heart pounded her rib cage as if seeking escape.

Samuel sat on the sofa, watching. Waiting.

Ellie's trademark smile froze into a grimace. She stared into Samuel's cool eyes, and her breath backed into her throat, choking her. He knew. Dear God, he knew.

Closing the book, Samuel stood, regarded her for a moment. "Good night," he said quietly, then turned off the gooseneck reading lamp, climbed the ladder and disappeared into the loft.

Ellie stumbled to the window, stared out at the falling snow. And she wept.

By noon the next day Samuel had nearly completed shoveling a path to the shed, his pace quickened by news that a new storm would descend by nightfall. Ellie watched from the back porch, her fingers scratching a nervous rhythm on the rough screening. "How about taking a break?" she called out. "I've made a fresh pot of coffee and whipped up a nice tuna salad for lunch."

A perceptible stiffness in his shoulders revealed that he'd heard her, but he kept shoveling.

"I even made pudding for dessert. Butterscotch. Of course, I've never made pudding with dried milk crystals before so the results might be kind of iffy, but—"

She bit her lip as he straightened and gazed over his shoulder with cool dispassion. "Maybe later," he said.

"You can't work without nourishment." The feeble argument fell on deaf ears. Samuel was already shoveling again.

Ellie returned to the kitchen, stored lunch in the fridge, then sat at the table, brooding about her next move. All morning she had repeatedly tried to slow Samuel's progress, but he simply would not be distracted. Whatever was in that shed—and when questioned, Samuel only itemized diesel fuel and tools for the generator—he was clearly determined to reach it. Today.

It was that very determination that disturbed Ellie.

That, along with the fact that he hadn't been able to look her in the eye all morning.

A cranky cry from the cradle indicated that at least one person around here was ready for lunch. Ellie was happy to oblige.

After Daniel had been fed, changed and put down for a nap, Ellie went to check Samuel's progress, and saw the path had been cleared all the way to the shed door, which now stood open. There was a flash of movement inside the shed. Samuel emerged with what appeared to be a couple of odd-looking tennis rackets tucked under his arm.

Ellie first frowned, then gasped in recognition. Snowshoes. He was carrying snowshoes.

Ignoring the blustery cold, she dashed outside without a jacket, met Samuel halfway up the path. His gaze hesitated, skipped over her shoulder to settle on a peak visible beyond a distant dip in the treed terrain. "You'd best get back inside," he said. "The temperature's dropping."

The chill had little to do with the convulsive tremors skittering down her spine. "Where are you going?" she whispered. When he didn't reply, she followed his gaze, recognized the faint outline of a wooden structure jutting above the trees. "The fire tower?"

He nodded. "I won't be gone long. A couple hours at the most."

She clutched his arm. "No, please. I mean, what if the storm moves in sooner than expected? It's too dangerous and besides, there's no reason for you to go, no reason at all."

Samuel's gaze shifted to her grasping fingers, lifted to settle on her face. A shadow darkened his eyes, the only indication that he was troubled. "The tower has a two-way radio,'' he said matter-of-factly. ''You might have to wait another day or so for the rescue chopper depending on the weather, but with any luck you and Daniel will be back home by the end of the week.''

''No!'' Ellie saw him flinch as she dug her nails into the sleeve of his jacket and forcibly loosened her grip. ''I mean, Daniel and I don't really have a home, at least not at the moment. My job at the lodge was just temporary, after all, and it's not like anyone is looking for us.'' Her laugh was high-pitched, frantic. ''Besides, we have everything we need right here. Daniel is thriving, and I know I haven't exactly been carrying my weight, but I will, I promise. I'll keep the cabin clean as a whistle, and I'll cook all your meals—''

She paused for breath as Samuel covered her convulsive fingers with his own gloved had. ''Ellie, you don't have to—''

''I'll even help you keep the paths shoveled,'' she blurted, unwilling to listen. ''I'm stronger than I look. I can chop firewood, too, you just wait and see. I'll keep the woodpile so high you'll need a ladder to reach the top—''

''Ellie, stop it.'' Dropping the snowshoes, Samuel grasped her shoulders with a gentle shake. ''Calm down.''

''I am calm,'' she babbled wildly. ''I'm perfectly calm, and I'm perfectly happy, and Daniel's perfectly happy so I don't see why you're so anxious to get rid of us, but if you want us to leave, we'll go, only you don't have to call anyone to come get us, we'll just get up and go, and, and...'' The foolish words condensed in the frosty air like frozen mist. Ellie swayed, saw shock in Samuel's eyes and realized that he thought her mad.

For an instant, she wondered if he was right. She

must be mad even to suggest snatching up a newborn infant and dashing through wilderness in the dead of winter. "I didn't mean that," she murmured, rubbing her head. "You know I didn't mean that."

His eyes flashed. "Didn't you?"

Ellie remembered the stormy afternoon she'd stumbled onto the cabin porch, half-frozen and nearly dead because she'd charged off in a blind panic without thought or reason. No wonder Samuel didn't believe her, didn't trust her. She wasn't certain she trusted herself.

Run. That's all she could think of when cornered, when faced by an obstacle that seemed too huge to overcome. Run. Escape. Get away.

But it wasn't just her now. Ellie had a child to think about, a helpless infant who needed her.

A trembling hand touched her mouth. It was her own hand. Turning away, Ellie bit her lip, felt hope drain away as if it were melting show. If she couldn't stop Samuel now, if she couldn't keep him from reaching that fire tower and calling for help, all that was precious to her would be lost forever.

He spoke softly, in a voice tinged more with concern than anger. "What is it, Ellie, what are you running from?"

Fear bubbled up like bitter bile. Desperate, she faced him, turned the question around, and clubbed him with it. "What about you, Samuel? Why does a man leave his job, his home and hole up like a hibernating squirrel in the middle of a frozen wilderness?" He vibrated as though struck, stumbled back a step, but Ellie was too frantic to care. "So you first, Samuel. Tell me what *you* are running from, then maybe we'll talk."

The most profound sadness flickered across his eyes, a grief so exquisite that it took Ellie's breath away.

Without a word, Samuel retrieved the snowshoes, hiked up the ridge of shoveled show and bent to fasten the woven, skilike objects to his boots. Behind him, Ellie called his name, but he blocked out the sound of her voice. Her words evoked memories that sickened him, scraped him raw inside.

"Samuel, please." The voice was closer now, sharp with panic. "I shouldn't have said that. I'm so sorry. *Samuel!*" It was a scream. "Don't go." It was a whisper.

A desperate whisper that turned him like a touch.

She was on her knees in the snow, only a few feet away from him. Her face was bloodless, her brown eyes huge with terror. She extended her arm, stiffly reaching, fingers straining to touch him, to touch safety, to touch life. The nightmare sprang to life, spinning through his mind.

Dark eyes. A reaching hand. A plea for help.

"Please, don't go," Ellie begged. "I'll tell you everything, I swear to God I will. Please, please, don't do this to me."

Samuel reached out, felt her fingers brush his gloved palm, then slip away.

Not again, he thought wildly. *Never again.*

Lurching forward, he collapsed on his knees directly in front of her, pulled her into his arms. She clung to him, trembling, sobbing uncontrollably.

"Hold on tight, honey." Samuel smoothed her tangled hair, tensed his body against the pull of a current that existed only in his mind. "We'll get out of this, I promise we will, just hang on. Don't let go," he whispered. "No matter what happens, don't ever let go."

Slumped at the kitchen table, Ellie felt numb and defeated. She closed her eyes, listened to the comforting cabin sounds. The strong scrape of Samuel's boots on the rough pine floor. The soothing gurgle of pouring liquid, a tinny rasp as the metal coffeepot scraped the iron burner. The cabin had become Ellie's refuge, a special place where the outside world and all of its pain was nothing more than a dim memory. She'd felt safe here. Protected. Cherished.

Now that would all change.

Samuel set a mug of steaming coffee in front of her, seated himself across the table. He studied her, watching as she sniffed, raked fingers through her tangled hair, grasped the ceramic mug to warm her icy hands.

Moistening her lips, she murmured her thanks, took a sip of coffee, then another. It was bitter. Samuel still hadn't figured out how to get the percolation temperature right. Across the table, he waited without comment until Ellie shuddered once, set the coffee down, stared into the mug hoping the answers she sought would be magically reflected in the swirling black brew.

They weren't. "I don't know where to begin," she said finally.

An awkward silence followed. Samuel shifted in his chair, cocked an ankle atop his knee and folded his arms loosely. Displaying no visible impatience, he simply waited.

After another sip of bracing, bitter coffee, Ellie took a deep breath. "I used to work for an insurance company. Actually I worked for several. Insurance is a cutthroat business, you know? People clawing their way up the ladder of success, trampling on anyone who gets in their way. I hate that." What she hated was the unpleasantness, the confrontation. "Life is too short for all that hostility, don't you think?"

She chanced a furtive glance, saw that his expression hadn't changed. Heaving a sigh, she propped her chin on one hand, ran the index finger of her other hand around the coffee mug rim. "Anyway, I'd just started a new job at a private insurance office. The people were happy, friendly folks—most of them were related to each other—and I just loved the relaxed atmosphere. We were always playing pranks on each other. Someone once put green dye in the hand-soap dispenser. That was a real hoot. Nobody ever got angry, though, not even when the boss hid an ugly rubber spider in the copier."

Ellie cut off the story, avoided Samuel's knowing stare. He wasn't smiling; he wasn't frowning. He was just regarding her with those piercing blue eyes that penetrated a person's soul, and laid private thoughts bare. He understood her well, she thought, and was not cheered by the realization.

"Talk all you want," he said quietly. "We both have plenty of time, and I figure you'll get around to the meat of the matter when you're ready."

Ellie flinched. Oh, he knew her, all right, had recognized her tendency to use unrelated jabber as a stalling tactic. That wasn't going to work with Samuel. He'd sit there until spring thaw, if necessary, but he wasn't going to let Ellie leave that chair until she'd told him everything.

Everything.

"There was a park across from my office," she said dully. "I jogged through it on my lunch hours. That's where I met Stanton."

A flicker of interest brightened Samuel's eyes. "Stanton?"

"Stanton Mackenzie." Suddenly exhausted, Ellie rolled her head, rotated her stiff shoulders, resisted the urge to lay her head on the table. "Politically connected president of a Sacramento computer-components firm, deacon of his church and upstanding pillar of the community. Of course at the time I thought he was just another fast-track yuppie on a fitness kick, but he had a wonderful sense of humor and we, well—'' Ellie studied a blemish in the oak table, gathered her thoughts. "We hit it off," she finished finally.

Samuel waited a moment, leaned forward to prop his forearms on the table. "What do you mean, politically connected?"

"His brother-in-law is one of the governor's aides."

"I see." He shifted back in the chair, drummed his fingers on his thigh. "So you and this Mackenzie started dating?"

She nodded. "It was casual, friendly stuff. Dinner, movies, the occasional Saturday at the beach. Neither one of us was looking for a serious relationship, so from my perspective, our friendship was perfect."

"But there came a time when it became not so perfect?"

"Yes." She raked her hair again, caught her fingers in a tangle. "I must look a wreck," she murmured, ineffectually trying to smooth the ruffled mess.

"What happened?"

"The snow got it, then the wind blew it into a mass of knots—"

"What happened with Mackenzie?"

"Oh." She'd known exactly what he meant. "I honestly don't know. One day we were laughing, making plans for a trip to an amusement park, then Stanton disappeared for a couple of weeks, and when he showed up again, he gazed at me as if I was the only roast beef sandwich at a picnic filled with starving men." Twitching nervously, Ellie scoured the hapless oak blemish with her thumbnail. "Before I could blink, I was being seriously wooed. Red roses on my desk and doorstep. Romantic dinners at restaurants with French names I couldn't begin to pronounce. Fancy hotel suites, with champagne and dipped strawberries. We, ah…'' She couldn't meet Samuel's eyes. "We became lovers.''

She chanced a look, saw his eyes warmed with understanding and a touch of sadness. "You were both adults,'' he said quietly. "It happens.''

"Yes,'' she murmured, swallowing a lump. "It happens.''

He nodded sagely, gave no hint of reproach or disapproval. "Somehow, I never did quite buy off on the artificial-insemination theory.''

A slow heat crawled up her throat. "I deliberately deceived you. I'm sorry.''

That didn't seem to be news to Samuel, although he didn't dwell on it. "Were you in love with him?''

"Stanton? Yes, I was.'' The edge in her voice took them both by surprise. "I didn't want to be. It just happened.''

"And Daniel, did he just happen, too?''

Ellie flinched. "Yes. That's not to say that I don't adore him. Daniel is the best thing in my life,'' she said fiercely. "I may not have planned to get pregnant, I may have even been scrupulous about using protection in the fear that I *would* get pregnant, but the moment I learned that I carried a life in my womb, everything changed. I wanted my baby. I wanted him more than I wanted my next breath.''

A warm palm covered hers as Samuel reached across the table. "You're a wonderful mother, Ellie. I never had a moment's doubt about your love for your son.''

Moisture gathered in her eyes, blurring his features. He was so infinitely kind, so dear, so very different from the man who had fathered her son.

When Samuel spoke again, his voice was edgy. "I

presume that this Stanton character was not as thrilled by the pregnancy as you were.''

Sucking in a breath, Ellie withdrew her hand from Samuel's comforting grasp and shook her head. ''On the contrary, he was absolutely elated. The first thing he did was make me an appointment with the best obstetrician in town and drive me there himself. He bought me tons of prenatal vitamins, called me six times a day to make sure I was eating properly, getting enough exercise, and generally taking care of myself. The only thing he didn't do—'' her voice caught ''—was be with me.''

Clearly, Samuel was surprised by that. He leaned back, his brow furrowed, his mouth grim. ''Are you saying that there was no further sexual activity after you became pregnant?''

''Nothing beyond a chaste kiss. It was almost as if he was relieved that a burdensome chore had been eliminated. I was hurt,'' she admitted. ''And confused.''

''I can see why.'' Samuel rubbed his face with his palms, peered over the fingertips. ''So this Stanton character wooed you, seduced you, was elated by your pregnancy, but he never once mentioned the word *marriage*.''

Ellie gave a limp shrug. ''He couldn't.''

''Why not?''

Tears spurted again, infuriating her. She angrily wiped them away. ''He couldn't marry me because he was already married.'' Ellie heaved a sigh, took a gulp of cooled coffee and ignored the hard stare Samuel was giving her. ''Please, don't look at me like that. I didn't know.'' She set the cup down, avoided his gaze. ''I found out when my boss invited me for lunch at a fancy restaurant. Stanton was there with a beautiful blonde. My boss was delighted. Seems he knew both Stanton and his wife from their chamber of commerce activities, and he couldn't wait to hustle me over for an introduction. Stanton was not pleased to see me, of course, and since up until then I hadn't a clue he was married, I wasn't particularly pleased myself.''

Samuel shrugged his lips, widened his eyes. ''No, I don't suppose you were.''

Ellie set the mug down with enough force to slosh its contents, dismissed the pity in Samuel's eyes with a flick of her wrist. ''Stanton called later that afternoon. I told him I wanted nothing to do with him, and he laughed at me. *Laughed*. He said I was carrying his child, and there was nothing on earth that could keep him out of my life. I thought he was crazy.'' Her lips quivered helplessly. ''But he wasn't crazy. He meant every word. I knew I was in trouble when I received the papers.''

That got Samuel's attention. ''Papers?''

Trembling uncontrollably, Ellie fisted her hands in her lap. ''A bunch of legal mumbo jumbo, the crux of which was that I would get a whole bunch of money if I gave up all rights to our child. I refused, of course, so Stanton came to see me. He admitted that because his wife was barren, he'd deliberately enticed me into an affair, then somehow managed to sabotage my birth control. He kept saying that I was young, that I could have more children, but this was his only chance. He cried. He begged. He pleaded. I kept refusing. Finally, he stood up, gave me a smile that turned my blood to ice, and said that he'd see me in court. The next day I got a summons. Stanton was suing me for sole custody of our child.''

Samuel's eyes glinted, his clamped lips were white with fury. He unballed a fist, regarded his flexing fingers as if seeing them for the first time.

"I was beside myself," Ellie said simply. "I went to a lawyer, who simply shrugged and said that the Mackenzies were rich enough and powerful enough to win. I didn't have the money to fight them."

Samuel took a steadying breath, stared her straight in the eye. "What did you do then?"

She returned his stare without flinching. "I did what I always do when things go wrong. I ran away."

"But he found you, didn't he?" Samuel leaned forward, touched her chin when she tried to turn away. "And after he found you, you ran away again, into the woods. That's how you ended up here."

A tear ran down her cheek, shifting course with her mute nod.

Samuel stood so quickly his chair fell over. He paced the kitchen, rubbing his temples, his face grim. Stopping, he looked over his shoulder. "Do you think Mackenzie is still looking for you?"

"I know he is," Ellie whispered, then pushed away from the table and burst into tears. "He'll never give up, never. Oh, God, Samuel, he's going to take my son away."

"No, he's not." Samuel lifted Ellie to her feet, hugged her fiercely. "I won't let him."

For a brief, sweet moment, Ellie almost believed him.

Chapter Six

Samuel cradled Ellie in his arms, stroking her hair, murmuring softly until her tears dried into his sweater. A ball of pure fury wedged into his gut. Ellie had been betrayed in the cruelest possible way by a man she'd loved, a man she'd believed had loved her. It had all been a lie, a deliberate deception so vile that even Samuel, who had spent years viewing the tattered remnants of violence people inflicted upon each other, was shocked.

Deep down he didn't want to believe Ellie's story, didn't want to believe that anyone could be capable of the sick abuse she'd described. But he'd seen genuine terror in her eyes, and a depth of sorrow that had shaken him to the core. He couldn't *not* believe her.

Tucked inside his protective embrace, she melted against him, all warm and quivery and soft. Then she shifted slightly, as if preparing to step away. Samuel tensed, held her tighter, reluctant to relinquish the fragile bond of trust between them. It was more than trust. It was an emotional joining, a dependence. A need.

Need. The word circled in his mind, spurted adrenaline straight to a jittering heart. Samuel feared being needed. More precisely, he feared his own inability to meet that need. He feared failure.

Loosening his grasp, he moved his hands to her shoulders, widened his stance as cool air rushed to fill the widening gap between them. Ellie shivered, sniffed, wiped her wet face with the back of her hand. "I'm okay," she murmured, although she clearly wasn't. He pulled out a chair, waited until she'd seated herself before bringing her a glass of water. She drank greedily, licked her lips, tried to smile. "You're so good to me."

"It's about time someone was." Regretting his sharpness when her expression crumpled, he exhaled slowly, recalled the photo he'd seen in her wallet and forced a gentle tone. "You have no family at all?"

Ellie's gaze skittered with guilt. "My parents live back East," she murmured. "But that's the first place Stanton would look for me. Besides, I don't want my son learning to greet every problem by tossing a melodramatic hand over his forehead and wailing, 'Aye, so much pain!'"

A simultaneous demonstration was theatrical enough to have been amusing under different circumstances, but neither Ellie nor Samuel were in a joking mood. Dropping her hand back to her lap, Ellie chewed her lip, gazed toward the cradle. "Don't get me wrong. I love my parents, and I know they love me, but they come with built-in guilt tentacles that snare a person's spirit and suck out the joy."

"So you don't get along with your folks?" The

thought saddened Samuel, who cherished his own parents with godlike reverence.

"We get along well enough. We just don't see things the same way." She sighed, rubbed the back of her neck. "I enjoy life."

"I've noticed." A grinning snowman outside the kitchen window bore mute testimony to that philosophy. "I presume your parents don't share your fun-loving nature."

She shrugged. "They have no sense of humor. Everything is a crisis to them."

"Some things really *are* a crisis, Ellie."

"I know that."

"You can't always run away from your problems." He squatted by her chair, sandwiched her fragile hands between his large palms. "Sometimes you have to face them head on."

"I'm not afraid of a fight." The statement was shaky, unconvincing. "At least, not a fair fight, but I can't win this, Samuel, and I'm not going to lose my son."

"No, you're not." It was an irresponsible assurance, he supposed, although he meant it from the bottom of his heart. Having saved both Ellie and her precious child from the icy jaws of death, Samuel had no intention of allowing them to be separated by the coldhearted cad whose cruelty had nearly destroyed them both. "You can't hide here forever, Ellie."

She glanced away, her lips clamped and colorless. "Just a few more weeks, until the roads are passable. Then maybe you could drive us somewhere, anywhere.... I'd pay you. I have money in the bank."

"It's not a question of money." Releasing Ellie's hands, Samuel stood, squeezed his nape and paced the small kitchen until Baloo wandered in to investigate the creaking floorboards. The dog eyed his somber master, then wisely returned to the comfort of his bed.

Samuel continued to mull possibilities in his mind. Running wasn't the answer. He knew it as surely as he knew his own name, yet he couldn't dismiss Ellie's fear of losing Daniel. This Mackenzie character was the child's biological father. If he was as wealthy and powerful as Ellie described, the courts would be impressed. Add to that the stability of a long-term marriage, and the ability to provide a two-parent home compared with a single mother barely able to make ends meet and the Mackenzies had a definite advantage.

"Samuel..." Standing now, Ellie braced herself against the table as if fearing her knees would buckle. "All I need is some time, just a little time. Please, can you give me that?"

The plea in her eyes broke his heart. He reached out, stroked her hair with his knuckle. "Yes, I can give you that," he whispered, and was surprised by a flood by relief. Deep down, he realized that he'd never wanted her to leave, not really. Ellie and Daniel had complicated his life, but they'd also brought him immeasurable joy.

They needed him. Need. He repeated the word in his mind; for once, it didn't frighten him.

That evening Ellie cooked venison meat loaf in a round cake pan, adding embellishment from a tube of squeeze cheese discovered behind a half-empty cracker box in the crowded pantry.

Samuel sat down to his meal, and found himself face-to-cheesy-face with a grinning meat loaf that bore suspicious resemblance to mysterious, smiling apparitions that appeared on the bathroom mirror after a steamy shower. Apparently Ellie had stumbled across the bottle of liquid defroster he used on his truck windows. The cartoonish creatures were harmless enough, and oddly amusing, although he'd certainly never admit that out loud. He did, however, look forward to his showers for no other reason than to view her newest creations. Ellie was nothing if not imaginative.

Now Samuel sliced the happy meat loaf without comment, served it with the protective dispassion of a man for whom emotion had become synonymous with pain. But deep inside, tucked away in a secret corner of his heart, a silent smile spread with healing warmth.

Initially Samuel had considered Ellie's constant cheerfulness to be the gift of a life untouched by sadness. How wrong that presumption had been. She'd suffered unspeakable sadness, endured the depth of deceit and betrayal heinous enough to destroy most people. But Ellie Malone wasn't most people. She hadn't been destroyed. Certainly she was frightened, terrified, even devastated, yet her inner joy had somehow survived.

Samuel didn't understand that, although he admired it, admired her. He was, in fact, intensely drawn to Ellie, to her vibrancy and enthusiasm, to her gleeful embrace of life, and the way she savored each delicious moment as if it were a gift of chocolate.

Beyond that, Samuel also felt a visceral connection to little Daniel with whom he had emotionally bonded from the moment of birth. Daniel was the child of his heart; Samuel loved him with frightening ferocity.

All of which was perfectly natural, he supposed, given the circumstance of proximity and interdependence. At least, that's what his rational mind insisted. His heart had other ideas.

Ellie's infectious humor had nourished Samuel's soul, enriched his life beyond measure. Every time he gazed into those dark, laughing eyes, every time the cabin vibrated with impulsive song, every time a cartoon appeared on a frosty windowpane or a happy-faced grin livened a meal, Samuel could almost forget past failure, and the trauma that had driven him to this isolated wilderness.

For those brief and shining moments, Samuel Evans was a happy man.

An icy sweep of February air rushed through as he ducked into the cabin, hunched forward with one arm cradling his midriff beneath the unlined leather. Baloo shot inside to prance worried circles around his master's legs, wailing mournfully and pawing the leather hem of Samuel's bulging jacket.

Ellie dropped the broom, hurried over as Samuel kicked the door shut with a grunt. "My God, what's wrong, are you hurt?" The frantic questions died on her lips as Samuel twisted awkwardly, withdrew his hidden hand to reveal a melon-size ball of fur sporting spiky, tufted ears. "Ooh, it's a bunny rabbit."

Baloo swung his head around, splashed a wet, lolling grin and gave an agreeable bark.

"'Loo found him." Samuel shrugged one arm out of the jacket, allowed Ellie to tug off the second sleeve after he'd gently transferred the terrified rabbit to his other hand. "It was trapped under a fallen branch."

After hanging the jacket on a peg, Ellie took a closer look at the tiny grayish white creature huddled in Samuel's gentle hands. A crimson smear stained its hindquarters. "Oh, the poor little thing is hurt."

"I figure he must have been grazing buck brush when the branch snapped in the wind, pinned his rear leg against a rock."

"Will he be all right?"

"I don't know." Samuel shrugged, headed to the kitchen table. "Do we have something to lay him on?"

Ellie ducked into the bathroom, returned with a fluffy blue bath towel that she folded into a soft pad in the middle of the table.

"There you go, little guy," Samuel murmured, nesting the trembling creature on the makeshift bunny bed. "Now, let's take a look at you." He frowned, continued to murmur softly as he examined the rabbit's hindquarters. "Bruising, swelling, some skin abrasion—" he probed with gentle fingers "—obvious soft tissue damage. No overt evidence of fracture, but he made no attempt to hop away when I moved the branch off him, so I've got to assume that his ability to use the leg has been severely compromised."

Ellie's gaze was riveted not on the bunny, but on the tender touch of the man who was tending it. Long, slender fingers, incredibly sensual, glided across the fragile furred creature with breathtaking ease, competent, knowledgeable, yet so achingly kind a lump raised in her throat. She remembered what it felt like, those knowing hands sliding across her own quivering skin, gentling her fear, soothing her pain, evoking the same trust she now saw in the frightened creature's eyes.

She remembered, and her heart quickened in response.

"Get down," Samuel muttered, popping the sensual image from Ellie's mind. Baloo dutifully hopped off a chair to sit dejectedly at his master's feet.

Before Ellie's pulse had slowed appreciably, Samuel's warm fingers slipped over hers, causing another spike in her palpitating heart rate. "Just keep him calm," he said, placing her hand over the rabbit's shivering body. "I'll get the med kit."

As he left the kitchen, Ellie stroked the animal's silky

fur, felt the frenetic stutter of its tiny heart. "It's all right, Snowdrift." She felt an empathetic kinship with the wounded animal. "You couldn't be in better hands."

"Snowdrift?" Samuel laid the plastic case on the table, muffled the snap with his hand so the sound wouldn't startle his skittish patient. "My brother and I once found a baby squirrel in the woods. Mom allowed us to take it in and nurse it back to health, but she wouldn't let us name it. She said it was God's creature, not ours." He retrieved a bottle of antiseptic, several tongue depressors and a roll of adhesive tape from the case and laid them beside the blue towel bunny bed. "Well, I was kind of an obstinate kid. I figured what the heck, God was too busy to notice one baby squirrel in a whole world full of critters, so I secretly christened the little fellow."

Ellie watched, smiling, as Samuel soaked a cotton ball with antiseptic and gently cleaned the animal's abrasions. "And what did you call your squirrel?"

"Fuzzy."

A snort of tickled laughter escaped. "Fuzzy? Oh, good grief."

He looked stung. "What's wrong with that?"

"It lacks a certain creativity, don't you think?"

"I was six years old."

"Well, in that case I'll cut you some slack."

"Thanks." Frowning, Samuel tossed the cotton ball aside, reached for a tube of ointment. "Anyway, the day we turned that squirrel loose was the day I finally understood why my mother hadn't wanted us to name him. While my big brother waved happily and hollered, 'Bye, squirrel,' I was bawling my eyes out screaming, 'Come back, Fuzzy. Come back.' It was pitiful, just pitiful."

"Oh, c'mon."

"It's the gospel truth."

"It's a pile of badger droppings and you know it." Suppressing a snort of tickled laughter, Ellie clutched her hands as if in prayer and launched into a comical parody. "Come back, Fuzzy, come back. Timmy fell down a well and you have to run get help! You'll be a hero, Fuzzy. They'll hang an itsy-bitsy medal around your neck and give you your very own TV show."

Samuel skewered her with a look. "Have you always been this cynical?"

"No, it's a relatively recent acquisition." She chuckled, handed him a gauze pad, noted the faint flush crawling up his earlobes. And quite attractive earlobes they were. "Truth time. There was never any Fuzzy, was there?"

Avoiding her gaze, Samuel completed dressing the rabbit's abrasions, turned his attention to creating a bunny-size splint out of the tongue depressors. "Would you cut a few adhesive strips for me? Three of them, about four inches long."

Ellie complied with a smug smile. She recognized an avoidance tactic when she saw one. "Well, Fuzzy or no Fuzzy, I'm naming this little fellow Snowdrift, so what do you say to that?"

"I say—" he paused to secure the tiny splint with one of the adhesive strips "—that when this bunny finally hops back into the woods under his own steam, you're going to be bawling on the front porch, and you'll wish you hadn't let yourself love him."

Sobered by a wistful catch in his voice, Ellie angled a glance upward and saw reverence in Samuel's eyes. And she saw pain.

Then he blinked and it was gone, replaced by a satisfied glow. "There you go, bunny. A couple weeks of bed rest and you'll be good as new." He stroked the animal's head with a fingertip, then lifted it gently and laid it in Ellie's arms.

"Where are you going?"

"I'll be right back," he mumbled, then headed out the back door.

An insistent whine caught her attention as Baloo placed his front paws on the table to sniff the interesting creature nested in Ellie's arms. "First me, now a wounded bunny. You're quite the rescue hound, aren't you, boy?" Baloo barked happily, swished his tail so fast his bony butt vibrated. "Maybe you're the one who deserves his own TV series." She flinched as a drippy tongue flopped out of the grinning muzzle. "On the other hand, maybe not. Ooh, calm down, Snowdrift. You're okay," Ellie whispered to the wriggling rabbit. "Baloo just wants to be friendly, that's all."

The silky little animal gazed up with moist dark eyes, twitched a velvet gray nose.

"You are just adorable," she told it. "And I don't care what Samuel says, I think Snowdrift suits you perfectly."

But as she spoke, Samuel's warning circled her mind. *You'll wish you hadn't let yourself love him.* A nervous weight settled in the pit of her stomach. It was a bittersweet prophecy, one that had come too late. But Ellie wasn't thinking of the sweet furred animal cradled in her arms; she was thinking of Stanton Mackenzie.

In twenty-six years of living, Ellie had never allowed herself to love anyone. Then she'd met Stanton, been swept into an affair both deceptive, cruel, yet she couldn't allow herself to regret it without regretting the issue of that relationship—her beloved son.

Daniel was the core of her universe now, the most precious person in her life. Ellie despised Stanton, despised the lies, despised what he was trying to do to her and to their child. But as much as Ellie regretted the nature of their relationship, she could never regret the precious result, a beautiful son to cherish and protect, even from the man who had fathered him.

The back door bumped open. Samuel backed inside carrying a good-size cage. "It's a 'coon trap," he explained, setting the cage on the table. "My father used it when raccoons raided the root cellar." He levered up the spring-loaded door, clipped it open with a snap secured to the top wire so he could arrange the blue towel inside.

Ellie eyed a peculiar spouted bottle hanging upside down inside the cage. "What on earth is that?"

"A hamster tube. I found it in a box of my brother's stuff out in the shed." Samuel unhooked the bottle, filled it in the sink. "Rory was big on gerbils. He must have raised three dozen of them."

"Rory is your brother, right?"

"Right."

Ellie had always wished for a sibling. "It sounds like you had a good relationship with him."

"He was a pain in the butt." The reply was startling, but issued with good humor. Samuel snugged the filled bottle inside the cage. "Rory was four years older, so he always got to do the fun stuff, like stay up late and go the park with his friends. I hated being left behind, hated the way he gloated that rank had privilege. As soon as I was old enough, I got even."

Reluctantly relinquishing the bewildered bunny, Ellie stood back as Samuel gently placed the diminutive animal inside its temporary home. "Dare I ask how you managed that? Getting even, that is."

"Hmm?" Samuel rubbed a fingertip between the rabbit's ears before lowering the spring-loaded closure mechanism. "Oh, I became my brother's shadow. If he went to the park, I went to the park. If he went to play baseball, I hung on the sidelines to laugh when he struck out. And when he went on his first date, I was in the movie line right behind him making kissy sounds until his face was red as a tomato. Say, would you get some of those newspapers from the screen porch?"

Ellie complied without comment, spread the newspapers beneath the wire-floored cage in that quiet corner of the living area. "Sounds to me like you were more of a pain to Rory than the other way around."

"That's what kid brothers are for. Making Rory miserable became my life's vocation. I was good at it, too." Samuel placed the cage on the newspapers, crouched to watch the confused rabbit hobble on its splinted leg to sniff out its new surroundings. "He'll need food. I'll gather buck brush leaves, and some other evergreens that rabbits graze in winter."

"There are carrots in the root cellar. I could chop one up for him."

"He might like that."

Baloo arrived at the cage site. The animal circled, sniffing madly, then came nose to twitchy nose with the caged bunny. The bunny scuffled backward. Baloo offered a helpful bark. The bunny spun on its splint, emitted a frantic squeal.

Samuel tugged on the old hound's collar. "You're scaring him, 'Loo." Baloo whined once, heaved a rejected sigh, then lumbered over to curl up in his bed for a well-earned nap. Samuel stood, rubbed the small of his back. "I'll start dinner."

"I've already started it."

"You don't have to cook every meal, Ellie."

"I like to cook." A flick of her wrist dismissed his protest. "We're sharing chores, remember?"

He frowned like a man unused to sharing anything. "You aren't nesting, are you?"

"Nesting?" Ellie laughed, shook her head. "Dang, you caught me. I've been fighting this overwhelming urge to shred newspapers, but decided to make tuna casserole instead." An image of gingham curtains brightening the rustic windows instantly flattened her smile. Maybe Samuel's observation wasn't so far off the mark after all. Ellie was comfortable here. She felt safe, far removed from the outside world and its dangers. In the five weeks since her arrival, the homey cabin with knotty pine walls had become her sanctuary.

It had become her home.

Twisting the hem of her borrowed flannel shirt, Ellie turned away, shifted uncomfortably. "Dinner will be ready in half an hour," she murmured, still trying to shake the gingham curtain thing. "Why don't you, ah, read or something?"

She could feel his perceptive gaze on the back of her head as surely as if those cool blue eyes were boring into her skull, reading her thoughts. Seeing the gingham.

All he said was, "Okay." Boots scuffled. The couch creaked. Ellie exhaled, couldn't stop herself from picturing a braided rag rug in front of the rustic woodstove. Earth tones would be particularly cozy. And fat clay pot, terra-cotta, with a few dried dogwood twigs. Some bayberry clusters for color. A couple of cushy throw pillows for reclining in front of the fire to relax in each other's arms. Her head on Samuel's shoulder, his lips brushing her hair, her face, her throat. Those long, healing fingers caressing her breasts, moving down to her bare thighs— She groaned at the sensual image.

"What's the matter?"

"Hmm?" Ellie glanced over her shoulder, met Samuel's suspicious gaze. Her voice squeaked like a startled mouse. "Nothing, why?"

"You groaned."

"Groaned? Me?" A high-pitched laugh bubbled like madness between her lips. "Heavens, no, not me, uh-uh, absolutely no groaning. My stomach must have growled, that's all. I'm totally famished. Are you? Famished, that is. What are you reading, that real-estate stuff again? The way you're studying, one would think you're preparing for some kind of a test. Are you? Studying for a test, that is. I could understand if real estate was, well, interesting. I suppose it *is* interesting to a Realtor, but you're not a Realtor. Unless you're planning on becoming a Realtor, which would explain why you spend so much time reading stuff boring enough to suck your eyeballs dry. Unless you really like it, but you don't seem to. Like it, that is. You always have this glazed expression on your face, kind of like the one you're wearing right now because I'm really not making any sense at all, am I?"

Samuel stared at her as if she had a bug on her nose.

"Well, better check that casserole," she chirped, then spun on her heel, hustled into the kitchen wishing the pine floor would heave up and swallow her whole.

It was past ten when Samuel finally laid the book down, rubbed his eyelids with a pained sigh. The generator, which had been humming for half an hour or so, suddenly turned itself off. The cabin fell silent.

Ellie looked up from knitting a cozy baby coat out of yarn unraveled from one of Samuel's old sweaters. "I told you that real-estate stuff would suck your eyeballs dry." When he made no response, she laid her knitting aside. "Tell me about it."

A startled glance bounced toward her, then away. "You're not interested."

"Neither are you."

His jaw set sharply, the muscles jittering beneath his ear. He said nothing.

"It's a waste, Samuel, a tragic waste of your talent and ability. You're a trained medic, able to react coolly in crisis, to calm fear with compassion. People instinctively respond to you, trust you." Her gaze fell on the cage on the far side of the room. "So do animals. You're a gifted healer, Samuel, so why are you holed up in the wilderness studying sell-points, mortgage terms and market analyses?"

Shoulders rippled, arms crossed tightly across a chest so rigid that it could have been carved in granite. His eyes focused on nothing, pinpoints of blue in an expressionless face. But deep within the blue depths a shadow of darkness emerged, a veil of pain so acute that Ellie's chest constricted in response. There was agony in those eyes, and the misery of the damned.

As if on cue, the fire flickered and dimmed. Samuel stood suddenly, put another log in the firebox, then bade Ellie good night and retreated to the loft.

Hours later, Ellie lay awake listening to his tortured moans, the sharp rasp of breath being forced into unwilling lungs. Nightmares had claimed him again. They were becoming worse, she thought. More frequent, more frightening. She didn't know what terrors persecuted his slumber, what horrors he relived in the private hell of his tortured mind. All she knew for certain was that Samuel Evans was emotionally wounded, a man at war with himself.

Ellie would have given anything on earth to understand why.

Chapter Seven

Samuel's pancakes grinned up at him. By now he was used to having his food wink and smile at him, so he merely plucked a raisin eye to dip in the happy half-moon of syrup.

Standing at the cookstove, Ellie balanced Daniel in the crook of one arm while flipping flapjacks. She was humming softly while her baby son gazed up, sheer adoration glowing in tiny eyes that grew darker by the day. At six weeks old, the baby was plump and happy. He smiled reactively now, followed movement with a wise and greedy little gaze. Daniel whacked his tiny hands when excited, puffed out a quivering lip when annoyed. He was developing a real personality. Samuel was nuts about him.

If he'd been honest with himself, he'd have recognized that he was also nuts about the child's mother, but being honest with himself simply wasn't Samuel's forte. Instead, he harbored personal expectations far harsher than those he attached to the rest of the world. When it came to emotion, particularly intense emotion, Samuel either rationalized his feelings or ignored them all together.

So as he gazed at Ellie, hungrily absorbing every nuance of expression, every quirk of the adorable dimple accenting a lush and alluring mouth, he chalked a queasy flutter in his chest up to guilt. Ellie was working. Samuel wasn't.

He pushed away from the table, leaving his own one-eyed meal cooling on the plate. "You sit down and eat. I'll finish cooking."

As she glanced back, a glossy swing of hair fell forward. She shook it away, waved the spatula like a scepter. "Nay, knave, for if thou touchest these priceless orbs, thy fingers shall feel the sting of my wrath."

"Which means?"

"Which means that if you come within ten feet of this griddle—" A vicious swish of the spatula provided adequate demonstration.

"That seems clear enough." Samuel stood warily. "At least let me take Daniel."

"You can't eat and hold a baby at the same time."

"If you can cook and hold him, I can eat and hold him. Besides—" Samuel eased the child from Ellie's grasp, tucked him in the crook of his own arm "—Daniel and I need some quality man-time."

"Man-time?" She chuckled, scooped a batch of completed pancakes from griddle to serving plate. "Is that requisite male-bonding stuff?"

"Hey, don't scoff. Psychological studies have proven that positive gender connection is crucial to a child's emotional development." The remark was issued lightly, without thought. Only when Samuel saw the sparkle drain from Ellie's eyes did he understand cruel implication in his clumsy comment. "That's not what I meant, Ellie."

"I know." She grabbed the batter bowl, turned away to spoon fresh batter onto the griddle, but not before Samuel saw the corner of her mouth quiver.

He shifted Daniel in his arms, instinctively snugged the child against his chest. "Lots of happy, healthy children grow up in single-parent homes. It all depends on how much they're loved. Daniel is loved, Ellie, deeply loved. That's what really matters."

The griddle sputtered with each poured circle. "I know that, too." She gave her head a bracing shake, set the bowl aside and wiped her hands on a tea towel. "Your breakfast is getting cold."

Fearing any further attempt to explain would simply make matters worse, Samuel settled Daniel in the crook of one arm, returned to the table and finished his meal in silence.

But his mind wasn't silent. Thoughts circled like vultures, worries about Ellie's future, and Daniel's. If there was any justice in this world, Ellie and her son would never be separated. Samuel knew the world wasn't just, life wasn't fair. Bad things happened to good people. Samuel had tried to change that. He'd failed.

Samuel wouldn't fail with Ellie, wouldn't allow Daniel to be taken away from her. At the moment he didn't have a clue how to stop that from happening. He just knew that he *would* stop it. Or he'd die trying.

With the aid of a small propane heater, the screen porch temperature hovered just above freezing. A bitter cold snap had turned the snowpack to ice, and the mountain itself into a tree-studded glacier. The clear February sky and crisp air was deceptive, cruelly inviting. Before taking Baloo out for a romp, Samuel had donned four layers of clothing, and wrapped a wool muffler around his face. Neither man nor dog seemed daunted by the frigid weather.

Ellie was most certainly bothered by it. Having spent most of her life in California's central valley with its killing summer heat and benignly mild winters, she was unaccustomed to cold intense enough to freeze spittle in midair.

Not that she'd tried to validate that colorful scenario. She'd take Samuel's word for it. Right now her biggest problem was completing the laundry chores without shivering herself into a muscle spasm. The portable heater helped, but not enough. The contrast of icy air on wet hands was brutal, and the soapy wash water, comfortably warm when she'd filled the tub, had rapidly cooled to barely tepid.

Teeth chattering, she hurried through her laundry chores, scrubbing garments against the ancient washboard, cranking them through a squeaky wringer bolted to the side of an old washtub resembling a relic from another century, then tossing wet clothes into a basket strategically positioned beside the heater to keep the damp laundry from freezing. After all that, she had to drain the tub, refill it with clear rinse water and repeat the grueling process.

By the time she lugged the basket of clean, wet laundry into the kitchen, her shoulders ached fiercely and her back throbbed like it had been flattened by a snowplow. She hoisted the basket to the table with a grunt, then dragged herself back to the screen porch to flip off the portable heater and save what precious fuel was left.

That's when she noticed that the washtub was still full of water. Perplexed, she checked the drain cap. It was open, but the water wasn't draining.

''Damn,'' she muttered, giving the tub a peevish kick. After bestowing a few descriptive adjectives on the hapless hunk of metal, she trudged outside to check the drain hose, and found exactly what she'd feared— a frozen ice spout attached to a completely clogged, utterly useless pipe.

Frustrated and freezing, she hurried back to the screen porch to consider her options. Leaving the wash tub full of water until the drain thawed was not one of them. Within hours the tub would be fit only as an ice skating rink for rodents, useless for days, perhaps weeks. Laundering diapers in the kitchen sink struck her as a bit unsavory, so she had little choice but to empty the tub by hand before the wash water froze solid.

A small bucket ought to do the trick. Ellie found one, and went to work.

Samuel bounced the pinecone on his palm. ''Third cedar from the clearing,'' he announced. Baloo eyed the target tree, issued a doubtful whine as his master prepared for the pitch. Samuel focused, lowered the pinecone to his chest, and had just raised his knee for a wind-up kick when a bloodcurdling shriek ripped the quiet mountain air.

''Help! Help me!''

Samuel dropped the pinecone. ''Ellie?''

''Samuel!''

''Ellie!'' He leapt forward, his feet slipped and he went down in a cursing heap. The surefooted hound dog issued a heroic howl and took off at a clumsy gallop leaving his frustrated master slipping and sliding on the icy crust.

Samuel finally skidded his way to the back of the cabin, and found Baloo frantically circling Ellie's prostrate form. His heart sank to his toes. ''Oh, God.''

He slid down the embankment to the shoveled shed path where Ellie lay on her side, twisted awkwardly and almost motionless except for one hand flailing wildly in a vain attempt to block the hound's slobbering assault on her face. "Stop!" she sputtered, pushing at the worried animal's muzzle. "Do you want to end up with your tongue frozen to my ear? Oh, for goodness' sake... Samuel, *help!*"

"I'm here, honey, I'm here. Where are you hurt?" Kneeling behind her, Samuel yanked the wool muffler away from his mouth, tried to lift Ellie's shoulders. She shrieked, but didn't budge. He yanked again. She shrieked again, then went into a sputtering fit as Baloo wiped a juicy canine kiss across her open mouth.

It took a moment before Samuel recognized the full extent of Ellie's predicament. He rocked back, sat on his haunches and stared in abject astonishment. "How in the world—?"

"Don't ask." Her shoulders vibrated either with a resigned sigh or silent laughter. Since her face was turned away from him, Samuel couldn't be certain, but when she spoke again, her voice quivered with unmistakable amusement. "Well, you're the expert. What does the rescue book say about silly people who freeze themselves to the ground?"

"I, ah, must have missed that chapter." After a cursory examination revealed that no portion of her skin had been frozen, and that she wasn't in pain or in danger, Samuel covered his mouth and pinched his lips together to keep from laughing out loud. What a sight she was, stuck like a human icicle with her clothing and even part of her hair encased in solid ice.

"I don't suppose you happen to have an ice pick in your pocket," she asked hopefully.

"Nope." Grateful that she couldn't turn her head far

enough to see his amused grin, Samuel latched gloved
fingers around Baloo's collar to drag him off the grunting woman. "But I could probably hunt one up somewhere, if the price was right."

She wriggled, heaved a sigh. "That's not fair. I'm
hardly in the position to bargain."

"Which makes for pretty good timing, don't you
think?" Enjoying himself immensely, Samuel patted
her head as if she was a recalcitrant puppy, and was
rewarded by her indignant huff. "Let's make a deal
here. You tell me how you got yourself into this ridiculous situation, and I'll figure a way to get you out of
it."

"You'll laugh."

"I'm laughing now."

"You'll laugh harder, and then you'll tell me I should
have known better."

"That's probably true."

"You don't have to sound so darned cheerful about
it."

"Aren't you the one who's always telling me to cheer
up?"

"Not anymore," she muttered.

Chuckling, Samuel spotted a bucket lying a few feet
up the pathway, then swung around to scrutinize the
frozen washtub drain. The image that popped into his
mind doubled him over, much to Ellie's chagrin.

She struggled to peer over her shoulder with adorably
narrowed eyes. "It's not *that* funny, mountain man."

"Oh, yes, it is." Gasping, Samuel stood, staggered
back a step, and laughed so hard his side ached. Clearly
Ellie had slipped and fallen while trying to bucket water
out of the washtub. "Keep an eye on her, 'Loo," Samuel said when he'd caught his breath. "Don't let her
wander off."

As the big hound accepted his mission with a happy yelp, Samuel went to retrieve an ice pick. Ellie was muttering to herself when he left and still muttering when he returned.

"Hold still," he warned. "Unless you consider body piercing to be an acceptable fashion statement."

She twisted her head as far as her frozen hair would allow, her eyes huge and worried. "Watch what you're doing with that thing."

"Quit staring. It makes me nervous."

"*You're* nervous?" She flinched at flying ice chips. "How do you think I feel?"

"Silly, I would imagine. My only regret is that I don't own a camera."

"There is a god," Ellie mumbled as Samuel hacked away the ice encasing her hair. When it was free, she raised her head with a moan of relief. "Oh, much better. My neck is so stiff— Ack! What's that?"

Samuel followed her horrified gaze to a few hairy brown tufts still stuck in the frozen path. "The good news is that layered haircuts are all the rage these days."

"I'm bald," she wailed, twisting her free arm to feel the back of her head.

"You've got plenty of hair," Samuel assured her as he chiseled at the frozen sleeve of her jacket. "A few strands are just a little shorter now. Roll forward so I can get underneath your elbow…that's better."

"Be careful. I'm partial to that elbow."

"I *am* being careful— Oops."

Her head swiveled around. "Oops?"

"Not to worry." His grin was deliberately sheepish. "There's a sewing kit in the cabin."

Ignoring her squinty-eyed glare, Samuel whistled a peppy jingle and hacked at the hem of her flimsy rayon jacket. When the garment was freed from its icy tomb, he sat back with a pleased grin.

Ellie levered up on one elbow, twisting her torso to examine the torn sleeve. "It could have been worse," she announced, then blew into her cupped palms to warm them. "Maybe I won't have to murder you in your sleep after all."

"Thanks." Smiling, Samuel removed his wool muffler, wrapped it around her face and ears so that only her eyes were showing. Her huge brown eyes, with amber lights sparkling like a sunset on a mountain stream, the kind of eyes that pierce a man's soul and haunt a man's dreams.

All at once Samuel's breath backed up in his chest. Blood roared past his ears, drowning the jackhammer thud of a heart suddenly gone mad. She was beautiful, perhaps the most beautiful woman on earth, but more than that, she was the most enchanting, most deliciously desirable woman Samuel had ever known.

He wanted her.

In that split second all the lies he'd told himself, all the excuses he'd made for longings he'd refused to recognize as real dissipated into a cloud of frozen steam.

He wanted her, wanted this woman more desperately than he wanted his next breath.

The realization scared him to death.

"Samuel?" The red wool flexed as she spoke, puffing softly, then pulling back to sculpt the outline of lips so lush, so familiar that he saw them in his sleep.

"You look pale. Are you all right?"

He blinked, forced his gaze from those intoxicating eyes. "Sure. I'm fine." Without looking up, he tugged off his gloves, held them out to her. "Put these on." The words broke harshly, an angry command. He didn't have to look up to know she was startled, but she accepted the gloves without comment.

From the corner of his eye he saw her slender hands disappear into tanned leather. "We're almost done, right?"

"Not quite." Exhaling slowly, he fastened his gaze on the portion of her left hip that was still firmly frozen to the path in such a manner that he'd have to practically press his face against her full, rounded bottom in order to chop her free. A dull throb in his groin elicited a groan that instantly caught Ellie's attention.

She stiffened, propped up on her elbow and struggled to peer down at the ice locked around her hip. "What is it, what's wrong?"

Samuel dared not look up, fearing he'd be forced to explain the bead of sweat oozing from his brow in freezing weather. "Nothing. It's just that we still have a lot of, er, territory to cover."

She followed his gaze and to his surprise, hooted with laughter. "That's one way to put it. Not very flattering, but probably more accurate than I'd like to admit." Settling back into a reclining position on her side, Ellie heaved a long-suffering sigh. "Do what you must before we both freeze to death."

Samuel swallowed hard, crouched forward and delicately jabbed the ice pick around the luscious curve of her hip. He worked carefully, methodically, forcing himself to focus on the chore rather than the fact that his forehead was pressed against her denim-clad bottom. She wiggled. His hands started to shake. Her hips flexed. Every drop of moisture evaporated from his mouth.

Each time he freed a few more inches of fabric, she wiggled, flexed and issued a soft, sensual sigh that damned near drove him wild with sexual hunger. By the time he chipped away the final shards of incarcerating ice, Samuel was in serious distress.

Ellie, however, was elated. With a gleeful whoop, she sat upright as Samuel parked the pick in the icy bank. Her happy arms encircled his neck as he helped her to her feet. "Free at last, free at last." Beaming, she reached down to pat the prancing hound's head with a floppy gloved hand. "I was beginning to feel like a fly in an ice cube." She turned to Samuel, rosy-faced and glowing. "My hero...again." Hoisting up on tiptoes, she pulled off the woolen muffler to brush her lips across his mouth.

The kiss was impulsive, a chaste expression of gratitude that exploded with nuclear heat. Light blasted his brain, a detonation of blinding brilliance that left him reeling, hungry for more.

He took more, urging her lips apart with a desperation that shook him to the marrow. Her response turned his knees to water, boiled the blood in his veins. A hot, sweet fire burned the pit of his soul. He tasted her deeply, drank her aching sweetness. It wasn't enough. He wanted to taste all of her. All.

It was Ellie who broke away, gasping, trembling, her eyes wide with shock, black with desire. She pressed her palms against his shoulders in an age-old signal of feminine retreat.

Samuel recognized the silent request; he simply didn't want to honor it, didn't want to feel her sweet warmth slip slowly out of his grasp.

But he did honor the request. Gritting his teeth, he sucked a breath of frigid air, and forced himself to release her.

Ellie stumbled backward until her calves bumped the shrinking snow embankment flanking the shoveled shed path. Her swollen lips moved without sound, then her tongue darted out to moisten them. Her gaze darted, her fingers slipped from his shoulders, tangled into a worrisome leather knot beneath her chin. "I, ah, don't know what to say."

Samuel's chest constricted. He felt ill. "I shouldn't have done that."

She angled a sideways glance, quickly refocused it on the screen porch door. "I think it would be more appropriate to say *we* shouldn't have done that." Her smile was forced, nervous. "I wasn't exactly kicking and screaming."

The memory of her heated response reignited the flame in his gut. He shifted, flinched at the painful pressure of jeans that were suddenly a size too small. "The responsibility is mine."

A light frown touched her brow, then was gone. She unlocked her gloved fingers, stuffed them into her pockets. "You're not responsible for everything in this world, Samuel. What happened, happened, but it wouldn't have if I hadn't wanted it to."

Their eyes met, sending and retrieving silent messages that both understood, yet neither was willing to acknowledge aloud. When she blinked and looked away, Samuel understood. They'd been alone together for weeks, isolated from the world by the intimacy of their cramped surroundings. They cared for each other. They nurtured each other. In a very real sense, it was natural for them to think about taking the next step, to consummate their emotional bonding with a physical bonding.

It was natural but it was wrong. Samuel's feelings were too deep, too jumbled. He had nothing to offer Ellie and Daniel because he had nothing to offer himself.

His shoulders stiffened reflexively. "It won't happen again."

Ellie regarded him for a moment before her eyes lightened, and a half smile lifted the corner of her mouth.

It would definitely happen again. They both knew it.

"Here you go, Snowdrift, your last home-cooked meal." Ellie slid a plate of carrot chunks and buck brush leaves into the bunny cage, lowered the spring door and sat back on her heels. She glanced over at the sofa, caught Samuel staring at her before he jerked his gaze back to the open book in his hands.

It wasn't the first time she'd seen him watching her when he thought she wasn't looking. Ellie certainly hoped it wouldn't be the last, but as always, she pretended not to notice. "Are you sure Snowdrift is ready to leave, Samuel? Three weeks doesn't seem like enough time for his leg to have healed completely."

He blinked up as if seeing her for the first time, lowered the book to his lap. "The rabbit is fine, Ellie. The splint has been off for a week, and there's no trace of a limp. I'm sure that if you asked, our hairy houseguest would agree that he's more than ready to go home."

"But it's so cold out there. Shouldn't we at least wait until the weather warms up?"

"It was cold when we found him. That's why nature supplied him with a warm fur coat."

She huffed to her feet, scowling. "You needn't speak to me as if I were a child."

"That wasn't my intent." Clearly it was, or at least so said the amused twitch at the corner of his mouth. "I'm well aware that only mature adults use terms like 'snooky-wooky, bunny-wunnums' in conversation with a flop-eared mute."

Ellie lifted her chin, issued a haughty sniff. "I'll have you know that Snowdrift understands every word I say."

"Ah, well, that makes one of us."

Chuckling, Ellie went to retrieve her fussy son from the cradle. "Women are supposed to be mysterious. That's part of the allure."

"In that case, may I say that you are one of the most alluring women I've ever met."

Even though she knew he was joking, her heart thumped a little harder. She pressed Daniel to her shoulder, rubbed his tiny shoulders as she gazed across the room. "Am I?" she asked softly.

Samuel's smile faded as a slow heat darkened his gaze. He didn't reply; he didn't have to. The longing in his eyes was all the answer she needed. Gooseflesh prickled her arms, tangible evidence of excitement she dared not reveal.

The kiss they'd shared earlier that day still weighed heavily on her lips, and in her heart. Ellie had been kissed before, but nothing had ever come close to the thrill of feeling Samuel's hungry mouth on hers.

Samuel wanted her. He just didn't want to want her.

The realization sent her heart into wild palpitations even as her rational mind signaled a frantic cease and desist order. Samuel was fighting his yearnings for the same reason that Ellie was fighting hers. They were both living a lie, a pretense of idyllic bliss that was destined to end, and end sooner than either of them cared to admit.

Despite her deep attraction to Samuel, Ellie knew all too well that the heart can be deceived. Love blinds, betrays. Having already learned that the hard way, the last thing on earth Ellie needed was another such lesson.

Yet Samuel Evans was as different from Stanton

Mackenzie as day is from night. A man of profound strength and exquisite sensitivity, Samuel exuded an aura of sadness that touched Ellie's soul. There was something powerful about his gentleness, something that affected her in a unique and most disturbing way.

But Ellie Malone was not ready to put her heart on the line again. Not now. Perhaps not ever.

Dawn broke clear and cold, a day so crisply blue that Ellie could have wept at its beauty. She bundled in layers of clothing, topped by the colorful rayon jacket with an ice pick tear in the sleeve, and went stoically to the front porch to bid a final goodbye.

From the steps she watched man and dog tramp the icy snowpack toward the forest beyond. Just before they stepped into the concealing woods, Samuel paused, turned to reveal the furry creature nested in his arms. He appeared to whisper something to the rabbit, hoisted it up for a moment in what appeared to be a final goodbye, then turned and carried the little animal into the forest.

Ellie watched until the final blur of movement disappeared behind the obscuring trees. A tear seeped out to freeze against her lashes. "Goodbye, Snowdrift," she whispered. "Have a happy life."

You're going to be bawling on the front porch, and you'll wish you hadn't let yourself love him.

Too bad her heart hadn't listened. Again.

Chapter Eight

Ellie descended the loft ladder clutching framed photographs found in a storage container beneath the unused cot. She took them to the kitchen where Samuel was hunched over the table scrawling study notes in a spiral notebook.

At the sound of her footsteps, he spoke without looking up. "Did you find anything you could use in that box of old clothes?"

"There were a few T-shirts, some flannels I can cut down to make nightshirts for Daniel and a couple pair of jeans that might fit me."

Her tummy, swollen and saggy for the first few weeks after Daniel's birth, had finally firmed back to relative normalcy, but there was no way her ample feminine fanny would fit into Samuel's slim-hipped jeans. She was sick to death of alternating between sweat pants and the maternity denims she'd been wearing when she arrived. When Samuel finally recalled that some of his brother's old clothes might be stored in the loft, she'd been as excited as a school girl on her first mall excursion.

Setting the framed photos on the counter, Ellie shrugged the draped garments off her shoulder, held up a faded pair of frayed Wranglers. "Wow, that's what I call roomy." Nonetheless thrilled by her find, Ellie laid the jeans aside to admire a pair of corduroys that was less worn, but just as large. "I may have to take them in a bit."

"Rory likes his beer," Samuel murmured, flipping a page. "Last time I saw him, he had the belly to prove it."

"Amazing, considering what a skinny kid he was."

After issuing a grunt of agreement, Samuel laid down his pencil. "How did you know that?"

Ellie glanced up from the extralarge flannel shirt she'd spread out to gage pattern dimensions. "Know what?"

"That my brother was a skinny kid."

"Oh, I almost forgot." Pushing the plaid fabric aside, she uncovered the framed photographs and brought them to the table. "I found these in with the clothes. That's you, isn't it?" Excited, she pointed to the smaller of two boys posing beside a rushing creek holding a fishing pole in one hand and a string of fat trout in the other. "Those serious eyes of yours are a dead giveaway."

Samuel lifted the photograph, studied it with a smile. "You'd be serious, too, if you'd just lost a month's allowance. Rory and I had bet on that day's catch."

Standing behind his chair, Ellie leaned forward until her breast inadvertently brushed his shoulder. She shifted quickly but not before she felt his reflexive

— PLAY —
L♥VE HEARTS
Scratch 'n' Match Game...

Place sticker here and scratch off silver circle opposite

How many FREE GIFTS can you claim with your LOVE HEART?

Scratch 'n' Match Claim Chart

   CLAIM 4 FREE BOOKS & A FREE MYSTERY GIFT

   CLAIM 4 FREE BOOKS

   CLAIM 2 FREE BOOKS

YES! I have placed my label from the front cover in the space provided above and scratched away the silver circle. Please send me all the free gifts for which I qualify, as shown on the claim chart above. I understand that I am under no obligation to purchase any books, as explained overleaf. I am over 18 years of age.

E8KI

MS/MRS/MISS/MR _____ INITIALS _____

BLOCK CAPITALS PLEASE

SURNAME _____

ADDRESS _____

_____

POSTCODE _____

THE READER SERVICE™ : HERE'S HOW IT WORKS

Accepting the free books and gift places you under no obligation to buy anything. You may keep the books and gift and return the despatch note marked "cancel". If we don't hear from you, about a month later we will send you 6 brand new books and invoice you just £2.50* each. That's the complete price – there is no extra charge for postage and packing. You may cancel at any time, otherwise every month we'll send you 6 more books, which you may either purchase or return – the choice is yours.

*Prices subject to change without notice.

quiver, heard his quiet intake of breath. The soapy scent of his freshly washed hair wafted up, delightfully dizzying, oddly erotic.

Ellie moistened her lips, exhaled slowly, waited for her pulse to slow before carefully reaching over his shoulder to touch the image of each fish on young Rory's string. "So he outfished you, hmm? Let's see, one, two, three—"

"Six," Samuel interrupted grumpily. "My brother caught six. I only caught four."

Amused that Samuel's irked expression was so similar to the one in the photograph, Ellie chuckled happily, gazed down at the somber young face that inexplicably tugged at her heart. "How old were you then?"

"I was eight or nine, I think, so Rory would have been around thirteen." He set the first picture aside, picked up the second, which was similar except that an older man with thinning but tousled hair and the same serious eyes had joined the boys. "That's my father. A moment after my mother snapped this shot, I accidentally whipped my string of fish into Rory's face and knocked him backward into the creek."

"Accidentally, huh? Sounds fishy to me."

When Samuel groaned at the pun, Ellie laughed, cheerfully ruffled his hair. The gesture had been intended as a good-natured teasing. Instead, her fingers paused without her permission, lingered to stroke and to caress. His hair was so much softer than she'd expected, and tingled the tips of her fingers with electric warmth.

She perceived rather than felt the subtle stiffening of his shoulders, his brief cessation of breath. Only after she'd reluctantly pulled her hand away did his chest heave to expel air. He was clearly affected by her touch. That pleased her, although she didn't care to speculate

why it should. They were friends, of course, dear and
devoted friends. In a different time, a different place,
perhaps they could have been more, shared more, but
not now. Now Ellie couldn't afford to unleash her heart
again.

But she couldn't seem to control it, either.

Struck by an overwhelming urge to wrap her arms
around his neck and nibble his earlobe, Ellie managed
to push away and totter around the table, where she
collapsed onto the chair before her watery knees buck-
led. A fevered heat radiated deep inside her, spreading
liquid warmth into places she dared not acknowledge,
yet couldn't possibly ignore.

It had been a long time since she'd been aroused by
the scent of a man. Longer still since she'd been unable
to tear her gaze from the subtle nuance of face and form
that had already seared a permanent scar in her mind.
She couldn't recall ever having been so emotionally be-
fuddled by a man's nearness that her pulse raced like
white lightning, and her heart pounded with such force
that she feared it might explode.

It was that kiss, she told herself, one glorious kiss
that had changed everything, charged the cabin air with
tension thick enough to slice. Nothing could be the
same between her and Samuel again. They had tasted
each other, a sample so achingly sweet it left them rav-
enous for more. Neither admitted that, but both knew.

Across the table, Samuel's eyes had dilated into blue-
rimmed orbs, and beads of moisture glowed over his
brow. He coughed, squirmed, stared intently at the photograph clenched in his white-knuckled grasp.

Ellie tested her voice. "Do you have any more? Photographs of your family, that is."

Puffing his cheeks, Samuel blew out a breath, and
laid the framed picture on the table. "There's an old

photo album around somewhere. My mother kept vacation pictures in it. It's probably in one of those junk boxes up in the loft.'' He flexed his fingers, avoided her gaze. The chair scraped as he pushed away from the table. "I'll go look.''

Suspecting he wanted a moment alone, Ellie neither protested nor offered to join him. She could use the time to recoup her own shaken composure.

Daniel had other ideas. A cranky squeak had Ellie heading across the room to check her awakening son. "What's the matter, sweet boy?'' she cooed, lifting the wriggling infant against her shoulder. The question was answered by a satisfying burp, after which the baby issued a relieved sigh and sagged like a deflated balloon. "Gracious, I'll bet you feel better now.''

Ellie rubbed his little shoulders, brushed her cheek against his silky scalp, and began to hum. Daniel yawned, bobbled his head against her shoulder as a song whispered quietly through the night. "Sleepy, sleepy little baby, precious little boy of mine. Sleepy, sleepy little baby, dreaming in a cradle made of pine.''

The loft ladder creaked. "Cedar.'' Samuel stepped down with a fat, leather-bound album tucked under his arm. "It's made of cedar, not pine.''

"I know, but cedar doesn't rhyme with anything useful.'' Ellie smiled, laid her drowsy son in the cradle. "Unless we're talking about someone named Peter, an avid reader—''

"Who designs meters,'' Samuel added helpfully. "And is some kind of, er, leader…''

"Peter, the meter reader leader?''

"Exactly.''

"And if Peter were to take up gardening, would he also be a seeder-weeder?''

Samuel's face went blank. "I'm not going to win this, am I?"

"Probably not. Ooh, you found the photo album." Ellie finished spreading the blanket over her sleeping son then joined Samuel on the sofa, and squirmed with excitement. She didn't know why a peek into this man's elusive past was so enticing, but she could hardly wait.

The moment he lifted the album cover, she spotted a buzz-haired youngster desperately hauling up the waistband of oversize swim shorts that dragged below his knobby little knees. She whooped gleefully. "Is that *you?*"

Samuel issued a curt nod, would have flipped the page had she not stopped him.

"How old were you then, five or six?"

"I guess so."

"Why are you screaming at the camera?"

"Because I was mad."

"Obviously, but why?"

He sighed. "If that picture had been taken two seconds earlier, you'd know why."

An amusing image popped into her mind. "Would such a photograph have shown a bit more skin?"

His grumpy expression faltered into a twitchy smile. "Let's just say that floppy swim trunks combined with swift creek currents and trigger-happy camera moms are a bashful little boy's worst nightmare."

"Ah, gotcha. Too bad she wasn't faster on the trigger, though. Just think what a keepsake your grandchildren would have." Grinning at Samuel's narrowed stare, Ellie kicked off her shoes, and tucked her feet up. "Okay, you can turn the page now."

For the next half hour, Ellie was treated to a rare glimpse into Samuel's childhood, a childhood filled with such obvious happiness that even reminiscence re-kindled joy in his eyes.

"This was taken while Dad was building the screen porch," Samuel said, pointing out a snapshot of his grinning father posed on a framed deck half-laid with planking. A blurred figure in the background was wielding a hammer. "That's Rory trying to help. His thumbnail was black for months."

"Aww, poor kid."

"Poor kid nothing," Samuel replied cheerfully. "Rory strutted around like a squashed thumb was some kind of heroic war wound."

She elbowed his ribs. "Do I detect a hint of jealousy?"

"Of course. I wanted a black thumb, too, but I certainly wasn't going to smash myself with a hammer when Mom had a drawer full of perfectly good felt-tip markers."

"You didn't."

He shrugged. "It was worth a shot. As it turned out, my folks thought the blatant bid for attention cute enough to warrant an extra helping of pudding."

"Which must have ticked your brother off royally."

"An additional benefit," he admitted without a trace of remorse.

"You can't fool me. You and your brother were crazy about each other."

A wistful reverence softened his reply. "Yes, we were."

A page was turned to reveal another year, another summer at the cabin. Ellie gazed at the snapshots, frozen moments of time, arranged with loving care to create a cherished book of memories.

The Evans boys were older in the next group of photos. Samuel, sporting the shaggy shoulder-length hair that had been fashionable two decades earlier, appeared to be at least twelve and Rory had sprouted into the throes of a gangly, awkward adolescence.

Someone else had joined the motley group of fishermen, too, a red-haired youngster with a face full of freckles. "Who's this?" Ellie asked, pointing.

Samuel's smile faded instantly. "Drake Jackson."

"He looks closer to your age than Rory's."

"We were friends," Samuel conceded, and would have turned the page if Ellie hadn't touched his hand. She questioned him with a look. "All right, he was my best friend. We were inseparable."

Something in Samuel's tone kept Ellie silent. On the next page, there were more photos of young Drake, but the pictures were different. They were larger, fluted at the edge, and taken with black-and-white film. But it was the content of those photographs that caught Ellie's attention. Samuel and Drake both looked distraught, as if they'd been crying. They were surrounded by strangers, men in uniform jumpsuits that were similar to military fatigues, with peculiar floppy backpacks dragging from the odd harnesses each man wore. In the background, the nose portion of some kind of aircraft was visible.

Ellie squinted at the snapshot. "Is that a helicopter?"

Instead of replying, Samuel flipped farther back in the album to reveal a large newspaper article pasted in place. A headline read Local Boy Injured In Fall. Below that was a news photo of a vaguely discernible figure on a rescue gurney surrounded by those same jumpsuit-clad men.

"Good Lord," Ellie whispered, studying the photograph. "Is that Rory on the gurney?"

Samuel stared at the blurred picture as if reliving the event. "The three of us were hiking in the ravine. Drake and Rory were on the path ahead of me. They were messing around, not looking where they were going. Drake slipped on a loose rock. Rory pulled him back onto the path, then lost his balance and fell over the side. I thought he was dead.''

His pain cut her like a knife. ''You must have been terrified.''

''Yeah.'' Samuel rubbed his eyelids. ''The volunteer fire department saved his life. They roared up, unloaded equipment and yanked him off the cliff so fast that Drake and I hardly knew what was happening. From that minute on, we both knew exactly what we wanted to do with our lives.''

The poignancy in his gaze made sense now. The skill of strangers to save his sibling's life had provided impetus for Samuel's future career as firefighter, paramedic and member of his department's elite rescue squad. ''That's why you became a rescue medic.'' She waited for an assenting nod. ''And Drake, did he follow in your footsteps?''

Samuel's smile was unnervingly sad. ''Drake was always ahead of me. I just tried to keep up. He was the department's best and brightest.''

''You both ended up working for the same department? You really were inseparable.'' A subtle tremor vibrated his arm, alerting Ellie that the conversation was veering into uncharted territory. She ignored the warning, was driven by an unquenchable need to know everything there was to know about this mysterious man who had first saved her life, then become a pivotal part of it. ''Is Drake still with the department?''

The album jittered against Samuel's fingers. He released the page, let it fall away. ''No.''

''Is that why you left, Samuel, because Drake did?'' Over the past weeks, Samuel had acknowledged only that he'd taken a leave of absence several months earlier, but he'd always changed the subject without offering explanation as to why he'd discarded a career that clearly meant the world to him.

He always seemed hesitant, as if he wanted to reply, wanted to purge himself of a dark, haunting secret. Despite repeated encouragement, he'd never done so.

This time, his eyes begged understanding, his lips quivered with need to relieve a secret burden. Ellie held her breath in anticipation. This might be the moment, she thought, the moment when his private torment would be revealed to her.

Instead, Samuel closed the album, laid it on the table. When he looked up, the familiar shuttered sadness clouded his gaze. There would be no revelation. Not tonight—perhaps not ever.

"I'm going to turn in now."

"Samuel—"

"Good night, Ellie." Samuel crossed room without a backward glance, climbed the ladder, and disappeared into the murky shadows of the loft.

Boiling water, brown with mud. The deafening thrum of engines. Clacking blades sliced air thick with screams. A day of destiny. A day of horror.

He pulled the swing cable inside the helicopter's bay door, fastened his harness to the rescue hook. A comrade tapped his helmet. The signal. He stepped into thin air, and descended into hell.

Below him the river churned like chocolate, crushed trees into deadly debris then swallowed it whole. He spun lower, dangled over the carnage on a woven thread of steel. His gaze was riveted on the target, a twisted log caught on the stoic branch of a partially submerged sapling.

The cable swayed, twisted, jerked, dropped him closer, closer, closer to the boiling flood.

And then he saw her. Huge, dark eyes, wide with fear. Wet brown hair. The small, outstretched hand. A thin voice, drowned out by the cacophony of terror, reverberated directly to his heart, words formed by colorless lips shivering with cold, and with fear. "Help me, please, help me."

She was only a child.

"Help me!" The little hand quivered, fingers desperately stiff, stretching upward, stretching out to him. To him.

He twisted on the cable, bucking his body forward and down, extending his hand to the drowning waif who clung so desperately to the wreckage of her young life. Pleading dark eyes. A small outstretched hand.

The cable jittered and swayed.

He could touch her now, feel the icy scrape of little fingertips brushing his palm. The battered log shuddered, twisted with the raging current. The small hand slipped from his grasp, and the huge, pleading eyes disappeared into the mud-swollen belly of the beast.

"No!" This wasn't happening. *"No!"* He wouldn't let it happen. *"No, no, no!"* Not again.

Dear God, not again.

"Samuel!"

A groan, a guttural cry. The earth shook.

"Samuel, wake up!"

He thrashed against the restraining hands. "No," he croaked. "She needs me—"

"It's a dream, Samuel. It's only a dream." The familiar voice was sweet, soothing. "You're all right now."

His lungs were on fire. He gasped for air, reared up and stared into darkness. A cool palm stroked his face.

He jerked reflexively and grasped her wrist. "Ellie?" The word scratched his throat, emerged in a dry sob. He released her, scoured his face with his palms. He was dizzy with fear, sick to the stomach with it. "Did I wake Daniel?"

"No." Her arms encircled him with comforting sweetness. "You're soaking wet."

He shivered. "I'm fine."

"You shouldn't sleep without—" her voice quivered "—without clothes. You'll catch your death."

Sweat dripped from his bare torso. Still disoriented, he glanced down, absently wiped his wet skin with the wadded sheet. "I can't stand anything tight around my chest," he mumbled, wondering why he felt compelled to issue such a banal comment. "I sleep in shorts." Why on earth had he said that?

"I know." She dried his back with the T-shirt he'd discarded the night before. Her touch comforted him, warmed him, yet he shifted away, eased the shirt out of her hand.

"I'm sorry I woke you." He cocked his head forward, used the wadded garment to wipe the sweat from his eyes. "Go back to bed, Ellie. I'm all right now."

"Are you?"

Samuel heaved a weary sigh, squeezed his eyes shut. A tingling warmth radiated from the crook of his arm as she touched him.

"You've carried this burden long enough," she whispered. "It's time to share it."

A lump wedged in his throat. God knew how much he wanted to do just that, to purge himself of the pain, the haunting memories. Fear had stopped him in the past, fear of seeing accusation in Ellie's eyes, the same cutting blame that stared back at him from the mirror. He couldn't bear that. Ellie meant too much to him.

Yet to withhold the truth would be akin to a lie. She meant too much to him for that, too.

Conflicted, emotionally drained, Samuel shifted, sat on the edge of the cot with his elbows braced on his knees. He waited until Ellie perched beside him. Still staring at the floor, he heard a stilted voice, recognized it as his own. "It was a clear spring morning," he said quietly. "It had rained the night before, just enough to wash the sky and leave everything smelling fresh and new. We were changing shifts when the call came in."

In his mind Samuel heard the tone blast. Three short, one long, the call for Station 12. His station. His call.

"We were rolling before dispatch radioed details."

Thunderstorms. Samuel remembered the warning crackling through his headset. Thunderstorms in the mountains, a wall of water surging from bloated ravines, crashing to the valley floor.

He took a shuddering breath. "A school bus had washed off the bridge."

Beside him, Ellie gasped. Samuel licked his lips, stared at the rough planking beneath his feet. "Shift A rescue squads took the land route to the river. My shift diverted to the chopper pad. By the time we'd suited up, the rescue copters were fueled and ready. We checked our gear en route, just like we'd done a thousand times before. When we reached the river it was—" A throat spasm silenced him.

Ellie touched his hand, said nothing.

After a moment, Samuel shivered and spoke. "It was the worst thing I'd ever seen in my life. The bridge was gone. The school bus was jammed against a frayed wooden pylon. All you could see was swirling brown muck trying to suck up a few feet of yellow metal and a couple windows. The kids—" his voice cracked "—the kids were everywhere. Screaming, sobbing, clinging to flooded trees and to each other. We pulled them out as fast as we could while the squads on the bank set snag lines across the current. There were so many kids, so damned many of them.''

Each detail of that horrible day was seared in Samuel's memory: the thrum of desperate chaos, the raw wind chafing his face, the helpless flailing of youngsters swept into the whirling vortex of the flood. One by one, Samuel had set his rigging, plucked child after child from the arms of murky death.

Then he'd seen her, a small, dark-haired figure clutching a log snagged on a submerged tree. He'd shouted at the spotter, pointed out the open bay door. The spotter nodded, the pilot banked left.

A moment later, Samuel had been lowered to the center of the raging torrent. The girl's hair was matted with murky mud, her dark eyes wide with terror. She'd pleaded for help, begged for her life. Samuel remembered her small hand reaching out, shaking with cold. He remembered the feel of her icy fingers brushing his palm.

And he remembered the sickness in his gut when she'd been swept into the raging torrent.

Ellie's fingers dug into his arm. ''It wasn't your fault,'' she whispered. ''There wasn't anything you could do.''

''There was one thing.'' His voice sounded dead as he related what happened next, how he'd done the one thing on earth that he'd been trained to avoid at any cost. He'd released his harness and plunged into the swollen river to grab the child.

The angry water had pummeled them, pulled them under. Samuel had clung tenaciously to the child, refusing to relinquish his precious cargo. He would save

her or he would die with her, but he would never let
her go.

"The current dragged us down. I held on to her, even
under water. I was so afraid to let her go...." Breathing
heavily, Samuel unclenched his fists, stared at the loft
floor until the planks blurred into the turbulent brown
mass in his mind. The swirling current, the putrid mud
stench, the battering debris. The taste of death in his
throat.

He remembered it all, relived it all.

One of the rescue squad's snag lines had caught
them, held them firmly against an inundated tree trunk.
Still clutching the limp girl, Samuel recalled grappling
with the line. He'd heard shouts from the bank, the
voices of his friends. The cable had arched against the
wind as a uniformed figure rappeled out to retrieve the
child and carry her to safety.

Barely conscious by then, Samuel had felt an im-
mense surge of relief when the child had been safely
transported to shore. But his strength had been waning
and he hadn't been able to maintain his tenuous grasp
on the snag line.

It had slipped from his grasp; the river had fought to
claim him.

A voice from the past circled his mind.

"Uh-uh, buddy." A safety latch had clicked onto his
harness. "You aren't getting away from me that easy."
Samuel could still remember Drake Jackson's smiling
face. "Hang on, my man. We're outta here."

Drake had never seen the massive raft of debris hur-
tling straight toward them. Before Samuel could croak
a warning, Drake had sensed danger, heaved forward to
block Samuel's helpless body with his own.

And with that single heroic act, two lives had
changed forever.

* * *

Ellie placed two mugs of herbal tea on the coffee table, then slid another log into the firebox before joining Samuel on the sofa. Her heart ached at the sadness in his face, at the taut set of his jaw and deep lines bracketing a face already roughened by pain.

Emboldened by darkness split only with light from the dancing wood fire, she laid a hand on his thigh. He flinched slightly, glanced away.

"You saved that child, Samuel, and you did it willingly without thought of your own safety. So did Drake. You both knew the risks. You both took them."

He wouldn't look at her. "I'm still whole. Drake isn't."

A sick heaviness settled into her stomach. The debilitating guilt in Samuel's eyes broke her heart. He'd told her about his friend's severe injuries, the crushed pelvis, the spinal damage that could bind him to a wheelchair for life. Even if Drake Jackson did walk again, which medical opinion considered unlikely, the poor man's firefighting career was over.

"What happened was tragic," Ellie said. "It's heartbreaking. I don't know your friend Drake but from what you've told me I can't believe he holds you responsible."

Samuel shrugged, rubbed his eyelids. "I hold myself responsible."

"Why?"

"Because I broke the rules. Drake was injured because I disregarded orders, and put my team members in jeopardy. If I'd followed departmental procedures Drake would never have been hurt."

"But a child would be dead," Ellie added softly. "Do you think Drake would have preferred that?" When Samuel remained silent, she continued. "Saving others is what firefighters do, Samuel. It's the reason you chose the profession in the first place. It's the reason Drake chose it. Both of you understood the risk involved, and it was a risk you willingly took."

Samuel set his jaw. "It's not the same."

"Of course it's the same. You risked your life to save a drowning child. Drake risked his life to save a drowning friend." For a moment, Ellie thought she might have gotten through to him.

Until he spoke. "We all understood that dealing with tragedy was part of the job," he said. "Every day we faced it, fought it, beat it and lost to it. Afterward, we never spoke about the bad calls, the ones we couldn't win. It was our way of keeping death a stranger." Samuel's chest shuddered. He stared into space as if reliving the terror all over again. "But on that day, in the eyes of that terrified little girl and the face of my very best friend, death wasn't a stranger anymore. I could touch it. I could smell it. It had a face. It was real." Samuel closed his eyes, opened them with exquisite sadness. "That's when I recognized the consequence of my failure. I couldn't let it happen again."

"Oh, Samuel." Tucking one foot under her, Ellie turned sideways on the sofa to cradle Samuel's face in her hands. She wanted to offer comfort, but knew that her words would be useless against the crushing weight a terrible guilt that only Drake Jackson could absolve. "You can't go on like this."

He reached for the mug, sipped the cooling tea.

"You'll never be able to go forward until you go back, Samuel. Drake needs you now, and you need him."

Samuel balanced the tea mug on his knee, regarded Ellie thoughtfully. "So you believe I should return to face the consequence of my sordid past?"

Unable to meet his intense gaze, Ellie flushed and turned away. She, too, had consequences to face.

A knowing smile revealed that Samuel also recognized the parallel of their lives. Each of them had avoided dealing with failure and confrontation, and in doing so had relinquished all hope of vanquishing their private demons.

They were so much alike, as two flawed halves of a perfect whole. Both were hiding from a painful past; Ellie trying to escape fear, Samuel trying to escape failure.

They'd escaped nothing. But they'd found each other.

And Ellie had found so much more.

A surge of moisture blurred her vision, brought a lump to her throat. She pressed her hand against his cheek, thrilled when he turned to kiss it. His lips stroked her palm so tenderly that goose bumps rose along her arm.

He took her hand between his, held it away as if studying universal secrets revealed in her palm. A subtle tremor vibrated through his touch. A spark of longing touched his eyes.

Ellie shivered, stood. "I think we should go to bed. Daniel will be awake soon. And by the way, I don't think you should sleep in the loft anymore. It's too cold up there for a man who prefers to sleep without, ah, constriction."

Clearly startled, Samuel also stood, watched her cross to the double bed in which she'd slept alone since her arrival. She nervously straightened her torn sleep top, wiped her moist palms on the matching fleece pants and slipped into bed.

Samuel still hadn't moved.

"Well?" She took a deep breath, patted the mattress beside her. "Are you coming?"

He shifted awkwardly, looked like a youngster being offered his first hot fudge sundae. "This isn't a good idea."

"Why not?"

"Because if I get into that bed with you, I'll want to make love with you."

"I'm counting on that," Ellie whispered. Then she drew down the covers invitingly, and held her breath.

Chapter Nine

A come-hither smile just wasn't doing it. Ellie batted her eyes, tugged at the torn sweat top and dipped a shoulder to expose a provocative hint of bare skin. "Well?"

Across the room, Samuel stood motionless, staring at her as if she'd completely lost her mind. "Well what?"

Her smoldering smile faltered. "Do I have to draw a squeeze-cheese picture on the pillow?"

An amber glow from the woodstove reflected his subtle smile. "If you're into innovative use of cheese products, I have a couple ideas that might interest you."

"Ooh, now that sounds intriguing." Breathless. She sounded absolutely breathless and a tad desperate. Of course she'd never seduced a man before—never needed to, never wanted to—but at the moment things were not going at all well.

She stroked the vacant place beside her, issued a

throaty purr designed to pique Samuel's interest. Samuel didn't move; Baloo did. The animal reared up, lumbered over to foist forepaws onto the mattress and gaze at Ellie with big, worried eyes.

A chuckle from across the room didn't help matters. "Looks like 'Loo thinks you swallowed a cat."

That was swell. Closing her eyes, Ellie hugged her knees, dropped her head and issued a frustrated moan that had the alarmed hound whining and pawing the bed. "I don't know," she murmured against her kneecaps. "I try to be a good person, really I do. I bathe daily, I'm nice to small animals and I never park in handicap spaces. What on earth am I doing wrong?"

A hesitant shuffle was followed by footsteps. "Go lie down, 'Loo." The animal whined a protest, but doggy toenails clicked a mournful rhythm across the room. Ellie felt rather than saw Samuel kneel beside the bed. "You're not doing anything wrong, honey."

Recognizing a slight advantage, she heaved a sigh, opened one eye far enough to angle a guarded glance. "There must be something. You think I'm a shameless hussy and your dog thinks I eat cats."

"I don't think you're a hussy. Shameless, maybe, but definitely not a hussy."

"So what about the cat thing?"

Samuel directed a look toward the contrite canine. "Consider the source."

"Good point." Ellie stroked Samuel's cheek with the back of her fingers. "I'm crazy about you."

The revelation clearly shook him. He grasped her hand between his own palms, held it away. "You don't owe me anything."

"I owe you my life." A fleeting sadness veiled his eyes, puckered his brow. "But that's not what this is about," she added quickly. "I'm not good at expressing myself. I know that. I always crack jokes to break tension and end up saying something completely inappropriate, so I'm probably going about this the wrong way.'' She held up her free hand, silencing his protest. ''I want to be close to you, Samuel. If you don't feel the same, that's okay.'' A lump clogged her throat at the thought. She coughed it away. ''Well, maybe it's not okay, but I can accept it if you just look me straight in the eye and say you don't want me.''

''It's not a simple question of wanting or not wanting.''

''Yes, it's exactly that simple.''

He shook his head, looked miserably away. ''I can't commit to you, Ellie. You know that.''

''Actually, I don't know any such thing.'' If the wild cadence of her heart would only slow down maybe her chest would stop aching. Maybe the tears poised on the edge of her lashes would evaporate before he saw them and realized how very close she was to losing control. ''It's irrelevant anyway. I'm not asking for commitment.''

''You should be. It's what you deserve, Ellie. It's what Daniel deserves.''

The very thought of commitment shook her to her soles. Whether she deserved it or not, Ellie had never wanted commitment, had always feared it, yet in some secret part of her soul, she suddenly craved it. That frightened her.

Clamping her lips together, she combed his thick hair with her fingers, smoothed a ruffled tangle at the crown into an appealing sexy tousle. ''You need a haircut. I'm pretty handy with a pair of scissors. Maybe tomorrow—''

He stopped her with a kiss.

Warm lips cherished her mouth softly, tenderly, trembling with leashed passion quivering below the surface like a rumbling volcano. The kiss ended as quickly as it had begun, and when Samuel drew away, his eyes glowed hot in the firelight.

Ellie touched her swollen lips, then used the same fingertip to trace the sculpted contour of his mouth. A hiss of breath warmed her skin a moment before he grasped her wrist, pressed his cheek to her palm. "This is a magical place," she whispered. "I never want to leave."

"I know." Samuel shuddered, stroked her wrist with his lips. "But none is this is real, Ellie. It's an illusion, a fantasy."

"It's real to me. I think it's real to you, too."

He sighed. "We can't hide from the world forever."

"Why not? What has the world ever done for us?" Desperate, foolish, completely irrational. She knew it. She didn't care. "There's nothing out there for either of us except grief. We can build our own world here, Samuel. We can build a life for ourselves and for Daniel."

"You won't feel that way when spring comes." He silenced her protest with another kiss, sweet and fleeting, then shifted from his crouched position and sat on edge of the bed. Gathering her in his arms, Samuel pressed her head to his shoulder and gently stroked her hair. "The only thing between us and the outside world is six miles of unplowed road. After the snow melts, it won't be safe for you here."

Ellie was well aware that. She just didn't want to hear about it. Yesterday had been the first of March. Snow flurries now dropped inches rather than feet, thawed faster than it fell. Jasper the snowman had melted into a skinny shadow of his former self. "Maybe Stanton has stopped looking for us."

"You don't believe that."

Her stomach tightened. No, she didn't believe that, not for one minute. There was nothing on earth Stanton Mackenzie wouldn't do to find his son. Nothing. Unless...

"I don't want to think about him."

"Honey—"

"I don't want to think about Stanton Mackenzie, or spring, or even tomorrow." Her voice cracked, clogged with emotion. She clung to him, tangled her fingers in loose fabric of his unbuttoned shirt. "All I want is tonight. I want to feel good again, I want to feel safe. I want to take away your nightmares, and I want you to take away mine. For now, please, just for now, I want to pretend this beautiful world we've created will never end. I want to love you, Samuel, and just for a little while, I want you to love me."

A sob humiliated her, and she buried her face against his throat. His pulse raced against her cheek. She felt it as surely as she felt his resistance melt in the heat of a fierce embrace. His breath warmed her face, whispered like mist in the chilly cabin air.

Words circled like soft butterflies, flapped frantically without form or substance. Desperate murmurs, prelude to love making. Ellie cherished the sounds, throaty, unintelligible rasps more thrilling than a sensual sonnet, more poignant than erotic poems of a bawdy bard. Sweet whispers touched her soul, stroked her starving spirit.

Samuel's hands were everywhere, a frenetic blur of movement and sensation. His mouth cherished her lips, her throat, the delicate flesh beneath her earlobes, the pale, pulsing curve at her shoulders. He tasted, he sipped, he drank greedily, drawing strength from her moans of pleasure, her startled sighs of delight and surprise.

The scent of him dazzled her. Erotic, fresh, musky arousal mingled with forest spice, a dizzying mixture of all that was natural, all that was male. She wanted him. Desperately, defiantly, beyond all whim or reason and with a passion beyond her experience. There was no time to rationalize, to sort out the jumble of sensation, the secret whispers in her mind. She knew that only this man and this man only had the power to heal her, to make her whole.

"Ellie...honey...are you sure?"

"Yes." It was a moan. "Oh, yes." She returned his kisses with frantic vengeance while her seeking hands roamed the slickened planes of his chest. She fisted the lose fabric of the shirt she'd insisted he don against the cold night air. Now she regretted that request, pushed at the offending garment until he shrugged it off and tossed it aside.

A satisfied sigh slid from her lips. She studied the beauty of his bare torso, sculpted and vibrant, glistening in the firelight.

"You're beautiful," she murmured. "So perfect."

He mumbled something against her throat, but made no attempt to quell her searching fingers. His skin was hot to the touch, stretched over taut muscles that vibrated beneath her fingertips like the oiled engine of a perfectly tuned machine. The power of his body, the strength of pulsing muscle, of steel-hard bone was incredibly exciting.

Ellie wanted to feel that strength, all of it. Around her. Inside her. Now.

As if reading her mind, Samuel withdrew slightly, and tugged the hem of her tattered fleece top. She raised

her arms, allowed him to remove it, then squirmed to
kick off her sweatpants. They, too, were brushed aside.

The chill air raised gooseflesh, along with a sudden
surge of modesty. She crossed her arms to cover her
swollen breasts, and the sturdy cotton bra concealing
them. "I, ah, I'm not as thin as I used to be."

Samuel's eyes reflected only wonder. "You're beautiful."

She flinched at the blatant admiration in his gaze,
recalling the last time he'd viewed her so intimately,
when he'd delivered her son. "In comparison, I suppose
there's been some improvement."

A startled blink, an amused chuckle. "You were
beautiful then, too, but considering the circumstance, I
thought it inappropriate to comment." Leaning forward,
he brushed a gentle kiss at the curve of her throat,
slipped a furtive hand behind to tickle between her
shoulder blades.

The bra sagged free, fell away. "Beautiful," he murmured, reaching out with a trembling fingertip to trace
pale blue veins of motherhood. "Sometimes I watch
while you're feeding Daniel, and I envy that closeness.
Before the two of you came into my life, I never
thought much about the bond between mother and child,
never considered its poignancy, its breathtaking
beauty." Ellie shivered as he slipped his palms beneath
her breasts to test their soft weight. "It's a miracle, a
gift of unconditional love. I never understood that before."

As Samuel bent to place a reverent kiss on each
dusky nipple, Ellie issued a soft cry, wrapped her arms
around his neck and drew his head to her breast. Grateful tears stung her eyes, moistened her cheek. Her heart
felt as if it would burst with happiness. This was a com-
plex man of strength and sensitivity, a man whose phys-

ical power belied a fragile heart and gentle soul. Every word, every gesture, every tender nuance of his being touched her on a level so deep she hadn't been aware it existed.

Samuel was a part of her, and she was part of him. She wanted him. She wanted him fiercely. She wanted him now.

The gentle embrace intensified, chaste kisses deepened. Lips tasted, tongues tested, probed. Fingers traced, touched, caressed, ignited a thousand tiny fires of passion and promise. Soft moans floated on giddy wings, dipped into delighted gasps, spiraled with shocking whispers, giggled replies.

Every tender stroke sent shock waves coursing through her body, every erotic caress pulled her closer to the edge of ecstasy. Her breath huffed like a freight train, her body vibrated like a well-tuned jet. Passion fogged her mind, sensitized her skin until she was so crazed with desire that she feared she might unzip the fleshy cover and leap right out of it.

She'd never been so crazed, so desperate for intimate contact. When her groping hands were thwarted by a denim wall, she cried out in frustration. Fumbling madly, she managed to open the zippered gate, only to find herself tugging vainly at the stubborn waistband. It wouldn't budge.

Samuel grunted, rolled over to fidget with the recalcitrant closer. A moment later he shoved the offending garment halfway down his thighs. Sweat glimmered from his face, dripped into eyes as glazed and bewildered as her own. "Wait," he croaked.

That was the last word on earth Ellie wanted to hear. She shoved a wet tangle of hair from her face, sucked in enough breath to speak. "Why? What's wrong."

He rolled to the opposite side of the bed, mumbling

and struggling to kick off the jeans bunched at his knees. The project hadn't quite been completed when he reached the edge of the mattress, kept on rolling and hit the floor with a thud.

"Samuel?" Scrambling to her knees, Ellie yanked up the bedclothes, dragging them with her. From the floor, sounds of struggle were punctuated by muttered curses. She peered over the edge just as the offending jeans were kicked free. "What are you doing?"

"Back in a minute," he assured her, then crawled over to retrieve something from the medical kit beside the nightstand.

As he tucked the item discreetly into his palm, Ellie caught the outline of a small square packet. "Condoms? I don't believe this. You brought condoms to an isolated cabin in the middle of nowhere? What on earth were you planning—? No, never mind. I don't think I want to know."

Slipping off his boxer shorts, he had the grace to look embarrassed. "It happens to be a very complete med kit. Now—" he bounced into bed with a sexy leer "—where were we?"

"We were just reaching condom point." Ellie made a grab for the packet, frowned when he held it out of reach. "Aren't you going to let me put it on you?"

"That depends on whether or not you're going to draw a face on it. I refuse to wear anything down there that's smiling."

The idea held a certain appeal. At the moment, however, Ellie much too anxious to bother. "Not this time."

After a moment's hesitation he relinquished the packet from which Ellie retrieved the little latex prize. With trembling hands, she managed to complete the process. He was every bit as gorgeous as she'd imagined, and touching him there had whipped her libido into renewed frenzy.

"Hurry," she whispered, but before he could move, she practically flung him on his back and straddled him. He lifted her up, teased her by rubbing himself against her thigh. It was the most erotic sensation she'd ever experienced in her life. She moved with him, shivering with delight. "Ooh, *ooh*— Uh-oh."

"Huh?" Samuel froze, followed her startled gaze. A pair of worried dark eyes stared back. Baloo sat beside the bed, whining, the tattered dog blanket clamped firmly in his mouth. "Oh, good grief. Go lay down."

The hound issued a disgruntled huff, then padded back to his own bed dragging the beloved blanket behind him.

"Sorry about that." Samuel's apology was dampened by a glimmer of amusement. "I guess he thought you were cold."

Steam rose from her sweaty skin. "I am definitely not cold."

"I'd agree with that." Wrapping an arm around her waist, he rolled over, taking her with him until he was firmly settled on top. "You're a lot of things," he murmured, yanking the bedclothes over their heads to form a privacy tent. "Cold is not one of them."

Ellie gasped as he pressed against her, wrapped her arms around his neck with a moan. His breath puffed moist and hot against her cheek as he rotated his hips slowly, sensually, easing himself into her slick warmth. She raised up to meet him, cried softly at the sweet ache of their joining.

He loved her tenderly, with a passion beyond anything she'd ever known. It was true, she thought in amazement, all that she'd ever read about the passion of true lovers was all true. Stars exploded. Bells rang. Two halves. A perfect whole. Complete now, and forever.

"Such a fussy boy," Ellie cooed, clapping Daniel's tiny hands together. "Yes, he is, a fussy little man. You want attention, don't you?" The baby smiled, emitted a happy gurgle. "How about if Mommy tickles that fat little tummy? Here it comes, ba-dum, ba-dum, ba-dum—" Feeling buoyant, well loved and profoundly satisfied after last night's passion, she lifted the baby's shirt, blew a noisy raspberry on her son's freshly bathed belly. Daniel reacted by flailing his hands and emitting a real, honest-to-goodness giggle. Ellie straightened, fried with excitement. "You laughed, you actually laughed! Samuel—!" She spun around, faced an empty cabin and remembered.

Samuel wasn't here.

Her excitement died instantly, replaced by a bubble of apprehension. He left two hours ago and should have been back by now. Unless something had gone terribly wrong.

Ellie bit her lip, scooped Daniel into her arms. "It's going to be all right," she whispered for her own benefit rather than her son's. "Samuel will be back any minute, and he's going to have wonderful news. I can feel it in my bones."

In truth the only thing she felt in her bones was sheer dread, but optimism was her crisis crutch, and she leaned on it now with a vengeance. "We're going to be free, Daniel, I'm sure of it. Samuel's going to tell us—"

A thud on the front porch spun her around. Footsteps, the familiar scrape of boots on rough wood. She held her breath. The knob rattled, turned. Baloo leapt from the sofa, sat by the front door, tail wagging, butt bouncing in excitement.

Only when the door swung open did Ellie dare breathe. "Samuel, thank God."

Shifting Daniel against her shoulder, she rushed across the room, jockeyed for position with the exuberant hound. A satisfying ear scratch had Baloo in the throes of an ecstacy he was clearly unwilling to relinquish. Ellie, however, would not be denied. She flashed an "excuse me" smile, gently hip-checked the startled dog aside and lifted her lips for Samuel's kiss. She was not disappointed. "Umm," she murmured. "Nice. I've missed that."

"Me, too." Smiling, Samuel nodded at the baby's bobbling head. "How's our boy?"

"He giggled, he actually laughed out loud."

"I wish I'd heard that." He wistfully stroked the baby's soft scalp, then turned away to shrug off his jacket.

Ellie waited anxiously, but not for long. "Did you get through to your friend?"

"Yes." On his way to the kitchen Samuel dug the fire tower key out of his pocket, returned it to the cabinet drawer. "If long-range forecasts and thaw rates match computer models, the high-country lakes will be open by the first of April."

Which meant that all the isolated access roads, including the one leading to the cabin, were expected to be clear and passable by then. "That gives us a couple of weeks. By then the snow crust should be thin enough to drive your truck out." She watched his expression carefully. It remained impassive, unreadable. "Assuming, of course, that we still have to leave. Do we, Samuel?"

He filled a water glass, drained it, then met her worried gaze. "Yes."

Her heart dropped to her toes, but she simply nodded.

Setting down the empty glass, Samuel propped a hip against the counter and crossed his arms. "My contact at the forest service says that a search team is scheduled for the first week in April. He asked if Baloo and I would be available."

The request didn't surprise her, since Samuel had mentioned that Baloo's one redeeming talent was an uncanny ability to sniff out lost skiers under conditions so poor that most rescue dogs couldn't even locate a scent trail. "They're still looking for me, aren't they?"

"Actually they're looking for a body."

"They think I'm dead?" The thought buoyed her spirits. "That's good, isn't it? If Stanton believes I'm dead, he'll stop searching and we can go on with our lives."

Samuel considered that. "Under the circumstances of your disappearance, Mackenzie clearly fears the worst, but without proof I doubt he'll accept it. From what I was told, missing-person flyers have been plastered all over the mountain, along with a photograph and a hefty reward offer. If we stay here, sooner or later someone will stumble up the road and recognize you."

"I suppose so." Deeply disappointed, Ellie laid Daniel in the cradle. "I never really believed that Stanton would give up, but when you mentioned there was a chance he hadn't pursued the search, I got my hopes up. That's why I asked you to, well, you know."

No response was given. None was expected. The trip to the radio tower had been Ellie's idea. Once she'd convinced herself there was a chance—however slim— that Stanton might have given up the search, she'd pleaded with Samuel to check it out. He'd agreed, deciding the information could be gathered under the guise of a routine weather check.

Now Ellie fussed with the rumpled receiving blanket, smoothed the downy fuzz of her drowsy son's scalp. Guilt pricked her. Life on the run was not what she wanted for her precious baby. There had to be a way to provide Daniel with a happy, normal childhood and still keep him safe. At the moment she had no clue as to how that could be done without losing him completely.

A whisper startled her. "He's getting big." Samuel gazed over her shoulder, slid his arms around her waist. "Look at those fat cheeks. He's beginning to look like a bald chipmunk."

Resting her head beside his cheek, Ellie relaxed against him. "My son is not bald. A little thin on top, maybe, but definitely not bald." A subtle tension seeped from his torso. "Samuel, is something wrong?"

A brief hesitation added to her concern. "No."

"Are you sure?" She turned in the circle of his arms. "Is there something you haven't told me, something you found out from your friend?"

"No, nothing." The cloud of uncertainty in his eyes was worrisome. "I'm just disappointed, that's all. I'd hoped—" He blinked, shuttered his gaze. "Never mind. It's nothing."

"What's nothing?" She reached out as he turned away. "Samuel, tell me."

Clearly disturbed, Samuel crouched to stroke Baloo's head. He spoke without looking up. "I just wonder if you're doing the right thing. You can't avoid Daniel's father forever. Sooner or later you're going to have to deal with him."

A frisson of fear fingered the base of her spine. "No, I don't, and I won't. Stanton Mackenzie is a liar, a cheat and a totally unprincipled cad. I won't let my son have anything to do with him."

Samuel sighed, stood. "You don't have the right to make that choice." He snagged her wrist as she turned away. "Listen to me, honey, I'm on your side."

She pulled away. "It doesn't sound like it."

"How long can you keep running, looking over your shoulder, putting your entire life on hold?"

"As long as it takes." An edgy bite in her voice made him flinch. She didn't care. "I won't give up my son, Samuel, not for you, not for anybody."

If she'd slapped him, he couldn't have looked more stung. "I'm not suggesting that, Ellie."

"Then what exactly are you suggesting? That I pit an empty wallet against a bottomless bank account, my overworked lawyer from the Legal Aid Society against Stanton's team of silk-suited barracudas, all in some futile, misguided hope that I might, *might* get visitation rights to my own child?"

"I'll get you a lawyer, Ellie, a good one. You won't lose Daniel. I've already told you I won't let that happen."

"How will you stop it, Samuel? Have you forgotten that I'm technically in violation of a court order? By this time Stanton's probably already been awarded temporary custody. I won't even be able to file a challenge until I hand Daniel over to him, and I won't do that. Do you hear me, Samuel? I will never, ever do that."

"Honey, please—"

"No!" She stepped back, hands raised like a shield. "I don't want to talk about this anymore."

Samuel dropped his arm to his side. "You can't solve your problems by running away from them."

"Why not?" she shot back. "You do."

The moment the words left her mouth, she wished

them back. It was too late. Samuel's eyes glazed with anguish, his expression crumpled into a mask of utter despair.

Ellie reached out. "Samuel, I—"

"We're out of firewood," he said quietly.

Then he took his jacket from the coat peg, opened the front door and was gone.

Chapter Ten

A cold wind howled from the east. Flurried snow stung like biting gnats. Samuel shivered, cursed his foolishness at having left his jacket inside the cabin. A flannel shirt was scant protection against the sudden arctic wind.

He trudged another hundred feet down the crusted road, paused to jab a tree limb into the iced snow. The measurement came up at eighteen inches, give or take, although he knew it would be deeper a few miles up the road where the forest thickened. Consistency below the crust was mushy. Spring thaw would be rapid this year. Creeks would rise quickly, the road would become a river of mud.

Their timing would have to be perfect.

Samuel tossed the limb aside, blew into his hands to warm them. The truck, a four-wheel-drive pickup already dug out and dressed in tire chains, could handle at least a six-inch snow crust, maybe eight. More than that would risk clogging the axle; less meant getting bogged down in a quicksand of oozing muck.

Spring could arrive unexpectedly in the mountains, and with amazing speed. Sometimes the sun showed itself without fanfare, and smiled warmly until fall. Sometimes snow fell until June. Late-season snow melted quickly, of course, which kept the creeks rushing at flood level and added to a watery rush of mud.

Yes, their timing would definitely have to be perfect.

Jamming his hands into his pockets, Samuel ducked into the wind and headed back toward the cabin. He shouldn't have walked out like that, shouldn't have been wounded by the truth. Ellie's words had sliced him to the quick, but she'd been right. Samuel, too, was running from reality, a gutless retreat based on motives considerably less substantial and more cowardly than hers.

Ellie was running from fear to protect her son; Samuel was running from failure to protect himself.

It was Ellie who had the most to lose, yet he'd blithely advised her to face Daniel's father in court and risk losing custody of her child when Samuel himself didn't have the courage to face the man whose life he had ruined. What arrogance.

All he could do now was apologize and beg forgiveness.

He hurried through the storm, pausing frequently to catch his breath and cough away an annoying tightness in his chest.

By the time Samuel reached the cabin, he was freezing and wheezing and desperate for warmth. He burst in the door, teeth chattering. As he entered the blessed warmth of the living room, he saw Ellie standing with her back to the open bathroom door, peering over her shoulder as if studying her reflection in the bathroom mirror.

Her eyes popped as he staggered to thaw himself at the woodstove. "Good grief, where on earth have you been?" She rushed to snag the comforter off the bed and wrap it around his shoulders, clucking and tsking like a mother hen. "Oh, look at you, your lips are blue and you've got icicles on your nose."

Samuel doubted the icicle part, but was fairly certain her assessment of lip color was accurate. "I forgot my jacket," he said stupidly.

"Well, duh." She jerked a thumb toward the occupied coat peg, her eyes flashing adorably. "No kidding. I ran out with it as soon as I saw it still hanging on the hook, but I couldn't find you anywhere. I was just about to take Baloo and hunt you down."

"Don't ever do that," he murmured between shivers. "If you put yourself at risk, you put Daniel at risk." He tugged the blessed comforter around his shoulders, saw Ellie's guilty flush as he turned to absorb the woodstove's radiant heat.

She licked her lips, avoided his gaze. "I'll get coffee."

As she turned, he touched her arm, stopping her. "You did the right thing, honey." When she shook her head, he folded a hand under her chin, urged her to look at him. He knew she'd been worried about him, and he felt bad about that. He also knew that she hadn't searched beyond the clearing because to do so would mean leaving her baby son alone. "Daniel is your first, your only priority. Don't ever jeopardize his safety for me, or for anyone else."

Her eyes darkened with conflict, but she simply nodded, smiled. "Now about that coffee…"

He stroked her cheek with the back of his hand. "Sounds wonderful."

Hoisting on tiptoes, she kissed his cheek, gave him a brief but fervent hug, then hurried toward the kitchen. Samuel watched the supple sway of her hips with a blended sense of enticement and confusion. Something was different. Her bottom seemed rounder, more sensually defined. "Are those my brother's pants?"

"Uh-huh." She set the pot back on the burner, carried the steaming mug of coffee back to the living area. "Here you go. Be careful, it's hot."

Nodding his thanks, he wrapped icy fingers around the warm ceramic mug and watched Ellie's perky pirouette as she modeled her newly tailored clothes. She spun around twice, then faced away from him, looked over her shoulder and smoothed a palm down her denim-gloved derriere. "I took in the waist, put a couple of darts in the seat and voilà!"

Samuel blew out a breath, shrugged off the comforter and took a burning gulp of coffee. There ought to be a law against that kind of sex appeal.

"Well, what do you think?"

He shifted the mug, loosened his shirt. "You don't want to know what I think."

Her face crumpled. "Don't you like the pants?"

"Oh, I like them, so much that all I can think about is getting you out of them."

A startled expression melted into a tickled grin. "First you're half-frozen, then you want to get naked. That coffee must have warmed you right up."

Samuel blinked a sweat bead out of his eye. His gaze was still riveted on her firm little bottom. "Coffee has nothing to do with the heat I'm feeling right now."

"Ooh, you silver-tongued devil." A flirty head toss, a twinkly, over-the-shoulder wink. "It so happens I just fed Daniel and put him down for a nice, long nap. Convenient, hmm?''

''Very.'' He followed her to the bed, reached out.

She skittered away with a laugh, returned a moment later with a goofy grin and a tube of squeeze cheese.

Samuel couldn't get his clothes off fast enough.

Ellie pursed her lips, fiddled with the hand-woven napkin holder in the middle of the table. ''It doesn't matter. Oregon, Idaho, wherever.''

Pushing the holder and a pair of trout-shaped salt-and-pepper shakers aside, Samuel spread out the map so Ellie could see it. ''I fought a wildfire outside Boise a couple of years ago. It's a great place, with great people, but it's too small-town friendly.''

''How can a place be too friendly?''

''When its citizens know everything about everyone in town.'' He studied the hodgepodge of color-coded roads, traced an interstate with his fingertip. ''You need someplace larger, more anonymous. Chicago?''

Ellie squirmed in her seat, stared at a blemish in her freshly tailored jeans to avoid looking at the map. ''Chicago is too urban. I want my son to grow up with his own yard, in a safe neighborhood where he and his friends can play on real grass. Besides, it's too far away.''

''I thought far away was what you wanted.''

''No...I mean, yes, but it's, well, *too* far. It would cost a fortune just to get there.''

''Let me worry about that.''

''I'm not taking money from you, Samuel. This is my problem, not yours.''

He regarded her thoughtfully. ''I'm not dropping you and Daniel off at the nearest bus station, Ellie. I'll take you wherever you want to go.''

Biting her lip, she pulled the map over, pretended to study it so he wouldn't see the moisture gathering in her eyes. "That isn't fair to you."

"I'll decide what's fair."

"You'd be putting your life on hold, your career—" She angled a glance upward, saw his jaw tighten.

"I don't have a career, remember?"

"You have a career, Samuel, you've just turned your back on it." Pushing the map away, she crossed her arms, frowned at him. "I still don't understand why."

A muscle beneath his ear twitched in warning. "I don't want to discuss it."

"I don't want to discuss hiding places either, but you insisted so here we are, staring at a stupid map when there's plenty of time to decide…. I mean—" Biting her lip, she struggled with the lie, fought against truth. She pushed away from the table, wiped her hands on her thighs as she stood. "So, what would you like for dinner? There's still a few pounds of ground venison in the freezer and a chicken. I saved a ham bone for soup—"

"Ellie." Samuel caught her arm as she passed by. "Honey, I know it's scary to think about leaving, but we can't stay."

"There's no rush," she insisted, sounding thin and unconvincing even to herself. There was a rush, and she knew it. The pantry was nearly bare, spring had officially arrived and the road could be ready to travel in less than a week.

Samuel wrapped a comforting arm around her waist, pulled her into his lap. "We can't stay here, honey, and we can't just point the truck and drive without knowing where we're heading."

She sniffed, wiped her wet eyes. *We.* She liked the sound of that even though the word sent guilty chills down her spine. "You'd better be careful of the *we* word, Samuel. It's beginning to sound like a commitment."

His smile was genuine, and a bit teasing. "Maybe I'm more committed than I'd like to admit." The smile faded, the sparkle died. "I won't let you go this alone, Ellie, not until you and Daniel are settled and safe."

"And then?"

He shifted, laid her head on his shoulder, ignored the hidden meaning of her question. "There are beautiful suburbs in the Chicago area. The city has a booming economy, lots of jobs available—" his gaze wandered "—a good real-estate market."

Ellie studied the sadness in his eyes. It hurt to see his pain, killed her to know she could do nothing to relieve it. "You'd make a lousy Realtor, Samuel."

The comment clearly startled him. "Thanks for the vote of confidence."

"That wasn't meant as an insult."

"Could have fooled me."

She sat up, swiveled on his lap to face him. "Look, I have nothing against Realtors. My mother put me through college selling properties, and she was wonderful at it. But you are not a salesman, Samuel. You're a firefighter, a paramedic, a saver of lives. It's what you do, it's who you are. Nothing else will give you the same satisfaction or sense of purpose."

He tensed, took a raspy breath. "Then I guess I'll have to settle for a life without purpose."

"Samuel, please—"

"I don't want to talk about this," he growled. Sweat beaded his forehead, and his cheeks were abnormally flushed. "You don't underst—" He coughed suddenly, turned away to cover his mouth and continued to cough while Ellie patted his back. Air wheezed into his lungs, and he finally straightened, breathing heavily. "Sorry." He wiped his tearing eyes, shook his head. "That snuck up on me."

"Are you all right? You were coughing in your sleep last night, too." She stroked his face, which seemed overly warm to her. "I think you have a fever."

"It's nothing." He turned his head from her touch, lifted her off his lap. "Probably just a virus. I've kept my distance from Daniel, and I shouldn't be breathing on you, either."

"If I recall, you've done a lot more than breathe on me." When he didn't respond to her teasing, she studied him with concern. He didn't look well. "You're really feeling ill, aren't you?"

"A little worn-out," he conceded. "Probably too much hiking yesterday."

Ellie flinched, went to retrieve a dampened washrag from the bathroom. "This is all my fault," she murmured as she sponged his face. "I never should have asked you to go to the tower."

"It's nobody's fault, honey." He eased the cloth from her hands, set it on the table. "I'm coming down with a cold, that's all. As drafty as this place is, it's a wonder we aren't all sick." He rubbed the back of his neck, and stood slowly, as if the movement caused him pain. "Maybe I'll take a couple of aspirins and lie down for a while."

A sudden surge of anxiety fluttered Ellie's stomach. "That's a good idea. I'll call you when dinner's ready."

"Don't fix anything for me. I'm not hungry."

"Samuel?"

He paused to look over his shoulder. "Is there anything I can do for you?"

He shook his head, issued a weary sigh. "I'm fine,

honey. Don't worry about me."

But he wasn't fine, and Ellie was worried.

Sterile. Antiseptic. The smell of agony and of death.
It turned Samuel's stomach. A white hallway undulated
ahead. Light sprayed from an open door.

He didn't want to go through that door, but knew that
he must. His feet dragged, step after reluctant step.
Blurred people hurried by, some dressed in white, some
in green, all were tense, rushed. They smelled like iodine.

Samuel was beside the open door now, close enough
to hear the groans from inside. Voices, stiff and professional. Cold and curt. Voices intoning possibilities,
probabilities, prognoses. Surgery. Risks. Paralysis.
Death.

Samuel moved away, backed down the hall, covered
his ears against the voice of cold dispassion.

Surgery. Risks. Paralysis. Death.

A scream. A terrible, agonized scream.

Samuel spun around, but there was no where to run.
Dark eyes, huge and pleading. An outstretched hand.

Help me.

Behind him, the agonized scream. Before him, the
pleading eyes. Surrounding him was failure. Failure.
Failure.

And death.

"Here, sip this." Ellie braced Samuel's shoulders,
eased him up against the pillows.

He blinked groggily, eyed the steaming mug.

"What is it?"

"Ham soup. Actually, it's ham bone soup, but it's
hot and it's nourishing and I want you to drink it."

"Not hungry," he mumbled, turning his head.

Ellie was nothing if not persistent. "Seems to me that

when I was in this situation, you made some kind of threat involving the use of a soda straw as a feeding tube.'' She smiled sweetly as he hiked a grumpy brow. ''The delivery mechanism is up to you, of course, but one way or another this soup is going to end up in that magnificent, washboard-firm stomach of yours.''

He stared woefully at the fragrant liquid. ''I'd rather have sex.''

The startling statement made her laugh, which in turn brought Baloo over to investigate. ''Isn't that typical?'' she asked the perplexed hound. ''The man can't hold his head up without help, but he can sure as the dickens get something else up on his own.'' The animal whined with appropriate chagrin. ''You see, even your dog is shocked by such a blatant conflict in priorities.''

''It's a guy thing,'' Samuel said with a weary smile. ''And you love it.''

''Yes, I do, so drink this—'' she wrapped his limp fingers around the mug '' —and get your strength back so I can jump your bones without feeling guilty.''

He issued a weak chuckle, pushed the mug back into her hands. ''Really, I don't want anything now. Maybe later.''

Pursing her lips, Ellie considered that for a moment. A brief moment. ''Perhaps I should sing to you.''

That got his attention. ''No! Er, I mean, you don't want to wake Daniel.''

''Daniel loves my singing. In fact, it always makes him eat better.'' She grinned at Samuel's forlorn expression, then launched into lusty song. ''Up on the moun-tain, mountain so high—''

Samuel groaned.

''Look toward the val-ley—'' Ellie didn't miss a beat when Baloo threw his head back and howled. ''Hear the wind si-igh.''

Baloo howled again. Samuel groaned again, covered his ears.

"Hear the wind sigh, dear—"

Howl. Groan.

"Hear the wind sigh, look toward the val-ley—"

"Enough!" Samuel croaked. "Give me the damned soup."

Triumphant, Ellie handed over the mug, watched happily as Samuel chugalugged the contents and wiped his mouth with the back of his hand. "There, don't you feel better?"

"Now that you've stopped singing, yes." He heaved a sigh, and let his head drop back on the pillow.

She laid a palm to his forehead, found it disturbingly warm. "I'll have you know that I was a lead vocalist in my high school choir. The music director was very impressed with my talent." Beside the bed, Baloo's muzzle split into a tongue-lolling grin, and his tail agreeably thumped the floor. "You see? Even your dog appreciates fine music."

"'Loo's been tone-deaf since birth," Samuel growled. He yanked irritably at the covers, bunched them under his chin. "Can't you put another log in the woodstove or something? It's colder than a well digger's fanny in here."

It was at least seventy degrees. "Sure."

"Thanks," he mumbled, then burrowed beneath the covers looking flushed and miserable.

Ellie dutifully added a log to the roaring fire, then retrieved a couple of aspirin from the bathroom cabinet. She brought them to Samuel with a glass of water. "Open your mouth."

He opened one eye instead. "Uh-uh."

"Don't be stubborn. This will make your achy muscles feel better, and help lower your fever."

After a suspicious squint at the small white tablets in her palm, he issued what Ellie interpreted as an affirmative grunt. She placed the pills in his mouth, held the water glass to his lips only to have him snatch the glass away with a cranky grumble. "I can hold my own damned glass."

"Whoa, sure you can, macho man. Didn't mean to threaten your masculinity." She laughed at his withering stare, waited until he'd swallowed the medication then took the glass and set it on the nightstand. "Men are such babies when they're sick."

The comment was given softly, with affection. No umbrage was intended, and Samuel took none. Instead he sniffed pitifully. "My head hurts."

"I know." She stroked his damp hair. "The aspirin should help."

He closed his eyes, and heaved a contented sigh. "You have soft hands."

"Thank you."

"And you always smell so good."

"Do I?"

"Umm." Shifting, he took a shallow breath, rolled his head against the pillow. "Sometimes the scent of you wakes me up in the middle of the night, and I want you so bad it hurts."

She combed his hair with her fingers, felt as if a giant hand were squeezing her heart. "I wake up wanting you, too."

He rolled his head back, used considerable effort to lift one eyelid. "Really?" When she nodded, he frowned. "You never told me that before."

"You never told me, either."

"No, I guess I didn't." The words were sleepily slurred. A moment later, his breathing slowed in slumber.

Across the room, a cranky wail filtered up from the cradle. Ellie bent to kiss her sleeping lover's cheek, then went to tend her baby.

It was a bad crash. Head-on, then over a steep embankment. Crushed metal, twisted steel. Limp bodies trapped in the carnage. A cry from the ravine. Someone was alive down there. Someone needed help.

Samuel shifted his gear, snapped the rappel rope through his harness clip. Just another call. A bad one, but he saw lots of bad ones. He saved those he could, wept for those he couldn't, went on to the next call. It was his job. It was his life.

The ravine was steep, treacherous. Halfway down now. Sharp twigs scratched at his eyes. Dirt and rock rained from above, a hailstone of pebbles loosened by his decent.

Three-quarters of the way down. The cry was weaker. He had to hurry.

The twisted wreck was right beneath him now, perhaps ten feet below. The rope wasn't long enough. As he dangled above the imprisoning mangle of metal, the cry diminished into a thin moan. Someone was dying in there, and he couldn't help because the rope was too short.

Too short.

Samuel reached for the harness. A voice in his mind screamed, "No!" It was Drake's voice, Drake's voice telling him not to release the harness. Samuel didn't listen. The cry from the wreckage had stopped now. He had to get there. Had to save a life.

He released the latch, and plummeted. Not ten feet. Not twenty feet. He plummeted a hundred feet, then a thousand, then a million.

He landed in a white hallway. Sterile. Antiseptic. The smell of iodine. A lighted doorway beckoned.

Voices, stiff and profession. Surgery. Risks. Paralysis. Death.

A scream. A terrible, agonized scream. Drake's scream.

He should have listened, shouldn't have released the harness. But the dark eyes were huge and pleading. The outstretched hand beckoned.

Samuel covered his eyes, but heard the scream. He covered his ears, but saw the reaching hand. No escape, nowhere to run.

Failure. Failure.

Death.

Chapter Eleven

"Samuel, wake up."

A soft voice, melodic, warm. He shifted, opened an eye. The most beautiful face in the world smiled down at him.

"How are you feeling?" Ellie asked. "You had a restless night."

"Did I?" Ignoring a wave of dizziness, Samuel pushed into a sitting position, flinched at a viselike tightness in his chest. After several shallow breaths, the room stopped swaying. "I'm sorry if I disturbed you."

"You always disturb me, handsome. Flatten your knees."

He complied without comment until she placed the breakfast tray in his lap. A bowl of raisin-studded oatmeal grinned up at him. His stomach lurched. "I'm not very hungry."

Ellie instantly burst into song. "Up on the mountain—"

Samuel snatched up a spoon.

"Good boy." She patted his head as if he were a paper-trained puppy. "Do you need anything else before I give Daniel his bath?"

When he shook his head, she brushed a breezy kiss on his cheek, scooped her son out of the cradle and hustled toward the kitchen sink, humming softly. Samuel's spoon hovered over the untouched cereal until Ellie turned on the faucet, then he placed the utensil quietly beside the bowl and issued a pained sigh.

"Mountain so hi-igh," Ellie sang without turning around.

Samuel muttered, retrieved the spoon and scooped up a generous portion of hot cereal along with one raisin eye. The singing stopped.

"Danged woman has eyes in back of her head," he muttered to Baloo, who gave a knowing whine and laid his chin on the mattress. He eyed the hound, slipped a furtive glance toward the kitchen. As soon as Ellie was distracted by Daniel's happy splashing, Samuel offered the heaping spoon to Baloo. The animal licked it clean in a flash. Samuel held his breath, waiting. When Ellie neither burst into song nor spun around to skewer him with a reproachful stare, he gave Baloo another bite, then another and another.

By the time Daniel's bath was over, Baloo was happily licking his whiskers and Samuel's bowl was empty.

"Wonderful!" Ellie exclaimed when she retrieved the breakfast tray. "You see, you were hungrier than you thought."

"Uh-huh."

"Would you like some more?"

"No, thanks, I couldn't eat another bite." Samuel patted his stomach to deflect attention from sounds of whisker licking and doggy lip-smacking. Ellie would have ignored Baloo entirely if the dog hadn't chosen that moment to deflate himself with a three-decibel burp.

"Goodness," Ellie murmured, turning toward the satisfied hound.

Samuel snagged her wrist. "I wouldn't mind some water, though, if it's not too much trouble."

"Oh, sure. Coming right up." She flashed him a sunny grin, took the tray into the kitchen.

Samuel pointed at the dog bed, mouthed the appropriate command. Baloo obediently lumbered past Ellie, who was on her way back with a filled water glass. Samuel accepted the glass, drank greedily and regretted it. With his lungs twisting in warning, he barely managed to set the glass aside before the coughing fit attacked, and continued until his face was afire and he was wheezing for breath.

It didn't help that Ellie was whacking his shoulder blades hard enough to knock his lungs out through his nose. He would have told her to stop, except it took another ten seconds before he stopped coughing long enough to draw even the shallowest breath. They were the longest ten seconds of his life.

By the time his head fell back against the pillow, Ellie was clutching his shoulders, her eyes huge with panic. "You're burning up."

"It's nothing." A weak wrist-flick did little to reinforce that proclamation, so he added a thin smile. "Really, I'm fine."

He wasn't fine. She knew it. And he knew it.

Her face was whiter than Snowdrift's ears. "I'll get the aspirin."

"No, please." There was no way he'd keep them down, but he didn't want to worry her further. "I, er, have to go to the bathroom anyway. I'll get them my-self.''

Ellie studied him for a moment. ''It might be better if I brought the bathroom to you, if you know what I mean.''

Samuel knew exactly what she meant. ''I am not go-ing to pee in a bucket.''

''It's not a terrible thing, you know. If I recall, you were quite helpful to me before I was strong enough to, well—'' she blushed adorably ''—you know.''

''That was different.''

''How?''

He folded his arms. ''It just was.''

''All right then, alpha man.'' Frowning, she stood back, swung her hand toward the open bathroom door less than ten feet from the bed. ''Go for it.''

''I will.''

''Fine.''

''Fine,'' Samuel mumbled, wishing the room would stop swaying long enough for him to get his bearings. He pulled back the covers, swiveled awkwardly around until his feet touched the floor. Every breath burned like fire, and his chest ached as if his lungs were pinched in barbed wire. He licked his lips, watched the target door undulate wildly. Puffing his cheeks, he sat rigidly for several long moments, then swung his legs back into bed and yanked up the covers.

Ellie sat beside him, rubbing his shoulder. ''You can't do it, can you?''

''I don't have to go anymore.''

''Samuel—''

''Baloo does.'' When her eyes widened in shock, Samuel nodded toward the front door where the hound was hopefully poised, wiggling in obvious discomfort. ''He's waiting for his morning walk.''

"He can wait a few more minutes."

"That's cruel," Samuel replied, managing to look both stung and reproachful at the same time. "It's not his fault he's a helpless animal depending on the kindness of humans for the basic necessities of life."

Ellie rolled her eyes, stood with a huff. "All right, I'll take him out, but you are not—I repeat *not* to leave that bed until I get back. Do you understand?"

"Perfectly." Of course, understanding and acquiescence were two entirely different things.

"I mean it, Samuel. You're a very sick man." With that, she opened the door for the exuberant hound, and left the cabin.

Samuel closed his eyes, breathing through his mouth to extract more oxygen with less effort. He was sick, all right. Damned sick, and if Samuel had correctly assessed his own condition, things would get a hell of a lot worse before they got better.

Jasper was just a formless bump of ice now. Samuel's precious Sacramento Kings hat and sweat shirt had been rescued weeks ago, when the poor shrunken snowman had become too fragile to support the garments.

Now Ellie stood beside the melted symbol of freedom and safety, mourning its loss even more than she'd mourned the departure of the bunny to which she'd become so emotionally attached. It was silly, she supposed, but she couldn't help herself. At least Snowdrift was alive and well, probably burrowed into a warm hole somewhere happily creating a new generation of flop-eared babies with a demure but ever-so-sexy Mrs. Snowdrift.

Yes, there would be more bunnies. There would never be another Jasper.

Ellie sighed, laid a hand over her heart as the melody

of "Taps" ran through her mind. "Spring has come," she sang softly. "Jasper's gone,/ From the snow,/ Don'tcha know,/ Seems so wrong—" A pinecone plopped at her feet.

She frowned at it. "What am I supposed to do with that?" Baloo wagged his tail, encouraged her with a yelp. "You want me to throw it?" Ellie doubted that the hound really nodded, but from her perspective, it looked as if he did. She shrugged and scooped up the pinecone. "Okay, boy. Go fetch." She flung the pinecone as hard as she could.

It bounced on the ground about thirty feet away.

Baloo whined.

"Go fetch, boy! Bring it back."

The hound gave her a dubious stare.

Ellie stared back. "Wait a minute. You don't expect *me* to go get the darned thing, do you?"

Baloo barked.

"Listen, bud, you are dog, I am human. Humans throw, dogs fetch. Those are the rules."

Saggy dog eyes blinked in disbelief.

"I take it this is news to you?"

Whining, Baloo shook his head, then wandered over to relieve himself on a nearby bush. Ellie noted the process with her own sense of relief. "It's about time you took care of business. Let's go inside now."

Ignoring the request, the dog lumbered to a particularly intriguing area at the edge of the clearing, sniffing and circling.

"I'm going inside," Ellie informed the indisposed animal. "Just scratch on the front door when you've finished your business."

Anxious to check on Samuel, she gave the melted snow mound a sad pat, heaved a regretful sigh and returned to the cabin, gushing about the beautiful weather before she'd even pulled the door shut behind her. "It is positively gorgeous today. The sun is shining, the sky is blue, and there are new buds on the buck brush—" Her gaze fell on the empty bed. "Samuel?"

Silence.

Her heart leapt into her throat, her voice was shrill with fear. *"Samuel?"*

The bathroom door was closed. Ellie dashed forward, pounded frantically. "Samuel, are you in there? Are you all right?"

Silence.

Modesty be damned, Ellie grabbed the knob, burst into the room and found exactly what she'd feared.

Cedar steam wafted from the simmering pot atop the woodstove. Ellie added fresh branches gathered from the forest, stirred the fragrant soup with a wooden paddle. Two days had passed since she'd found Samuel unconscious and bleeding. Two long, grueling days during which his condition had continued to deteriorate. Ellie was petrified.

In the cradle, Daniel cooed happily, blissfully unaware that the direction of his young life, and indeed his entire future rested on decisions his mother would soon be forced to make.

Ellie shuddered, absently petted the worried hound that now followed her like a four-legged shadow. Animals instinctively understood crisis. Unfortunately they couldn't deal with it any better than their human counterparts. At least Baloo couldn't. The heartbroken hound hadn't eaten in two days, and was practically paralyzed with grief.

The dog followed Ellie into the kitchen where she tried to console him with some hand-fed kibble. The offering was refused with a pathetic whine. "There's no sense in all of us starving," she told the reluctant animal. "Samuel would be very upset if he knew you weren't taking proper care of yourself."

The admonition wasn't given in a particularly stern tone since Ellie's appetite hadn't been any better than Baloo's. She forced herself to eat, but only to maintain a sufficient supply of nutritious breast milk for her son.

Heartbreak had never been so painful.

She glanced at the awful fish-shaped wall clock, then went to awaken Samuel as she'd done every two hours since he'd passed out in the bathroom and struck his head on the sink.

She sat on the edge of the mattress, felt tears sting her eyes. He was so very pale. The rugged creases that had once seemed so virile now looked like sunken chasms in gray rock. She stroked his dear face, smoothed hair that was no longer glossy, but felt dry and brittle to the touch. His breathing was labored, shallow. Gurgling.

She bit her lip, buried her fear with gentleness. "Wake up, Samuel."

A quiet groan slid from his slack lips.

"I know," she soothed. "I know, but you have to wake up just for a few minutes."

His eyelids fluttered, refused to rise.

Ellie moistened a cloth in the basin by his bed, cooled his face with it. "There, doesn't that feel good? I think your fever has gone down. You don't feel nearly as warm today."

True enough, although that gave her little solace since he seemed to be having even more difficulty breathing. The cedar steam that had been so beneficial in Daniel's first days of life didn't appear to have any effect now.

Samuel's chest vibrated as he sucked a noisy breath, and painfully opened his eyes. Hollow eyes. Dead eyes.

It took every ounce of strength she could muster to keep from weeping. "Good morning," she whispered. "Again."

He blinked, focused. A small glow of recognition sparked in his eyes. "Hi." The word was forced out with great effort.

On the other side of the bed, Baloo hoisted his forepaws to the mattress and sniveled. Samuel turned his head to acknowledge the animal. "Hey, boy. How's—" a breath "—it going?"

The hound licked Samuel's wrist.

Samuel turned away coughing, too weak to protest as Ellie raised his shoulders, held him until the spasm had passed. She fluffed the pillows, settled him back into the semisitting position that seemed to ease his breathing.

"Can you take a little water?" When he nodded, she retrieved a glass from the nightstand, held it to his lips. He sipped cautiously, made no attempt to hold the glass himself. When he turned his head, she exchanged the glass for the med kit penlight which was also on the nightstand and forced an airy tone. "It's time for me to practice all the neat medic tricks you taught me. Open your eyes for me." He complied and she shined the light into each eye. "Everything is dilating nicely. Still no sign of concussion."

"Lucky me." There was no edge to his voice, only profound sadness.

Ellie swallowed hard, managed a bright smile. "Actually you really are lucky, considering the size of that blue golf ball on your forehead. I was afraid you'd fractured your darned skull."

"Too thick."

"I'd agree with that." She returned the penlight to the nightstand, picked up the stethoscope.

Samuel raised a weak hand, shook his head. "Don't bother—" A coughing spasm cut off his breath. When it was over, he looked like death on a stick.

Ellie laid the stethoscope aside without argument, used the damp cloth to sponge his face. She didn't have to listen to his chest again to know that every breath he took sounded like the ocean being sucked through a straw. "You have pneumonia, don't you?"

At first he gave no indication that he'd heard. After a moment, he nodded weakly.

The confirmation was no surprise, but still hit her like a fist in the gut. Pneumonia was serious, damned serious. People died from it.

She set the cloth aside, fearing the frantic trembling of her hands would reveal her terror. "All right, now that we know what we're dealing with, how can we treat it?"

He shook his head again, looked away.

Ellie stood suddenly, spun to focus on the med kit in the corner. She rushed to open it, dug through the contents with hysterical abandon. "Antibiotics," she mumbled stupidly, tossing ointment tubes and bandages onto the floor. "There must be antibiotics in here somewhere."

"Ellie—"

"There must be!" Ignoring Samuel's thin plea, she heaved an instrument tray out to root beneath it. "You have everything in here. Dear Lord, you even have latex gloves and condoms." The items in question hit the floor along with a pack of tongue depressors and several rolls of over-the-counter antacids. "You have everything in here, everything—" Her fingers clamped around an official-looking prescription-type bottle. She read the label. "What's this?"

Samuel sighed. "Allergy medicine."

Ellie was already shaking tablets into her palm. "Take them. They might help."

"No—"

"Take them!" She stumbled to the bed, thrust the handful of pills at him. "Please!"

Somehow he mustered the strength to lay a hand over her wrist, speak brokenly between strained breaths. "There's nothing you can do...has to run its course." His eyes were calm, determined. Weary. "Do something...for me."

Ellie clutched his hand. "Anything."

He gave a tired nod, licked his lips. "Take Daniel and go."

The implication of his request didn't sink in right away. "Go where?"

"Anywhere. Chicago, Boise—" He turned away, coughed, took a shuddering breath. When he could speak again, he sounded like a man resigned to his fate. "It's time, Ellie. It's time."

A cold terror settled in the pit of her stomach. "I'm not leaving you, Samuel. I'll never leave you."

"You have to. For Daniel."

"No." She stood, spun away. Her fingers absently clawed her scalp, her feet moved without permission, and she paced the cramped cabin like a caged animal. "You're getting better every day." She fervently believed that. She had to believe it. "We'll leave when you're well, Samuel, and we'll leave together. All of us. Together."

"The drawer," he whispered.

Ellie jerked to a stop, looked over her shoulder. His eyes were sunken, bruised, like lumps of coal in a colorless, winter-white face. Like a snowman melting in the sun, dying before her eyes. She was helpless to stop it.

"Kitchen drawer," he repeated, paused to lick his lips. "Truck key. Take it."

Unable to speak, Ellie refused by shaking her head.

"My wallet. Credit cards. Take them, too."

Tears slid down her cheeks. She wouldn't leave him. She wouldn't.

Samuel's soft voice echoed as if reading her mind. "You have to leave."

Panic cracked inside her, shattered into stinging shards of hopeless terror. Blood rushed to her brain, whooshed like a roaring river, drowning thought, drowning logic, drowning everything but the hideous fear. It was pulling her under, squeezing her lungs until she wanted to scream from the searing pain. But she couldn't scream because she couldn't breathe.

You have to leave.

No, she wouldn't. She couldn't.

For Daniel.

No.

It's time.

The room spun wildly. Air rushed into her starved lungs. Tears spurted from her eyes. All her life she'd dealt with problems by running away from them. It had been easier that way because she'd never wanted anything badly enough to endure the pain of confrontation. Never until now.

For the first time, Ellie was willing to stay, to confront, to pay any price, endure any anguish to save the man she loved more than life itself. And she did love Samuel Evans, desperately, irrevocably, with every fiber of her being, every atom of her soul.

She wouldn't leave him. She couldn't leave him.

But if she didn't leave him, she could lose her precious son forever.

"Ellie."

The weak whisper caught like a cruel hand, spun her around. Samuel was ashen, his eyes dark with desperation. She hurried to his bedside, clasped his icy hand between her palms, pressed it to her heart.

He coughed weakly, tried for a thin smile. "Thank you."

"I haven't done anything."

"You brought joy into my life." His fingers contracted as if he'd tried to squeeze her hand. "So much joy, so much laughter. Thank you for that."

Still clutching his hand with both of her own, Ellie dipped her head to wipe her wet face on the shoulder of her shirt. It was a delaying tactic allowing an extra moment to gain composure, to steady the emotional crack in a voice over which she barely had control. She licked her lips, focused her mind, faced him with forced reproach. "I will not allow you to give up on yourself, Samuel. Not this time."

He hiked a brow, managed a small smile. "Low blow."

"Dammit, Samuel, I'm not kidding. You are going to get well, do you hear me? If you don't, I'll...I'll sing to you. Yes, yes I will, I'll sing so loud and so long that you'll leap out of that bed for no other reason than to shut me up."

A puff of air slid from his lips as he closed his eyes. "Take 'Loo."

Startled, Ellie released his hand. "What?"

"When you leave. Take 'Loo. Please."

Reality hit like a sledge. That lazy old hound dog meant the world to Samuel. From the day Samuel had chosen the animal from the litter of scampering ten-week-old pups, Baloo had been his constant companion. Nothing had separated them. Nothing could.

Nothing except—

Ellie stood, jammed her hands on her hips. "I'm not taking your dog, Samuel, so you're just going to have to get better so you can care for him yourself."

"Protection."

"Protection?" Ellie stared at the lazy, saggy-eyed hound and didn't know whether to laugh or weep wildly. "Are we talking about the same animal that hid under the bed sniveling because there was badger on the porch?"

But Samuel didn't respond. He was asleep.

A sudden chill raised the flesh of her arms. She rubbed herself, wandered toward the cradle where Daniel was just awakening for lunch. "Don't worry, precious boy," she murmured, lifting him into her arms. "Mommy won't let anything bad happen to you, and she won't let anything bad happen to Samuel, either."

Daniel gurgled, gave her a trusting grin.

Ellie's heart sank. In the course of her life she'd made many promises, broken most of them. She'd never taken responsibility for not keeping her word, because she'd always had perfectly good reasons for not having done so. Flexibility was the key to survival. If situations change, one has to change with them.

Ellie's mother hadn't understood that, and had spent a lifetime of misery because of a promise, a wedding vow that she'd refused to break no matter how intolerable the marriage had become, or how incompatible its participants. Ellie had been determined never to let promises destroy her life. She always took on friendships, jobs and relationships with the highest of hopes, but if things changed, she was out of there. No fighting. No confrontation. No guilt, no emotion, just the flexibility to recognize one's error and move on.

So she'd always told herself, convinced herself that life was a gift to be experienced and enjoyed. But Ellie hadn't been experiencing life, she'd been avoiding it—avoiding the pain, the angst, the emotional commitments, avoiding all that was precious, all that made life unique.

She considered that as she settled onto the sofa to breast-feed her baby. There was a decision to make, a decision over life and death and the future of her beloved child. "Your father isn't a nice man, Daniel." Speaking aloud helped organize her thoughts. "But he wants you very much, and I know that he'd never do anything to hurt you." Daniel, who was more interested in a meal than a discussion, suckled happily.

Ellie smiled down at her baby, wondered if she could survive without him. She doubted it. Daniel was the light of her universe; Samuel, however, was its emotional core.

She loved them both. How could she choose?

It would take hours for her to drive to the nearest phone and more hours before help could be sent. It was only an hour's hike to the fire tower. By the time she returned, help would be on the way. If she left now, as Samuel had asked her to do, she and Daniel would be safe, but the man she loved could die. If she stayed, Samuel would live, but she could lose her son forever.

The decision circled like an impatient vulture, pecked her heart out.

Save her lover. Lose her child.

Long after Daniel had fallen asleep against her breast, Ellie was still fighting the vulture, still shielding her heart. In the end, the decision swooped on wings too formidable to ignore.

Hugging her sleeping son's warm body, she nuzzled his scalp, and gently tucked him into his cradle. He'd sleep for at least two hours now. She went to the kitchen, saw the firetower key in the drawer.

There was only one choice, only one. Ellie made it.

Chapter Twelve

A raw wind buffeted Samuel's face as he twisted over the ravine. Below him, the mangled wreck of a vehicle creaked and yawed. Each cry for help rose up weaker than the last. There wasn't much time.

Samuel's fingers clutched the harness hook. If he released it, perhaps he could rescue the trapped victim.

Perhaps he'd become a victim himself, the instrument of death for one of his colleagues.

The voice from below haunted him. It was a familiar voice, one he recalled from his childhood.

Drake. It was Drake. Trapped in that wreck.

Samuel frantically yanked at his harness. The lock froze, refused to release. He dangled helpless, unable to reach the man who'd been like a brother to him, the man who had destroyed his own career to save Samuel's life.

A guttural cry rose from his own throat. He clawed

at the harness, bucked madly in midair. He had to free himself, had to save Drake.

Blood pounded past his ears. A rhythmic rush, like a heartbeat. Like a whirling blade. *Chucka-chucka-chucka*. Like a helicopter.

Squinting into the distance, Samuel saw the teardrop silhouette move out of the clouds. A rescue chopper with the life-cable dangling beneath its belly. A figure was harnessed to the cable, a figure signaling the pilot to move closer to the wreck. Closer. Closer.

So close Samuel could see the face of the man strapped to the life hook, a man with tousled hair and lake blue eyes. It was his own face.

He watched himself being lowered to the wreck, grasping the arm extending from the vehicle's shattered windshield. He watched himself struggle to extricate the victim.

Chucka-chucka-chucka.

He moaned as a brilliant ray of sun blinded him, heating his skin, boiling his blood.

Chucka-chucka-chucka.

A baby fussed in the distance. Daniel…was it Daniel?

Chucka-chucka-chucka.

Samuel moaned, thrashed. His eyes flew open. He wasn't dangling from a rescue cable. He was in the cabin. In bed.

Chucka-chucka-chucka.

But the sound was real, the helicopter was real. It moved closer, closer. Closer. The vibration shook him, surrounded him.

Rubbing his eyes, he heaved a tortured breath, rolled his head and saw Ellie standing by the living room window. She was wearing her bright rayon jacket and holding Daniel in her arms, staring outside with a gaze both sad and noble, her lips loosely resigned.

Chucka-chucka-chucka.

Pine needles slapped the window, blown by a sudden vortex of wind. The helicopter had landed. In the clearing. By the cabin.

In the space of a single, agonized heartbeat, the haze lifted from Samuel's mind. He realized what Ellie had done, understood the sacrifice she had made for him. And his heart wept.

The deputy was tall as a sequoia and just as rigid. He tipped the brim of his tan flight cap, gazed through oval aviator glasses with reflective lenses. The patch on one sleeve of his sharply creased uniform presumably announced the law enforcement agency to which he was aligned, but any detail beyond his imposing stature was not likely to be noticed. A stern, authoritative tone completed the impressive image. "Eleanor Elizabeth Malone?"

Staring at her mirrored reflection in the sunglasses, Ellie was mildly amused by the rebellious tilt of her chin, the boldness of her gaze. She looked like a cornered cat—back curved, hair raised in defiance even as its pupils dilated in terror. Not trusting her voice, she hiked her chin another notch and nodded.

The reflective gaze dipped to the infant in her arms. "A lot of people are looking for you." When Ellie made no comment, the man shifted. "I'm Deputy Shaeffer, ma'am. I'll have to ask you to come with us."

"Am I under arrest?"

Instead of replying, he gazed past her to the front porch, where paramedics were rolling the gurney out of the cabin. Baloo followed, yelping, circling in bewil-

derment as strange men wheeled his beloved master toward the waiting chopper.

Shifting Daniel in her arms, Ellie moved quickly
across the thin snow crust. "Samuel? Samuel—"

Neither of the attendants glanced up or slowed their
progress. When the gurney wheels caught on the slush,
the men lifted it without missing a beat, hustled past
Ellie without the slightest indication that they'd seen
her. She would have followed but for the hand clamped
on her shoulder.

Ellie jerked to a stop, hugged Daniel to her breast
and watched as the gurney was loaded into the helicopter's open side door. "Will he be all right?"

"The medics are doing everything they can," the
deputy replied.

Of course they were. Samuel was one of their own.

He took hold of her elbow. "We should go now."

She automatically tightened her grip on her son.
"There's a navy blue backpack and a duffel inside the
cabin, by the front door. Would you get them for me?
My baby's things..." Her voice broke, the ground
swayed. She bit her lip, locked her knees to keep them
from buckling.

Deputy Shaeffer wavered, seeming afraid to release
her lest she bolt into the woods. He glanced at the surrounding forest, then at the helicopter with its blades
spinning and the frantic hound trying to leap into the
exposed belly through an open door too high to reach.

Finally the pressure on her elbow dissipated. "All
right," the man said quietly. He cast a final furtive
glance, then disappeared into the cabin.

The forest beckoned. Ellie gazed at the concealing
trees, inhaled the woodsy perfume, imprinted the scent
and the sound and the sight of this precious haven that
was safe no more.

These weeks, these precious months had been magnificent, but it was over now. All that mattered was Samuel. He would be all right. He had to be. Ellie refused to consider the alternative.

She took a final, bracing breath, then walked bravely toward the waiting chopper, shifting Daniel to the crook of her arm and using her free hand to retrieve Baloo's leash from her jacket pocket. The frantic animal dived toward her when she called, tail wagging wildly as she knelt to snap the leash on his collar. "It's okay, boy," she soothed. "Everything's going to be okay."

Baloo whined as if he knew better.

"We can't take the dog."

Ellie stood, spun around as the deputy marched toward them carrying her stuffed backpack and an old duffel she'd found in the loft. She squared her shoulders. "If Baloo doesn't go, I don't go."

The man's eyes narrowed. "I'm under orders to escort you back to Sacramento." Apparently taking umbrage to his sternness, Baloo bared his teeth with a snarl, forcing the deputy to step back and gentle his voice. "We'll send someone back for him."

"Before or after he starves to death?" Clenching the leash in her fist, Ellie stared at the furious woman reflected in the man's sunglasses. "Just contact Fire Station 12. I'm not sure which district it's in, but Samuel has friends there. One of them will pick Baloo up at the airport and care for him until Samuel is well."

"There's no room in the chopper."

She scanned the big fellow up and down. "You take up more than your share."

"Now see here—"

"No, *you* see here." Ellie interrupted with ice in her voice and fire in her eye. "We're not talking about some ordinary, run-of-the-mill house pet, although even if we were, I think your attitude stinks. The point remains that this particular animal is a legend around here because he has saved more lives than you could count without taking your shiny boots off. Now, do you really want the thankless task of explaining to public officials how there wasn't enough room in your precious little chopper for the most decorated animal in the state's canine rescue unit?''

Finishing her exaggerated spiel with a flourish, Ellie mustered an indignant glare and was rewarded by a flustered stain crawling up the big man's throat.

An amused chuckle from the cockpit signaled the battle had been lost. The deputy knew it. Heaving a resigned sigh, he flung Ellie's bags into the cargo hold.

When the chopper lifted off ten minutes later, Deputy Shaeffer scowled from the rear jump seat holding the heroic hound on his lap.

Voices circled his head, buzzed like annoying gnats. He knew he was in a rescue chopper. He knew the medics were tending him, recognized whispered vital signs that were being checked and rechecked every few minutes. Heartbeat. Pulse rate. Blood pressure. Rising, falling, stable. All duly noted.

Something pinched his arm. Stung. An IV needle. Fluid drip. Saline.

Beeps. Familiar beeps. Monitor. Portable EKG.

Chucka-chucka-chucka. Helicopter blades.

Over the din, a baby fussed. Daniel. Daniel was here on the helicopter. Ellie must be here, too. They were taking her back, taking them back. To him.

To him.

Beep, beep, beep, beep… ''Pulse erratic, blood pressure's up.'' A flurry of activity, the chill of smooth metal against his bare chest. Strained voices, orders issued.

A jarring bump followed by more activity, more orders. The chopper had landed. The belly door rumbled open. Night air swept in, dark, sweet, cool. The gurney was moving, bumping, jumping, gliding in air, rolling on asphalt. He had to stop it.

Had to stop—"Ellie." A croaked whisper, his own. He raised a hand, clutched the closest object, which happened to be a masculine forearm. "Got to—" a coughing spasm cut him off.

The annoying voices took on an urgent tone. In the distance, a dog was barking. Baloo. Where was Baloo? Where was Ellie?

Samuel fell back, wheezing. *Ellie.* His mind screamed; his voice was momentarily useless.

A cool palm touched his brow, soft. Fragrant. "I'm here, Samuel. Baloo is okay. A friend of yours is here to take care of him."

A friend? Samuel had no friends, not anymore. He forced his eyes open, saw her blurred image, again realized the sacrifice she'd made for him and was overcome by emotion. "Shouldn't have…" was all he could say.

"I had to, Samuel, I had to. Any other way would have taken too much time. I couldn't leave you alone that long, I couldn't risk losing you."

Two fuzzy figures loomed beside her. Men in suits, Samuel thought. One spoke. "Ms. Malone, come with us, please."

"No!" The word burst from him with astounding force. He reached out, clung to the hem of her jacket. "No."

Still cradling her blanket-wrapped son in the crook of one arm, Ellie bent close enough for him to see tears glistening in her eyes. "It's all right," she whispered. "You'll be fine, Samuel. They're going to take good care of you."

"Don't...go."

The tears slid down her cheek. "I have to."

"Ellie—" But she was moving away, flanked by the men in suits who ushered her toward a dark sedan parked at the edge of the tarmac. Samuel struggled to raise his head, struggled to reach out a hand.

She turned, extended her free hand as if trying to touch him. The distance was too great. "I love you," she whispered.

He mouthed the words, "I know."

Then she and Daniel were hustled into the big, dark sedan and disappeared into the night.

Ellie stared straight ahead, gazing absently over the front seat headrests, past the driver, through the tinted windshield as familiar landmarks blurred by.

The back seat was heavy with silence, thick with the scent of tailored wool and expensive cologne. Slick money, she thought, and wondered if they were politicians or lawyers, or both. Stanton was well connected with the former, and surrounded himself with the latter. Either way, there was nothing she could do to save herself.

But Daniel would be all right. No matter what happened, Ellie knew that Stanton would care for his son, would supply every material necessity and luxury that she could never realistically expect to provide.

Yes, Daniel would have a good home, a home in which he'd be loved and nurtured and cherished. Despite Stanton's many faults, he was a man who desperately wanted children. Ellie had no doubt that he would try to be a good father to Daniel. She prayed he would succeed.

The sedan slowed, paused at the entrance to the exclusive gated community where the Mackenzie home was located. The driver slid a plastic key into the slotted card reader. The gate yawned open, the sedan hummed through.

Manicured streets, shaded by dozens of mature trees. Clean sidewalks. Mansion-size houses. A good place to raise children.

The thought gave her little solace. Her chest felt hollow, empty, as if her heart had been surgically removed. She squeezed her son to her breast so tightly that he squirmed in protest. Fear clawed inside her throat. She knew where they were taking her, and she knew why.

The sedan rolled into a massive driveway, hummed to a stop. A porch light flickered on, illuminating a huge entrance dripping with baskets of blooming flowers. Beneath a crescent of arched glass, oversize double doors opened slowly. A woman stepped out with perfectly coiffed blond hair, wearing an extravagant hostess gown. Jewels twinkled at her throat, dripped from her ears. A perfect picture of extravagance and sophistication.

Marjorie Mackenzie, beautiful, sophisticated, wealthy and barren. Marjorie Mackenzie, who wanted a child so desperately that she was willing to overlook her husband's faults and infidelities, to use all of her family's wealth and power, to do anything and everything, even if it meant ripping a baby from its mother's arms.

There was no doubt in Ellie's mind as to why she'd been brought here tonight. The Mackenzies had the law on their side. They were going to take her son away now. There was nothing she could do to stop them.

* * *

Beep. Beep. Beep.

It was driving him crazy.

Beep. Beep. Beep.

He couldn't think.

Beep. Beep. Beep.

He had to clear his mind. The emergency room staff had aspirated his lungs so he could breathe easier, and rehydrated him with fluids so he felt stronger, but his mind was still a muddle. Samuel was desperate to think, to figure a way to save Ellie and Daniel from Mackenzie's Machiavellian clutches.

But the monitor, the damnable EKG monitor kept beeping and beeping until his skull reverberated with obnoxious noise. Disconnecting the thing would only result in a piercing death wail that would scramble every nurse on the floor. That was the last thing he needed. If he could just turn off the audible alarm switch—

He twisted against the pillows, swore under his breath. Even in the darkened room he could tell the monitor controls were out of his reach. A small cabinet lamp and light spraying through the open doorway provided the private room's only illumination. Still, the monitor was only a few short feet away.

Beep. Beep. Beep.

It was driving him stark raving mad.

Panting with effort, Samuel eased back the covers, paused to catch his breath. Oxygen blew softly from a flexible tube positioned beneath his nostrils, gave him strength. Two steps, two flimsy little steps and he could silence the dratted machine, clear his groggy mind.

He shifted painfully, hung an ankle over the edge of the mattress.

"Going somewhere?"

The voice was familiar, but the crooked stance of a

slender silhouette looming in the doorway was not. The shadowy figure dipped low on one side, as if leaning askew. Samuel squinted at it, felt the hairs on his nape prickle.

The figure shifted, chuckled, moved awkwardly into the room with a peculiar *thunk-swish* sound. "I told the floor nurse not to turn her back on you. She seemed to think you were sick enough to be docile." *Thunk-swish*. "Even nurses are wrong once in a while."

Shallow breath backed up in Samuel's clogged lungs. He wheezed, fell back against the pillows, gasping.

"Easy, my man." The voice softened. Samuel felt his dangling foot being eased back onto the mattress. "You're not ready to run a marathon yet." *Thunk-swish, thunk-swish*. A shadow fell across the lighted monitor, and the abominable beeping stopped. "That what you had in mind?" Another soft chuckle. "You always were an impatient sort."

Samuel swallowed, licked his lips. "Drake."

"You sound surprised." He pulled a chair beside the bed, hooked a walking cane over the backrest. As he gingerly lowered himself into the chair, light from the cabinet lamp reflected from a ruffled shock of fiery hair, illuminated a pale, freckle-studded face.

Drake grimaced with the effort, then relaxed, gave the familiar crooked smile that haunted Samuel's dreams. "I'm not a ghost. You can pinch me if you want. Of course, I'll be forced to retaliate just like when we were kids, so it might be kind of difficult to explain how you got a black eye lying in a hospital bed—"

"You're walking."

He cocked his head. "I told you I wasn't going to spend the rest of my life in a wheelchair."

"After the surgery—" Samuel drew a tortured breath "—I heard the doctors. They said—"

"I know what they said." Drake shifted, turned his entire upper torso, skewered Samuel with a look. "They were wrong. You just didn't hang around long enough to figure that out."

Samuel rolled face away to avoid his friend's reproving stare. "Couldn't face you."

"Why?" The shock in Drake's voice brought Samuel's head back around. "What does any of this have to do with you?"

"What does—?" Samuel moistened his lips, sucked a wheezing breath. "My fault."

"Your fault?" The chair scuffed as Drake stiffly changed position. "How in hell do you figure you're responsible for the worst flood in two decades and a damned runaway log?"

"If I hadn't...dropped the harness—" Samuel moaned, coughed, fell back panting.

A strong hand gripped his arm. "If you hadn't dropped the harness that little girl would have died. You saved her life, Sam-man."

Samuel's lungs were on fire. "You saved mine."

"So what? You'd have done the same."

True enough, but beside the point.

"By the way," Drake added cheerfully, "you owe me seventy-five bucks. I know the bet was only fifty, but when I went to collect, you'd already skipped out so the rest is for sheer aggravation. Better yet, make it an even hundred."

The bet in question, whether or not Drake would be on his feet by Christmas, was made under duress and before the surgery which from Samuel's perspective had crushed all hope that his friend would ever walk again.

But he *was* walking.

Even as Samuel's eyes stung with moist gratitude, he wondered if this was some kind of cruel dream. "I don't understand. The doctors—'' he paused, took several shallow breaths ''—I heard them. Fractured spine, fused vertebrae.'' Another pause, another shallow breath. ''Disk damage, nerve damage, possible spinal—'' pause, gasp ''—cord separation.''

Drake nodded slowly. ''All true. That's why I get to wear this nifty back brace, and use this really cool cane. JoAnn's kids think it's pretty awesome. They call me their bionic buddy.''

''JoAnn?''

''JoAnn Martin, my physical therapist. She's a sadistic beast who gets off on howls of agony and firmly believes the word *can't* should be banned from the English language.'' A telling flush stained Drake's freckled cheeks. ''We're, ah, getting married in June. Want to be my best man? Assuming your lazy butt is out of bed by then.''

''Married?'' Samuel was certain he'd misheard. ''You?''

''Why not me?'' Drake asked, seeming stung. ''There's uglier men in the world. Some walk even funnier than I do.''

''You always said—'' Samuel bit off the thought.

Drake finished it for him. ''I always said I was married to my job.'' He shrugged, cast a sad glance into thin air. ''Just because the job divorced me doesn't mean my life has to come to a screeching halt. Stuff happens, y'know? It was an amicable parting, irreconcilable differences and all that rot. The guys gave me a party.'' A twinge of pain crept into his voice. He coughed it away. ''I've been accepted into medical school. I start next semester.''

Samuel was certifiably stunned. ''A doctor?''

''Yeah.'' Drake's wistful gaze brightened into a silly, boyish grin. ''The way I see it, we'll still be a team, only you'll be hauling 'em in, and I'll be sewing 'em up. Pretty cool, huh?''

The room spun, jiggled to a queasy stop. Samuel closed his eyes, said nothing.

Chair legs scraped the floor. Plastic creaked in relief. A familiar *thunk-swish* signaled that Drake was on the move. Leaving. He was leaving.

Suddenly panicked, Samuel swung his head around. "Wait."

Drake's torso revolved stiffly. "Why, to watch you lie there feeling sorry for yourself?"

The blood drained from Samuel's face, icing his skin, fogging his focus. "What?"

Leaning on the cane, Drake shuffled around to face the bed. "You gave it up, Sam-man. Our hopes, our dreams, our plans for the future—everything that was snatched away from me, you just handed over without a whimper. You ran out on it. You ran out on me."

"I—" Protest died on his lips. "I know."

Drake regarded him thoughtfully. "You took leave from the department. Why?"

A bitter taste flooded Samuel's mouth. How could he explain failure to a man who'd never known defeat, the debilitating fear of second-guessing oneself when mere seconds meant the difference between life and death? Drake Jackson was a mountain of confidence, of sheer grit and courageous determination. He could never understand the crippling doubt, the horrifying realization that one flawed choice could snuff out a life.

"Couldn't do it anymore," Samuel said simply.

"Couldn't or wouldn't?"

Samuel shrugged. Semantics didn't matter. "Either, both."

The cane shifted. "So you just gave up."

"Yes." Samuel stared across the room, his gut

twisted in knots. It sounded so cowardly when truncated to the marrow. *So you just gave up.* "I had to," he murmured. "I had to."

"Because you froze?"

Samuel's head snapped around. A coughing spasm erupted when he sucked in a shocked breath. When the attack eased, he wiped his eyes, wheezing, and saw Drake again sitting in the chair.

His friend's eyes were warm, understanding. "Captain told me what happened at the ravine. It wasn't your fault, Sam."

The nightmare formed in his mind. Twisted wreckage. Charred metal. A rappel rope too short. Panic. Indecision. A cry for help from the mangled car. Shouts of encouragement from his teammates up the hill. Samuel remembered his mind going blank. He'd struggled to remember department procedures, had known that if he broke them again, someone else could be injured, someone else could die.

He'd committed those procedures to memory, drawn upon them a thousand times. Then suddenly he hadn't even been able to remember his own name. Above him, his teammates had shouted at him, but Samuel hadn't been able to respond, hadn't been able to recall the signals. He'd been ripped by indecision, paralyzed by fear.

The old Samuel, the confident Samuel, had boasted instinctive, split-second decisions that had always been correct, always been successful. Always. Until the flood. Until Drake.

As he'd dangled over the mangled wreck in the ravine, instinct remained ominously silent, washed away in a flood of indecision, of fear, of self-doubt and shattered confidence. For the first time in his life Samuel hadn't known what to do, so he'd done nothing. He'd hung there like a useless side of beef while his teammates made the decision for him, and pulled his shaking, cowardly carcass out of the ravine.

Samuel had known then that his career was over. He couldn't be trusted, couldn't trust himself. He'd frozen. He'd put lives at risk.

"It happens," Drake said softly.

Samuel blinked, looked Drake in the eyes. "Not to me."

"What makes you so special?" The question was issued kindly, with the edge of a smile old friends use with each other.

"I'm not." The bedclothes vibrated, a nervous shuffle of his own feet that he barely noticed. "People are."

"What's your point?"

"People depended on me. I let them down." He paused for breath, closed his eyes, whispered, "I let *you* down."

For several minutes, Drake was silent. When he spoke again, his voice was tough, unyielding. "If that's how you feel, I guess we've got nothing more to talk about."

With some effort Samuel focused his gaze, wishing he could say something, do something to erase the disappointment in his friend's weary eyes. There was nothing. The past couldn't be erased.

Drake stood. "I've got to go. Baloo's in the car. He's probably eaten half the upholstery by now."

"'Loo?" Samuel levered up on one elbow. "You've got 'Loo?"

"Apparently your lady friend didn't want that lazy hound of yours ending up at a shelter. She insisted the pilot call the station to have someone meet the chopper. The station chief knew Baloo and I went way back, so he gave me a jingle." Drake regarded him slyly. "Your friend seems to think a lot of your dog."

"Ellie," Samuel whispered, remembering her tearful smile, the men in suits hustling her into a sleek sedan. She'd sacrificed everything for him. He'd let her down, too.

"So," Drake said. "How about it?"

"How about what?"

"Will you be my best man?"

Medication fogged Samuel's brain, making him feel even more despondent, even more helpless and unworthy. "You could do better."

Drake's jaw tightened, his eyes flashed. "Yeah, you're probably right." He limped to the doorway, then turned his torso for a final glance into the room. "By the way, since you don't have anything better to do than rehash old news in your head, try thinking about how I got out of that damned river after the log hit."

With that, Drake was gone, and a cold sweat coated Samuel's brow. He didn't want to think about the day of the flood, had pushed it out of his mind. If only he could push it out of his nightmares.

Try thinking about how I got out—

Samuel squeezed his eyes shut. No. He couldn't control his nightmares, he could control conscious thought.

Try thinking—

He didn't want to try, didn't want to remember.

Try—

The memories rushed in, chaotic, terrifying. Boiling brown water, the reeking stench of mud. Dark eyes. A reaching hand. The sweeping current pulling him under as he clung to the drowning child. Drake's face, calm and courageous. The debris raft bearing down on him. A cry drowned out as Drake sank beneath the tangle of deadly wood.

Samuel had dived under the raft. He remembered clutching Drake's clothing, dragging him to the surface.

His own lungs had been burning. Darkness clouded his eyes, but he'd refused to pass out, refused to lose consciousness. Clutching Drake in a death grip, Samuel had hung on until the rescue team converged to drag them both out of the churning flood.

The next thing Samuel remembered was lying on the bank, gasping for air. There were voices. "Turn him loose, Sam. We've got him. He's safe now. Let go."

They'd had to pry his fingers loose.

Images of the flooded river dissipated. Samuel was in a dark hospital room, bewildered and alone. Conscious memories of that horrific day were different than the distorted terror of slumber. His nightmares always ended when the log hit. It was as if life had suddenly ceased at that moment, the life he'd known, the life Drake had known. Samuel once believed nothing beyond that moment mattered.

But it had mattered.

Because just as Drake had saved Samuel's life, Samuel had also saved Drake's. The knowledge didn't really change anything. It wouldn't spare Drake the agony he'd suffered, or return his lost career, but it did give Samuel some small measure of peace, a sense of purpose about his part in events played out that fateful day. That mattered. It mattered to Samuel.

Just as Drake had known it would.

The blonde studied her coolly. "You're quite lovely. I can see why Stanton was attracted to you."

Praying her terror didn't show, Ellie stood in the polished foyer clutching her squirming son to her bosom. She said nothing, made no reply to the woman's observation. Above her, a chandelier twinkled like a thousand crystal stars. Behind her, the stiff-suited men guarded the massive entry door like a pair of wool gray pit bulls.

Marjorie Mackenzie's gaze dropped to the fussy bundle in Ellie's arms. Her gaze softened, her red lips curved into a gentle smile. "He's so beautiful. I knew he would be."

Ellie's stomach twisted, tightened. "Why am I here?"

The woman's mascaraed lashes fluttered to reveal an emerald gaze that was sharp and wily.

Ellie gave her chin no permission for the defiant lift, but felt it rise anyway. A curt nod of her head gestured toward the men at the door. "If these pinstriped goons had any legal authority, they'd have taken me straight to the police station. Since I'm clearly not under arrest, I insist you allow me to leave immediately or I'll notify the police."

The woman's crimson smile twisted into a smirk. "You're free to leave any time you like."

Ellie licked her lips, pivoted around. The gray-suited men snapped to attention, and blocked the front door. She looked warily over her shoulder, saw that the woman's smile had flattened.

"You may leave," she said quietly. "Not the child."

With those ominous words Ellie's worst fears were realized, and her entire world collapsed.

Chapter Thirteen

Fear dripped like ice water down her spine.

Something was very wrong. In her haste to save Samuel, Ellie hadn't focused on the details of how her own legal battle would evolve. Given the Mackenzie's wealth and political power, she'd realized that she could, and probably would, lose physical custody of Daniel eventually, but had been too distraught to consider how or when that would occur.

Now she realized there was nothing legal going on here. She had no representation. These gray-suited men were not officers of the court. There was no judge, no child-welfare authorities, no social services' reports, none of the official procedures as explained by the harried legal services aid with whom she'd conferred prior to her desperate escape.

This was not the court-sanctioned service of a custody order. It was a kidnapping.

Terrified, she pressed Daniel to her shoulder, turned on wobbling knees to face the men who had escorted her here. One of them seemed vaguely familiar, as if she'd glimpsed him in a public forum too generalized to recall. His sandy hair was professionally cut in the cleanly conservative style favored by politicians; emerald eyes, so like those of her ex-lover's wife, shifted in silent communication with the blond woman to whom he bore striking resemblance.

As Ellie studied him, he shifted on nervous feet, mumbled something to which his more distinguished companion issued an amiable nod, then the green-eyed man hurried through the foyer, automatically sidestepping a lushly intrusive houseplant placed attractively but inappropriately close to the walkway. Emerging into a spacious living area, Ellie's view of which was partially obstructed by the expansive curving staircase, the man was met by a well-dressed woman with huge, frightened eyes. The woman gazed at Ellie, bit her lip and might have spoken had the green-eyed man not grasped her elbow and hustled her away.

There was something peculiar about the couple. Rather, there was something peculiar about their presence here and their familiarity with the house itself. Ellie scanned what she could see of the living area, noted photographs arranged atop a baby grand piano beside a yawning bay window. Family photographs, with children and a dark-haired woman that looked very much like the woman who'd just been escorted away.

Ellie's conclusion was as obvious as it was disheartening. This was not the Mackenzie home. Clearly, Stanton had gone to great lengths to ensure that she and Daniel would not be easily found.

Assuming, of course, that anyone was looking.

Forcing an impassive expression, Ellie returned her

attention to the man still positioned in front of the front door. With thinning, chrome-colored hair and a glittering diamond on his manicured pinkie, the statesmanlike gentleman exuded an air of distinguished confidence and regarded Ellie with something akin to sympathy.

A small advantage. Ellie took it, gazing hopefully into eyes reflecting the same silvery sheen as neat brows curved above them. "Please, can you at least tell me where am I?"

"That's not your concern." A melancholy tone, an air of resignation, as if responding to a role he found distasteful but sadly necessary.

Still, his empathetic eyes made him the closest thing to an ally Ellie had, so she focused her attention on him. "Am I a prisoner?"

It was Marjorie who replied. "Of course not, dear. You are our guest."

The crisp response iced air, sent a chill down Ellie's spine. She glanced over her shoulder, saw what she'd expected in the woman's frigid gaze. "It's my understanding that guests are allowed to come and go as they please," Ellie replied.

A grim twitch of crimson lips. "And where would you go?" the woman asked with deceptive courtesy. "Would you force a helpless infant to spend the night on a filthy park bench, a cardboard box in an alley filled with winos and junkies? That sounds like child abuse to me, Ms. Malone. Child abuse is a crime."

"So is kidnapping." With her knees shaking so hard she feared they'd buckle, Ellie confronted the diamond-pinkie man who continued to block the front door. "You don't want to be an accessory to this, I can see it in your eyes. Please help me, help us." Her voice cracked as she hugged Daniel to her breast.

The man wavered, slipped a glance past her shoulder

as if seeking a clue from the icy blonde at the base of the stairs, then met Ellie's frantic gaze with one of sad resignation. "There are no illegalities here. We offered you transportation. You accepted and accompanied us of your own free will."

"I was misled." Her voice cracked. She fought to steady it. "You brought me here under false pretenses."

"We made no representations false or otherwise. You have absolutely no basis for either civil litigation or criminal complaint."

"That sounds like lawyer talk to me." When he offered no reply, Ellie confronted him directly. "Are you an attorney?"

He hesitated. "I am."

"Then you should know better."

Clearly unhappy about the situation, his tone softened from crisply professional to compassionate. "I understand your concern, Ms. Malone, but sadly, the discomfort to which you've been subjected has been necessitated by circumstance."

"What circumstance?"

"All will be explained in due time," he assured her, then was distracted as his sandy-haired companion returned. The two men conferred briefly before the returning man nodded curtly and left through the front door.

A perfumed breeze brushed past Ellie as Marjorie Mackenzie moved to confer with the attorney. They whispered a moment, casting an occasional rueful glance toward the frightened, unwilling houseguest, and coming to apparent agreement just as the first man reentered the foyer carrying Ellie's backpack and duffel.

"Of course," Marjorie murmured, scraping Ellie with a faux-bright hostess smile. "You must be exhausted, poor thing, and famished. We'll have the cook prepare you a meal."

Before Ellie could refuse, Daniel began to wriggle and fuss. She shifted him in her arms, shushing him softly.

Marjorie's eyes lit like neon. "He's awake." She hurried across the slick foyer as fast as her stiletto heels would allow, gasped in delight as he focused his tiny eyes on her. "Oh, how sweet, how utterly adorable. He has your eyes, doesn't he? Rather exotically shaped and quite handsome."

Something in Marjorie's wistful tone kept Ellie from backing away. Instead, she studied the woman's luminous eyes, was struck by their instantaneous transformation from glacial to glowing.

"Oh, look at his tiny hands. How perfect they are." Clearly entranced, Marjorie reached out a smooth, crimson-tipped finger as if to stroke the flexing baby fists. She hesitated, raised a questioning glance. "May I touch him?"

For reasons Ellie couldn't begin to fathom, she allowed it, and was deeply affected by the exquisite wonder in the woman's expression as she caressed the infant's delicate arm.

"I had no idea baby skin was so soft, like freshly opened rose petals." Daniel chose that moment to yawn, which sent Marjorie into a frenzy of delighted laughter. "Oh, my! That was a big one! Did you hear the precious little squeak he made?" She laughed again, looked up with surprise and such genuine jubilance that Ellie found herself smiling back. "He seems so healthy and happy," Marjorie cooed. "And look at those adorable fat cheeks. He must eat very well."

"Daniel has always had a good appetite."

"Of course, he would," the woman gushed, hesi-

tantly touching the silken fur on his bare scalp. ''Culi-
nary expertise runs in the family. Stanton has always
been quite the gourmet. Look! I do believe he has Stanton's mouth, don't you think? Yes, yes, I'm sure of it.''

At the mention of her ex-lover, Ellie's stomach tightened. She licked her chafed lips, took a wobbly step
backward, reinforced her wariness. Throughout her ordeal, Ellie had been vaguely aware that a major player
in this sad drama had yet to make an appearance.

As much as she'd dreaded facing Stanton Mackenzie,
she now realized that he represented her last hope. If
she could plead her case directly, perhaps she could
convince him how detrimental separating a child from
its mother would be. After all, she and Stanton had been
close once. Before they'd become lovers, they had been
friends, close friends. Friends sharing thoughts and feelings, hopes and dreams, even some secrets, although
clearly not all.

Ellie's gaze settled on the wife Stanton had never
mentioned. Although the man she remembered had always been arrogant and somewhat self-indulgent, he
had also been reasonable, logical and basically well-
intentioned. The man for whom Ellie had once cared
deeply would never sanction what was happening now.
He'd certainly had his faults, a lot of them, but he'd
never been deliberately cruel, and he'd have never con-
doned any behavior that could result in physical or emotional harm to a child.

In her panicked mind, Ellie found herself rationalizing the cruelty of Stanton's initial betrayal by reminding
herself that he loved children. She went a step further
by presuming the discovery that his wife couldn't provide children must have been a bitter disappointment,
bitter enough to muffle his conscience and corrupt an
already duplicitous nature with an act so vile, so dia-

bolically immoral that the man Ellie had known could never have conceived it.

At least, not on his own.

Marjorie Mackenzie's rapt fascination with her husband's child gave Ellie pause. The woman was beyond enamored; her eyes glowed with the reverence of one worshipping a small god. For the first time, Ellie wondered if Stanton also might have been a victim, the willing pawn of a wife so desperate for children that no crime was too sinister, no circumstance too heinous in pursuit of her maternal goal.

It was all speculation, of course, with no proof beyond the chilling adulation in eyes capable of shifting from reverent to frigid in the space of a single heartbeat.

Ellie stepped back, held Daniel beyond reach. The woman's smile faded, her gaze cooled. A sick heaviness settled in the pit of Ellie's stomach, although she forced a light, conversational tone. "I'd like to speak with Stanton now."

The chill drained from Marjorie's eyes, replaced by an emotion that Ellie couldn't quite identify. "Of course. This way, please." Pivoting sharply, she glided toward the stairs, mounting them with practised sophistication so that the swishing hem of her flowing silk gown drew attention to well-turned ankles and shapely calves. She paused where the staircase curved, glanced down to see that Ellie had made no move to follow. "I thought you wished to see my husband."

Ellie tightened her grip on Daniel. "Where is he?"

"Waiting for his son," Marjorie replied quietly. She spoke softly, with polished calm, but her gaze reflected a turbulence of emotion so profound it defied description. It could have been sadness; it could have been madness.

Whatever her shuttered gaze concealed, Ellie instinctively knew there were answers at the top of those stairs, answers to questions that had haunted her for months, answers that would change the course of her life—and Daniel's—forever.

The woman was adamant, impatient, clearly annoyed. Samuel didn't care. After two days of futile searching, he'd finally connected with the deputy who'd escorted Ellie and Daniel from the cabin and wasn't about to hang up the telephone just because a harried floor nurse with the girth of a sumo wrestler had chosen that moment to take his blood pressure.

Shifting the receiver to his right hand, he flung his left arm out to pacify the frustrated woman, then returned to his conversation with Deputy Shaeffer. "Look, Deputy, I've already discovered that the custody case was dismissed months ago, as was the failure to appear warrant, but you told the chopper pilot that you had orders to escort Miss Malone and her son back to Sacramento. What I want to know is who gave you those orders, and under what authority were they issued?"

A faint rustling filtered through the wire. "I'm not in a position to reveal that information."

Samuel's knuckles whitened around the receiver. "Yeah, yeah, I've heard that before, from your boss and his boss, and just about everyone else involved in this dirty little scheme. The thing is, Deputy, no one has seen or heard from Ellie and her baby since you handed them over to those goons at the airport. If anything happens to either of them, heads will roll, and yours is going to be first on the block."

There was a startled hiss, as if the deputy had sucked a sharp breath. "No one has seen them since they left the airport?"

Samuel didn't reply. He couldn't. A boiling terror throbbed just below the surface. Shaeffer had been his last hope of finding Ellie and Daniel, and clearly the bewildered deputy didn't have a clue where they were.

After having pulled every string he could get his hands on, besieging every contact he'd ever made on the job, Samuel managed to have a squad car check the Mackenzie residence only to discover the home was vacant except for a servant who'd informed the officers the Mackenzies had left a few days earlier, ostensibly for an extended European vacation.

Now there were no clues, no sightings, no leads to follow. Ellie and Daniel seemed to have dropped off the face of the earth.

A frantic voice dragged Samuel's attention back to the telephone. "I was just supposed to escort them back," Shaeffer was saying. "That's all. I'm so far out of the loop I don't even know where the rope is tied."

"Tell it to the grand jury," Samuel snapped. "Because I'm going straight to the district attorney, the justice department. Hell, I'll go to the White House if I have to, whatever it takes to find Ellie and her son, and frankly I don't much care who ends up being the scapegoat when this mess makes front page news."

Clearly shaken, Shaeffer's tone mellowed from belligerent to contrite. "Look, I was told my boss got a call from his boss who got a call from someone with serious political clout." The deputy lowered his voice. "I don't know the whys and wherefores, but it seems that the lady had some folks in very high places looking for her. My job was simply to escort her back to Executive Airport and turn her over."

"Turn her over to wh—"

"Mr. Evans, please!" The aggravated nurse yanked his arm flat, skewered him with a hard stare.

He ignored her, shifted the phone. "The men in suits who put her in the dark sedan, who were they?"

"I don't know their names, but—" Shaeffer's whisper echoed as if he'd cupped his hand around the mouthpiece "—the car had Capitol tags."

Samuel blinked in comprehension. Capitol tags. A legislative vehicle. Ellie wasn't kidding when she'd said that Mackenzie knew all the right people. He swore under his breath, pounded a fist on the mattress as the nurse was trying to inflate the pressure cuff.

"Mr. Evans!" Using hands the size of meat hooks, she ripped off the cuff, glaring at him. "I have other patients."

"Sorry," he muttered, wishing she'd attend to those other patients and leave him alone.

The frustrated woman readjusted the pressure cuff muttering to herself, nodded at the stripe-suited young woman who'd just entered to remove Samuel's untouched supper tray. "Might as well take it," the nurse growled to the startled aide. "Mr. Evans here has been so danged busy flapping his mouth there's no time to use it for anything else."

As Samuel returned to his phone conversation, the nurse suddenly stuffed a thermometer in his mouth. He spit it out, gave her a frigid stare. "Look, just leave everything. I'll take my own vitals and update the damned chart when I'm done here."

She snatched the thermometer off the bedclothes, folded arms the size of small boulders. "I suppose you want to take your own blood sample, too."

"Sure, whatever." He turned his back on her. "Did either of the men who took Ms. Malone mention where they were going, or who they were working for? Did you note the license plate number? Can you tell me anything, anything at all?"

"Well…" The deputy paused as if glancing around to ensure he wouldn't be overheard. "You didn't hear this from me, but scuttlebutt is that one of them is a muckety-muck in the governor's reelection campaign."

"The governor?" Everything fell into place like a line of kicked dominoes when Samuel recalled Ellie mentioning that Mackenzie's brother-in-law worked in the governor's office. "Listen, Shaeffer, I think I know where Ellie and Daniel are being held. Send a unit over to— Ouch!" He yanked his stinging arm away as the smug nurse laid a hypodermic aside. "What the hell was that?"

"You need rest." She plucked the phone from his limp hand, hung it up looking quite pleased with herself. "Doctor prescribed a stronger sedative."

"No, wait—" The room was spinning darkly.

"Next time your lady friend calls, I'm going to tell her what a cranky boy you've been," the nurse said cheerfully. "Now, let's try our blood pressure again, shall we?"

"Lady friend?" Samuel fought the encroaching dizziness, grasped at the nurse's nimble fingers. "Someone has been calling?"

"Twice a day since you arrived. Never asks to speak with you, never leaves her name, but she certainly sounds concerned about you."

Ellie. It had to have been Ellie. "Call police…trace call…" The sedative grabbed him by the throat, choking him into unconsciousness. "Stop…you don't… understand…"

A relieved chuckle. "Nightie-night, Mr. Evans."

It was the last thing Samuel heard as he drifted into a stuporous slumber.

The night sky was clear, peaceful, awash with thousands of twinkling stars nested in a stellar cradle.

Beyond the isolated window through which Ellie gazed, a glittering neon shawl, sewn with freeway ribbons of crimson and white, wrapped the city's shoulders. The city wore plaid, she realized, a luminescent version of the flannel shirts Samuel favored.

Samuel. God, she missed him. Her fingers flexed over the nightstand phone before she withdrew them. He was sleeping now, or so the floor nurse had told her an hour ago. The same nurse had also reassured Ellie that Samuel's condition continued to improve. He might be released this weekend.

She smiled, thinking that he must be going stir-crazy. Samuel hated to be sick, hated to be constricted by circumstance. During the weariest days of their confinement, when storms had raged for days on end and the knotty-pine walls seemed more prison than sanctuary, Samuel had prowled the cabin like a caged animal.

At the time, Ellie's own sense of peace and contentment prevented her from understanding how trapped he must have felt. She understood it now. She understood everything now. She even understood herself.

Too bad that the knowledge had come too late. Too late for her, too late for Samuel. Certainly too late for Stanton.

If only she'd known—

Cutting off the wish with a sigh, Ellie turned from the window of the plushly appointed lace-and-silk room she'd occupied since she'd arrived three nights ago, when the gray-suited men had whisked her off in a dark sedan, and turned her entire world upside down.

If onlys were useless. Ellie knew that. Wishing didn't change the way things were, and blame had no power to heal. It wouldn't bring back the past, recreate the time she'd wasted running from reality, running from herself.

Fear of confrontation had created both redemption and ruin, a life of refusals leading to destruction and bitter loss.

If only she'd known.

But she hadn't known, hadn't given herself the chance to know, because she'd followed the only course of action she'd understood at the time, behaved as she always had when confronted by a problem. She'd fled without considering the reasons behind Stanton's desperation or the dire consequence of avoiding that which she could not, would not understand.

Ellie knew the truth now, understood everything. Everything except how to live with the pain. And the loss.

And the guilt.

"Strip those pants off, mister. I want your butt bare, and I want it in bed."

Huffing and hopping, Samuel shoved a foot into the denim tube, yanked, zipped, scraped the scowling nurse with a look. "You took my phone."

"You weren't getting enough rest."

As if to prove her right, Samuel staggered back a step, sat on the edge of the bed, winded and wheezing. He took a strained breath, reached behind his head in a vain attempt to unfasten the hospital gown tied at his nape. Panting, he gave up, eyed the tank of a woman blocking his only exit. "I'm checking myself out."

"Not on my watch." The nurse strode into the room, flexed her impressive biceps and cut him with a stare cold enough to freeze meat. "Are you going to take them off, or am I?"

Samuel narrowed his eyes. "I'll pay you to go away."

An amused twinkle flashed, disappeared. "You

wouldn't make it to the bank, hon. They'd be scraping your cold, dead body off the pavement.''

As much as he'd like to argue the point, he knew she was probably right. He was weak as a kitten, dizzied even by the insignificant effort of trying to dress himself. Since he couldn't argue on a logical basis, he returned to the original complaint. ''You took my phone.''

''Get those pants off.''

''No.''

''I'm not a patient woman.''

''Either I get my phone back, or I'm out of here.''

''So you want to play rough, huh?'' She heaved a sigh, crossed her arms beneath breasts so large that Samuel could imagine the unrestrained version as lethal weapons. Her grin was positively maniacal. ''Fine with me. I like 'em feisty.''

Samuel didn't doubt that for a minute.

Lacing her fingers, she straightened her arms to crack all of her knuckles at once, then advanced with a grim leer. ''I'm going to enjoy this.''

He didn't doubt that, either. ''Wait.''

Startled, the woman stopped, stared at his upturned palm as if she'd never seen one before.

Samuel sucked a breath, flinched at the pain. His lungs were clogging again. Breathing was becoming more difficult. ''Please. I have to have a phone. It's a matter of life and death.''

''You'll have to do better than that,'' she muttered, flicking her wrist as if swatting a pesky fly. ''This is a hospital. Everything is a matter of life and death. Now strip bare, bucko, or you and I are going to share an intimate moment.''

Desperate, Samuel yanked the hospital gown across his lap knowing the flimsy cotton cloth was scant protection from the polyester-clad clutches of a woman who ate puny patients for breakfast and picked her teeth with their bones.

"You don't understand," he wheezed. "I know where they've taken her."

"Taken who?"

"She's in danger."

"Who's in danger?"

The room was moving again. Samuel was infuriated by his weakness. "They're trying to steal her baby. I have to stop them."

"Uh-huh." The nurse eyed him as if calculating size for a psychiatric restraint garment. "Sure you do, hon."

"It's my fault," Samuel moaned, frustrated that he couldn't make her understand. "She risked everything for me, everything. Now she's in trouble and I know where she is. I have to find her, I have to—" A ghostly specter appeared, rendered him mute.

At first he thought it was a figment, an illusion caused by illness and fear. Only when the nurse acknowledged the pale presence with a glance did Samuel realize that the specter was real.

Ellie was real, all right, but she didn't move, didn't speak, simply stood in the doorway, white as death. Her eyes were red. Her arms were empty. And she was crying.

Chapter Fourteen

From his unsteady perch, Samuel hunched on the edge of the mattress, his weakened lungs crumpling in upon themselves. He couldn't breathe, couldn't speak, could only stare in horror at the wan figure hovering in the doorway, empty arms hugging her own thin torso.

With a shuddering breath Ellie rushed across the room and threw herself upon him. Whimpering, sobbing, crazed with emotion, she kissed his face, his neck, hugged him fiercely before drawing away to study him so intently he felt as if she could see straight through him. Moist eyes darkened, soft fingers traced the jagged planes of his face, caressed a jaw slackened by shock.

Apparently satisfied that he was indeed alive, she sat back on her heels, clutching his limp hands. "You look so much better. Thank God."

The sound of her voice forced out a single word from him. "Daniel?"

It was a harsh croak, nearly inaudible, but she heard, squeezed his hands in response. Mute lips moved, were moistened with the tip of her pink tongue. She closed her eyes as if in prayer, uttered a choppy reply. "Marjorie has him."

A fission of fear chilled him to the marrow. He searched his memory. "Stanton Mackenzie's wife?"

"His widow." A fresh spurt of tears brightened her red eyes. "Stanton died last night."

If she'd told him space aliens had invaded the White House, Samuel couldn't have been more shocked. "Mackenzie is dead?" She avoided his gaze. "How? I mean, was there an accident?" A horrible thought struck him. He released her hands, gripped her shoulders. "Has Daniel been injured, is that why he isn't here? For the love of God, Ellie—"

"Shh, Daniel's fine, Samuel. He's just outside." She cupped his face with her palms, met his panicked gaze with one of intensity and truth. "I asked Marjorie to wait in the lobby while I spoke to you. I wanted to explain…" Words failed. A helpless shrug, and her hands dropped soundlessly to his lap. She absently scratched the coarse denim stretched over his thighs, fingered the faded hem of the flowered hospital gown. A trace of a smile touched lips pale enough to be worrisome. "A fashion statement?"

A voice boomed from across the room. "Hurumph. More like a scream, I'd say." The nurse, who'd been watching events unfold with uncharacteristic silence, stepped forward, focused on Ellie. "Maybe *you* can get this stubborn fool's pants off." She scraped them with a squinty stare. "My guess is that it wouldn't be the first time."

Ellie blinked. "I'll, ah, see what I can do."

"All righty then, I'll leave you to it." A brusque nod

and, from the doorway, a grim warning that Samuel took to heart. "When I get back, I want to see you naked."

"Yes'm," he replied meekly.

Ellie ducked her head. When she looked up, the doorway was empty and her lips were still quivering. "It's nice to know you're in competent hands."

The only hands that interested Samuel belonged to the beautiful woman crouched before him, the woman who loved him so much that she was willing to sacrifice all that was dear to her on his behalf. Samuel took those trembling hands, stroked the delicate knuckles with his thumbs, repeated the process with his lips.

He kissed each of her fingers, then tugged her hand lightly, urging her to rise and sit beside him on the bed. "I'm sorry, Ellie." His throat spasmed with emotion, nearly choking him. Stanton Mackenzie was dead. That news was shocking but Samuel wasted no grief on it. Instead he was shaken, shattered, by the sorrow in Ellie's eyes. No matter what faults the man had, he'd fathered her child and she'd loved him. Perhaps she still did. The thought chilled him.

Not knowing what else to say, he repeated himself. "I'm sorry."

"You have nothing to be sorry for, Samuel."

"I'm sorry for your loss." He noted the subtle shift in her gaze, was inexplicably wounded by it. "And I'm sorry for all that you gave up because of me."

Ellie's gaze snapped back, widened in surprise. "Gave up?"

"If not for me, you and Daniel would be safe now."

"We are safe." Her mouth wobbled again, although not in amusement. Emotion jittered through her eyes, twitched her raised chin as she spoke. "There was so much I didn't know, so much I wouldn't allow myself to know because I ran away from it." She paused, touched her lips, struggled to speak. "I always ran, you know. Every time an obstacle appeared I turned my back and ran like hell, rationalizing that every challenge was too difficult to overcome, and convincing myself that life was too short to waste with unpleasantness. I thought I was being sensible. In fact, I was simply being a coward."

Samuel blinked, trembled inside. He, too, had run away from life, turned his back on those who needed him. He'd drowned himself in guilt rather than exhibit even a fraction of the courage that Drake Jackson had shown. Ellie wasn't the coward; Samuel was.

"You changed me, Samuel." Ellie's gaze softened. "You showed me that life is about confronting and overcoming problems, not running away from them. If I'd listened to you sooner, Stanton might have—" She bit off the words with a shudder, fortified herself with a cleansing breath. "Perhaps I should start from the beginning."

Samuel didn't like the sound of that but squeezed her hand in encouragement.

She nodded, gazed across the room. "When I first met Stanton, he was energetic and flirtatious, an outrageously arrogant but basically decent man who was considerate to the needs of others. He never pressured me, never tried to coax me into more intimacy than I was prepared for, and when I was ready for our relationship to change, he was gentle with me, and he was kind."

Samuel couldn't prevent his spine from stiffening. "A kind and decent man doesn't seduce a woman without mentioning his marital status."

Ellie met his gaze without blinking. "There's no

doubt that Stanton was a philandering cad. I'm not defending that.''

"It sounds like you are.''

"I suppose it does.'' Easing her hands from Samuel's grasp, Ellie stood, hooked her fingers behind her neck and avoided his gaze. "Marjorie knew the kind of man her husband was. She knew, and she loved him anyway. My heart aches for her. She's been through so much.'' Ellie's eyes clouded briefly, cleared with a blink. "But I'm getting ahead of myself.'' Samuel waited as she cleared her throat, tangled her fingers as studied them as if she'd never seen them before. Eventually she continued, sounding small and weary. "Anyway, there came a point when Stanton disappeared for two or three weeks. When I saw him again, he was different.''

Samuel recalled Ellie mentioning Mackenzie's sudden change in demeanor at the cabin, when she'd first revealed the truth about Daniel's father and the brutal betrayal that sent her fleeing in fear. Now he said nothing, waited for Ellie to continue.

After a moment, she did. "There was an urgency about Stanton then that I'd never noticed before. He seemed tense, preoccupied, almost desperate even when we were—'' a flush stained her cheek "—together.''

Concealing his clenched fists beneath crossed arms, he willed an impassive expression. He didn't want Ellie to see his pain, to know how the image of her with Stanton Mackenzie ripped his heart out.

But she did see. She did know.

Ellie saw the pain in Samuel's eyes, and it shattered her. But she couldn't stop, couldn't conceal the truth from him no matter how deeply wounding that truth might be. She'd seen the devastation avoidance had caused. Although she feared Samuel's reaction, she was nonetheless determined to see this through to the bitter end no matter how painful, regardless of consequence. The time for running was over.

And so she went on. "I'd always known Stanton wanted a child, but suddenly becoming a father was an obsession with him. He begged, he pleaded, he told me that I was the only woman on earth with whom he wanted to share the Holy Grail of parenthood. I refused because I wasn't ready to settle down, and I certainly wasn't ready to be a mother." Ellie's heart was pounding so hard she paused for breath. Beside her Samuel waited in a shroud of silent misery. A dry edge flattened her voice. "But Stanton had become a man who would not take no for an answer."

A subtle flinch was all the emotion Samuel revealed. "You've told me all that. You also said he'd sabotaged your birth control."

"Yes."

"Do you know how?"

"No, but at least now I know why." She shuddered, faced him. "Stanton had learned that he was dying of cancer."

The bed vibrated. Samuel looked as if he'd been struck.

It was too late for retreat. Ellie stared at her own twitching, tangled fingers and forged on. "Stanton believed having a child would provide a ticket to immortality. It became an obsession to him, and eventually to his wife as well."

Incredulous, Samuel could only stammer. "His wife was in on this…this obscenity?"

A lump formed in Ellie's throat. She remembered that final night, remembered holding the shattered widow in her arms, offering scant comfort as her husband took his final breath. It had been a night of bereaved tears, of grief, of exquisite sadness and haunting guilt. It had also been a night of redemption.

Now Ellie blinked away her own tears, ducked her head to wipe her wet cheeks with her sleeve. "Marjorie didn't know anything in the beginning. Stanton only confided in her after I became pregnant. Can you imagine that?" she murmured, misinterpreting the sadness in Samuel's eyes as empathy for the betrayed and bereaved wife. "That poor woman had barely recovered from the shock of learning the man she loved was terminally ill when she was hit by news of his most recent infidelity, and the fact that another woman was carrying the child *she* had been unable to conceive. I think the pain and the guilt must have driven her mad."

"Guilt?" Samuel's derisive snort shocked Ellie, as did the bitterness in his voice. "What in hell did she have to feel guilty about? She wasn't the one running the streets boffing anything that smelled good and felt warm." As Ellie drew back, Samuel sucked a ragged breath, squeezed his nape in frustration. "I'm sorry. I didn't mean that."

Ellie was fairly certain that he meant every word, but simply patted his hand without reproach. "Don't you see, Samuel? Marjorie felt as if she'd driven her husband into the arms of another woman because she couldn't give him the family he craved. Oh, she understood Stanton's faults, knew that he'd been cheating on her long before I came along, but she accepted his duplicity because she loved him, and because she blamed his behavior on her own failure to produce the family he so desperately wanted."

"That doesn't make any sense."

Ellie laid a gentle hand on his thigh. "It might, if you were a woman."

"This isn't a gender thing, Ellie, it's an issue of right and wrong."

"A week ago I would have agreed with you, but a week ago I hadn't met Marjorie Mackenzie, hadn't seen the agony in her heart. She's been through hell this past year, Samuel, a hell that you and I can't possibly understand."

"You're right. I can't understand." A glint of anger, a flash of bared teeth. "The woman tried to take your child away from you. She kidnapped you, for God sake—" Anger slipped into dark suspicion. "Or did she?"

"Technically, I suppose, although it was her brother and Stanton's lawyer who drove me from the airport."

"I knew it," he muttered. "I knew it had to be him."

"Him?"

"Stanton's brother-in-law. By the time I'd figured out they were holding you at his place, Attila the Nurse had given me a double dose of knockout drops, and when I woke up, she'd stolen my damned phone." His expression crumpled in remorse. "I tried to find you, honey. God knows how hard I tried—"

She touched his lips, silencing him. "I'm glad you didn't find me, Samuel. I needed to go through these past days to understand. And to forgive."

"Forgive? How on earth can you possibly forgive what those people have done to you?"

"I can forgive because I understand the despair and desperation that drove them to it. Marjorie knew that Stanton's plan to take custody of Daniel was wrong, but she went along with it out of guilt and grief and because she wanted a part of her husband after he was gone. After I ran away from the ski lodge, it was Marjorie who convinced Stanton to drop the custody suit."

Clearly Samuel still did not consider the aggrieved

widow a candidate for sainthood. "She had no qualms about directing her family to pull every political string they had to get Daniel back."

"They were desperate," Ellie repeated quietly. "Stanton didn't have much time left. They wanted him to see his son before he died."

A veil lifted, as if Samuel suddenly understood at least a small part of what she was trying to convey. "So you weren't being held against your will?"

"No, not after I learned why Daniel and I had been brought there." That damnable lump of emotion wedged into her throat again, bringing fresh tears, unbearable pain. "Stanton spent the last few hours of his life gazing on the face of his only child," she whispered. "If I hadn't run from my fear and my responsibility to Daniel's father, he could have spent months with his son. I kept them apart. I'm not sure I can ever forgive myself for that."

The fingers in her lap blurred. She bit her lip to keep from crying. So much wasted time, so much unnecessary pain. It shouldn't have happened. She shouldn't have let it happen.

A warm arm encircled her, pulled her close. Samuel pressed her face to his shoulder, murmured against her hair. "It's all right, honey. You didn't know."

"I wouldn't let myself know." She sobbed against his throat. "I just took off without considering how others would be affected. All I could think about was getting away. All I could think about was myself, and a man died without having a single moment of quality time with his only child."

"Stanton saw Daniel." Samuel lifted her chin, gazed into her eyes. "He spent his last days with his son. That has to count for something."

"It's not enough, don't you see?" Sniffing, Ellie

fought panic, fought the crushing blame. "Stanton was so weak at the end, he couldn't even hold him— couldn't even hold his own child. It's all my fault—"

"Stop it, honey, don't do this to yourself." He shook her mildly, waited until she'd stifled her sobs and focused her attention. "We can't change what was, Ellie. Believe me, I know. If there was any way I could go back to that flood and make things different, I would, but I can't go back, and neither can you. Yesterday is gone, tomorrow is a gift waiting to be opened. All we ever have is today, right this minute. That's what we have, that's what counts."

Ellie clung to him, caressed his face, had never loved him more than she did at that moment. There was knowledge in his eyes, a sense of resignation, perhaps even peace, that she'd never seen before. "Something else has happened, hasn't it?"

"Drake was here."

"Here? At the hospital."

"He was walking, Ellie, upright and on his own two feet."

"Oh, Samuel." A breath, a thankful smile at his reflected pride. "That's wonderful."

The smile faded, the pride dimmed. "I should have been there for him, but I wasn't. He had to go through it alone because I couldn't face him, couldn't face what I'd done."

"He doesn't blame you, Samuel."

"No, he doesn't." His brow quirked. "But how could you know that?"

"Wild guess." Heaving a contented sigh, she nested her head in the curve of his throat. "I guess we're more alike than either of us would like to believe."

"Not really. I sing a lot better than you."

"Heck, Baloo sings better than me." She chuckled.

"You, on the other hand, have absolutely no snowman-sculpting ability."

"Ah, but I do weave a mean cradle."

"Yes," she whispered fondly. "You certainly do."

Samuel stroked her hair, kissed the top of her head. "Do you remember what you said to me at the airport?" He paused, waited for her affirmative nod. "I just wanted you to know that I, er, I do, too. Love you, that is."

Ellie's heart thumped. "I know."

They sat there for several long moments, embraced in love profound enough that it need not be spoken, then Ellie withdrew, smiling. "Would you like to meet Marjorie now?"

Samuel frowned just a little. "I'd like to see Daniel."

"I know that, too."

His frown eased. "You know just about everything, don't you."

"Of course. Haven't you learned that by now?" A giggle of pure happiness bubbled from her throat. Samuel loved her. She'd always known it, always felt it, but now it seemed more tangible somehow, as if she could reach out and cup it in her palm. "First I think we'd better get those pants off and get you tucked into bed." She reached for his fly.

He pushed her hand away. "I don't want to take my pants off."

"Tough. The pants are history, bud. Either I do it, or Nurse Attila does it. Up to you."

It took less than a minute for him to decide.

Daniel's burp was manly and satisfying. His head bobbled against Ellie's shoulder, tiny body twisting as he gazed up at his mother's smiling face. He focused on her, gave a baby grin and uttered something that sounded like, "Ooghmum."

Ellie chuckled, pressed a kiss to his silky, fuzz-covered scalp. "I love you, too, snookie-wookie."

In the hospital bed, Samuel shifted against the pillows, reached out to tickle between the baby's shoulder blades. "Kid's got an appetite like a linebacker." His gaze clouded, withdrew.

Pulling up a chair, Ellie nestled her son in the crook of one arm, used her free hand to massage the yellowing IV bruise on Samuel's wrist. "You're thinking about Marjorie, aren't you?"

He turned his hand, laced his fingers with hers. "She shouldn't be alone this afternoon. Making arrangements is difficult enough, and when she was here she seemed so... I don't know. Vulnerable, I guess."

She understood what he meant. Marjorie had spent less than thirty minutes in the hospital room, but it had been long enough for Samuel to see the grief in her eyes and the regret. "Marjorie won't be alone. Her brother will be with her."

"What about later, when she returns to her own home?"

"I'll be there." Ellie avoided his gaze. "It only makes sense. I have nowhere to stay at the moment, and Marjorie doesn't want to be alone." When he made no comment, she glanced away to study a peculiar fold in the bedclothes. "When visiting hours are over, Daniel and I will take a cab to Marjorie's place, and spend a few nights with her. Just until she's feeling better."

Samuel tightened his grip on her hand. "And then?"

A weak shrug, a nervous smile. "I haven't thought that far ahead, actually. You won't be released for several days, so..." She licked her lips, let her words drift into thought. The truth was that she hadn't thought beyond Samuel's release from the hospital, but had simply presumed that wherever he went, she and Daniel would go, too. Now she realized that such a presumption was, well, presumptuous.

For Ellie, home was a drafty cabin tucked on top of a snowy mountain. She wondered if she'd ever see it again.

"Honey?" Samuel touched her chin, urged her to look at him. "Why are you crying?"

She sniffed, blinked, tried for a quivering smile that felt more like a grimace. "Just tired, I guess."

He considered that. "Were you still in love with him?"

The question shocked her to her toes. "With Stanton? Oh, no, Samuel. How could you think such a thing?"

"His death has hit you pretty hard."

She couldn't deny it. "Yes, it has but not because I was in love him. In fact, I'm not sure I ever truly loved Stanton Mackenzie." The confusion in Samuel's eyes hurt her, so she looked away. "I've had some time to think over these past months, and I realize that my attraction to Stanton had been based on his initial refusal to commit, which was perfectly suited to my own fear of emotional entanglement. When everything changed and he began pursuing me, I was frightened. I didn't want permanence. I didn't want commitment."

Samuel sucked a quick breath. "And now?"

And now the past still haunted Ellie, but she'd gained the strength to deal with it, and with her own culpability in a relationship that had been flawed from the outset. She hadn't understood Stanton; she hadn't understood herself. Despite considering herself fiercely independent, Ellie now realized that she'd always run from her weaknesses and lied to conceal them. During those weeks in the cabin, the dichotomy of her self-image had been shattered, first as she'd relied on Sam for her very existence, then as he'd relied upon her for his life. The woman who'd prided herself on being neither needy nor needed had discovered that she was both.

She'd learned to trust. She'd learned to love.

Ellie smiled at this man who was everything to her. "And now everything is different."

Relief flooded his gaze, softened his shoulders. "Has anyone ever told you what a kind person you are?"

That startled her. She'd been told that she was funny, flighty, even self-indulgent and a little odd, but never kind.

Samuel studied her intently. "Watching you comfort Stanton's widow touched me, Ellie. This is a woman who has done nothing but cause you grief, yet you consoled her, let her cry on your shoulder, gave her emotional support and comfort. That's what kind people do, Ellie. They care about others."

She squirmed at the praise, retrieved her hand from Samuel's grasp so she could absorb the warmth of her sleeping child with her palm. His tiny chest rose beneath her hand, rhythmic little breaths that were more comforting to a mother than all the world's riches. She realized Samuel was right. She *did* care about others now. She cared about her beautiful baby. She cared about Samuel. She even cared about Marjorie Mackenzie, who had endured such heartache and pain. "Maybe I've finally grown up," she murmured. "My mother would say it's about time."

"You're grown up, all right." Samuel reached out, waited until she'd taken his hand. "You're a full-grown woman, Ellie, the finest I've ever known." He hesitated, seemed strangely nervous. "These past few days, I've had a lot of time to think, too."

"Think about what?"

"Things." A moist sheen gleamed along his upper lip. "Things about you, mostly. And Daniel, and me. And you and me. And you and me and Daniel." Stuttering now, Samuel sucked a wheezing breath, muttered a frustrated curse. "I mean, I've been wanting to talk to you about—" He straightened, blinked, stared past her toward the open door.

Ellie anxiously tugged his hand. "What, Samuel? What did you want to talk to me about?"

He pointed. "Did you see that?"

Irritated by the interruption, Ellie tossed a haphazard glance over her shoulder, saw nothing but a shadow in the hall. "Just someone walking by. Now, what were you saying?"

A rumble from the hallway grew closer. A moment later, the front edge of a gurney paused in the doorway. There was a sheet-covered lump on the gurney. Ellie stiffened. "What on earth—?"

A vaguely familiar face peered inside, cracked into a grin, then disappeared. Before Ellie could turn for a better look, the gurney rolled into the room followed by a half-dozen uniformed paramedics and the owner of the grinning face, who limped in with the aid of a cane.

The freckle-faced civilian leaned over the gurney, whispered something to the covered lump, which instantly vibrated, reared up. Chaos erupted. One of the paramedics pulled off the sheet. Baloo leapt off the gurney, woofing madly.

Samuel lit up. "'Loo!" It was all he could say before the joyful animal scrambled onto the hospital bed, threw himself into his master's arms and covered Samuel's face with happy dog kisses. The animal paused long enough to climb over Samuel's lap, sniff Daniel, kiss Ellie, then circled the bed, barking in excitement.

"He's been sulking for days," the civilian said cheerfully. "I told him you were too damned mean to die, but old Baloo has to see everything for himself."

The hound emitted an agreeable yelp, then went back to licking his laughing master's face while uniformed crew members surrounded the bed, chattering non-stop.

"Hey, man!"

"'Bout time you got back."

"Where've you been, Sam?"

"The department's gone to hell without you."

Everyone was talking at once, including Samuel, who responded to each of his co-workers as if such pandemonium was a normal part of his life. All Ellie could do was hug her sleeping son to her breast while her gaze darted from each of the chattering paramedics to the rumpled gurney abandoned at the doorway.

A kind voice emanated from beside her. "For some odd reason, the hospital has rules about pets visiting, so we had to be creative." The civilian smiled, held out a pale hand spattered with rust-colored freckles. "You must be the infamous Ellie Malone."

She took his hand, returned his smile. "And you must be the notorious Drake Jackson."

He flashed a mischievous grin. "Aw, who told?"

"Let's just say that you haven't changed much since you were ten."

"Ouch." Drake flinched, yanked an invisible dagger from his heart. "Sam must have pulled out the old photo album, hmm?" His laugh was warm, inviting. "I'd like to think I've changed a little since those days. At least I'm taller." When Ellie agreed that he was indeed taller, Drake's voice took a more serious edge. "If it wasn't for you, Sam wouldn't be here."

"If it wasn't for him, *I* wouldn't be here, nor would my son."

"Yeah, I heard." Drake's gaze wandered to the

baby's face, so peaceful in slumber. He shifted, clutched the cane with both hands and leaned forward. "Anyway, I've been wanting to thank you for, you know, taking such good care of him."

Ellie touched Drake's wrist. "I've been wanting to thank you for the same thing."

Startled, he glanced over, studied her for a moment, his pale eyes warmed with understanding. Beyond them the chaos of male voices and laughter became an indistinguishable hum of white noise. "I guess we both kind of like the guy, hmm?"

"No accounting for taste, I suppose."

Drake laughed. "Y'know, you're all right. I approve."

"Funny, I was thinking the same thing about you."

"What is *this?*" A mass of white polyester fury loomed in the doorway, returned Baloo's happy yelp with a horrified stare. "A dog? A *filthy animal?* This is an outrage!"

"Uh-oh," Drake whispered from the corner of his mouth. "Dragon lady caught on. We'd better boogie before she turns us into surgical cadavers."

Blue uniforms blurred into motion as the angry nurse sputtered and spouted hideous threats. The gurney was grabbed, Baloo was leashed, goodbyes were hollered above the crashing din while the crew and their canine stowaway were unceremoniously ushered away.

Drake winked from the doorway. "Later, man." He paused when Samuel called out to him. "Yeah?"

Samuel heaved a nervous breath, slipped an arm around Ellie's waist as she stood beside the bed. "You know that thing you asked me to do for you?"

A perplexed frown furrowed Drake's amber brow. "What thing?"

"The, er—" Samuel cleared his throat "—best-man thing."

"Yeah," Drake replied warily. "What about it?"

"I was just wondering, I mean, if you haven't found anyone else—"

"I haven't."

"Well, I'd kind of like to, ah—"

"Your tux has already been ordered." A smile crinkled the corners of his mouth. "You didn't think I'd let anyone else stand up for me, did you?"

Samuel's fingers tightened at Ellie's waist. "No more than I'd want anyone else to stand up for me. That is, if you'd be willing to return the favor."

It took a moment for Ellie to interpret Drake's smile of surprise. "Hey, man, congratulations! When's the big day?"

"I, ah—" Samuel angled a sheepish glance upward, met Ellie's shocked gaze with a question. "That all depends on the lady. If she'll have me, that is."

Clinging to Daniel, Ellie felt her knees wobble dangerously. "Samuel Evans, are you asking me to marry you?"

"Uh-huh." A wary cloud veiled his eyes. "Will you?"

A warm mist of happiness blurred her vision. She blinked it away, laughed out loud. "You don't think I'd sing to anyone else, do you?"

A warm chuckle emanated from beyond the empty doorway, while the familiar *thump-swish* dissipated down the hall.

They were alone now, Samuel and Ellie and Daniel, alone to cherish the memories of yesterday, the joy of today and the gifts that tomorrow promised. Ellie knew that Samuel would be all right, both physically and emotionally. By releasing his pent-up grief, he could put past defeats in perspective and savor the victories by remembering those whose lives he had touched and restored.

The demons of their past were behind them now. They could live again; they could love again. Their new life had just begun.

Epilogue

"Mama, Mama, Mama!" Daniel Mackenzie Evans stretched out his chubby arms, danced an impatient jig inside the custom-hewn canopy crib that was a gift from his godmother. Rumpled feathers of brown hair tweaked from his sleep-dampened scalp, and a pressure mark from the mattress reddened his left cheek. "Uh-uh-uh," he grunted, flexing fat little fingers as his mother approached.

Ellie scooped him up, laughing. "Did Mommy's precious snookie-wookie birthday boy have a good nap?"

"Joose," Daniel said.

"Oh, you're going to have juice and cake and ice cream and so many presents that you won't know where to begin. Won't that be fun?"

The baby stuffed both hands in his mouth, giggling madly. "Joose."

"First we have to spruce up for our guests. You've got to look particularly spiffy today." Spinning him around until he shrieked with delight, Ellie finally settled her son on the changing table and went to work. "Birthday boy," she crooned. "Mommy's joy, he turns one today. Birthday boy, he's so coy—"

A mournful howl drowned out the final stanza. Ellie skewered Baloo with a look. "I suppose you can do better." The hound threw back his head, howled like a bereaved coyote. Ellie flinched, angled a worried glance toward the hallway beyond which guests were congregated for Daniel's party. "Okay, okay, I concede. Pipe down before you scare everyone away."

Baloo fell silent, gazed up with a triumphant, tongue-lolling grin while Ellie dressed her son in a natty little sailor suit and tidied his ruffled hair with a silky soft brush. "There, you look positively adorable." Daniel clapped his hands, emitted a jubilant screech. "Okay, handsome, let's greet our adoring public. Whoa, you are getting heavy."

Shifting the squirming baby on her hip, Ellie gave his drooly mouth a final wipe and headed to the living room of the small two-bedroom home that she and Samuel had rented last spring.

As they emerged from the hallway, Samuel stepped from a group huddled by the buffet table. "There's my man." Two steps and he'd dodged the twinkling Christmas tree to scoop Daniel out of Ellie's arms. "Hey, buddy, how's it feel to be the big one-oh!"

"Da-da," Daniel squeaked, then plopped a wet, open-mouthed kiss on his adopted father's grinning face. "Joose."

"How about ice cream and cake instead?" Samuel shifted his son, bent to brush a kiss on his wife's cheek, then carried Daniel over to the fawning group of party-goers that included Drake and JoAnn Jackson, her two children from a previous marriage and several of Samuel's colleagues from the department, including the psychologist with whom Samuel had been working to establish a counseling program for traumatized rescue workers.

Samuel glanced down just as Baloo hoisted up to investigate the tempting aromas wafting from the buffet table. "'Loo, no! Go lie down." The banished hound whined, slunk to his doggy bed and curled up on his raggedy blanket, bright eyes on the lookout for any tasty morsel that might slip from a hapless guest's plate.

A glance at the clock sent Ellie heading toward the kitchen to retrieve Daniel's birthday cake from the safety of a dog-proof cupboard. The round layer cake sporting a grinning, smiley-face caricature was placed on the buffet table amid appreciative murmurs from the guests.

"Umm, chocolate. Ow!" Drake yanked back his slapped hand, gave his frowning wife a hangdog look as he sucked icing off the tip of his finger. "That's what I love about physical therapists," he whispered in a sexy purr. "They're so physical."

JoAnn flushed to her roots while Drake's comrades guffawed, but she would have no doubt issued her own snappy comeback if the front door hadn't flown open with enough force to startle everyone in the room.

"Gracious, such traffic! Honestly, Ellie, you really must move to a better part of town. It's miles to the nearest mall." Marjorie Mackenzie, fresh from her latest therapy session, breezed inside in a cloud of perfume, swishing fur, tossing her glistening blond mane and carrying a large gift wrapped with gold foil and Irish lace. She thrust the package at the nearest body, which happened to belong to the assistant fire chief, who stared at it as if it were a bomb.

Shrugging out of her mink, Marjorie flopped the thick garment against Drake Jackson's chest, then spun around, gushing. "Where is he, where is my handsome godson?"

"Ma-mar!" Daniel shrieked happily, thrusting out his fat little hands.

"There he is! Oh, my sweet, precious boy!" Marjorie hurried forward, plucked the giggling baby out of Samuel's arms to cover his tiny face with kisses and crimson lipstick.

Ellie and Samuel exchanged a knowing smile, then Samuel took the mink from Drake and hung it in the hall closet while Ellie retrieved the extravagantly wrapped gift from the startled chief and placed it with the other presents. There was no doubt that the contents of the gilded package would be as extravagant as the wrapping. Marjorie had always been extremely generous with Daniel, almost painfully so.

Ellie and Samuel had set no limits on her gifts because she adored the child so, and because the feeling was mutual. Daniel was too young to understand material items his godmother provided, but he certainly wasn't too young to understand that she lavished him with love. Marjorie Mackenzie had become a big part of Daniel's life.

Despite a flamboyance emerging after her husband's death and used, Ellie suspected, to conceal a lingering grief Marjorie refused to acknowledge, the two women had become extremely close over the past year. Daniel adored her, Samuel was amused by her and Ellie considered her a dear friend.

She was, however, a bit on the self-indulgent side, and a little scattered when it came to details, such as remembering one's driver who was hovering uncomfortably in the doorway holding a huge pink bakery box.

Marjorie spotted the poor man as she spun the giggling baby around for the fifth time. She jerked to a stop. "Oh! Danny, look what else Godmommy brought for your birthday." She plopped the baby into the nearest set of arms, which again happened to belong to the long-suffering assistant fire chief, then hurried to retrieve the bakery box. "That will be all, Wilkins."

"Yes'm." The relieved man issued a polite head bow, then beat a hasty retreat, presumably to relax in the car until called back to duty.

"Perhaps Wilkins would like some refreshments?" Ellie suggested.

Marjorie blinked up as if startled by the thought. "Of course not, dear. I've given him the afternoon off. He's going to take his granddaughter to the zoo."

From the corner of her eye, she saw Samuel apologetically retrieve their son from the bewildered chief. "That was nice of you, Marjorie."

The woman shrugged off the praise, flipped open the box with childlike excitement and displayed a massive sheet cake decorated with intricate frosting sculptured toys. "Isn't this simply the most splendid cake you've ever seen?"

Samuel peered over Ellie's shoulder. "It's nice, Marj, but Ellie already made a—" He grunted as his wife's elbow poked his ribs.

"It's lovely," Ellie assured her. "Why don't you put it in the kitchen until I can find a nice platter for it?"

Marjorie beamed, swished off with her prize while

Ellie headed for the buffet table to conceal the grinning, smiley-face cake with an inverted salad bowl.

Moments later Marjorie returned, party hats were distributed, happy birthday songs were sung, JoAnn's children played pin-the-tail-on-the-donkey and a rollicking good time was had by all.

Finally it was time to cut the cake, which Marjorie insisted on retrieving herself. Only when her distressed shriek silenced the entire room did Ellie glance at the empty dog bed. Her heart sank. Following her gaze, Samuel's eyes widened in horror. They simultaneously bolted toward the kitchen, where Baloo sat politely at the kitchen table licking frosting off his face. The fancy, extravagant sheet cake had been reduced to a half-eaten pile of gooey crumbs.

Marjorie wailed. Baloo burped.

Gasps and chuckles emanated from the crush of guests gathered at the kitchen door. Samuel heaved a sigh, pasted on a bright smile. "Well, I guess it's time to haul out the emergency backup cake."

The assistant fire chief stepped forward to escort a shaken Marjorie into the living room. As they passed by, Ellie heard him whisper, "What is that scent you're wearing, Ms. Mackenzie? It's quite appealing."

Marjorie replied with a throaty laugh, tucked her slim, crimson-tipped fingers through the crook of his arm. The cake incident was clearly the last thing on her mind.

Samuel shifted Daniel in his arms, leaned over to nuzzle his wife's ear. "I love you, Mrs. Evans."

Ellie smiled. "I know."

As Samuel rejoined their guests, Ellie stood in the doorway, savoring the moment, the miracle of her precious son, her beloved husband and a dozen dear and devoted friends, each with their own story of triumph over adversity.

In a corner of the living room displayed in a place of honor, the hand-woven cedar cradle brimmed with brightly colored birthday gifts, a poignant reminder that for those with the courage to accept it, love is the greatest miracle of all.

* * * * *

SILHOUETTE

›SPECIAL EDITION‹

COMING NEXT MONTH

CHRISTMAS BRIDE Marie Ferrarella

That's My Baby!

Despite the fact that Toni has separated from her husband, Derek, she hasn't had the heart to tell her family. What's worse, she hasn't told Derek she's expecting his baby! So spending Christmas together is asking for a holiday miracle....

WILD MUSTANG WOMAN Lindsay McKenna

The Donovan Sisters

Circumstances have kept Kate Donovan apart from the strong, rugged man of her dreams, Sam McGuire. Now, after many long years, can Kate depend on Sam to save her family home?

THE LITTLEST ANGEL Sherryl Woods

And Baby Makes Three

Angela Adams refuses to have anything to do with her unborn baby's reluctant father, much less marry him! However, now the shock has worn off, Clint Brady is determined that nothing should come between him and fatherhood—not even stubborn Angela!

MARRIED...WITH TWINS! Jennifer Mikels

Daddy Knows Last

Finding themselves suddenly the parents of twin toddler girls just days before their divorce, Valerie and Lucas Kincaid have to instantly adjust. Will they stay together and could this be the second chance that they need to save their marriage?

CHRISTMAS MAGIC Andrea Edwards

The last thing self-confessed Scrooge, Mike Burnette, wanted was a houseguest over Christmas, much less the unbearably enthusiastic Casey Crawford. Can Casey melt his icy heart and instil the spirit of Christmas into his life?

SECOND CHANCE DAD Angela Benson

When Dillon Bell is suddenly introduced to a son he never knew he had, he has a hard time believing ex-girlfriend Monique. After all, she has betrayed him before. But the more time he spends with his son, the more he wants to become a permanent fixture in Monique's life, too.

COMING NEXT MONTH FROM

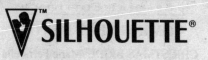
SILHOUETTE®

Intrigue
Danger, deception and desire

A CHRISTMAS KISS Caroline Burnes
THE LONG-LOST HEIR Amanda Stevens
UNDERCOVER CHRISTMAS B.J. Daniels
THEIR ONLY CHILD Carla Cassidy

Desire
Provocative, sensual love stories for the woman of today

A BABY IN HIS IN-BOX Jennifer Greene
THE NOTORIOUS GROOM Caroline Cross
THE SURPRISE CHRISTMAS BRIDE Maureen Child
SANTA COWBOY Barbara McMahon
A HUSBAND IN HER STOCKING Christine Pacheco
THE BEST LITTLE JOEVILLE CHRISTMAS Anne Eames

Sensation
A thrilling mix of passion, adventure and drama

THE PROPOSAL Linda Turner
ONE CHRISTMAS KNIGHT Kathleen Creighton
YULETIDE BRIDE Rebecca Daniels
A FAMILY FOR CHRISTMAS Rina Naiman

RACHEL
LEE

CAUGHT

Someone is stalking and killing women, someone with
a warped obsession. And with loving devotion the
stalker has chosen Kate Devane as his next victim.
What he hasn't realised is that Kate is not alone. She
has a lover. A lover she has never met.

*Rachel Lee takes readers on a "sensational journey
into Tami Hoag/Karen Robards territory."*
–Publishers Weekly

1-55166-298-1
**AVAILABLE IN PAPERBACK
FROM NOVEMBER, 1998**

MIRA®

HEATHER GRAHAM POZZESSERE

Never Sleep with Strangers

Jon Stuart watched his wife plummet to her death.
Although cleared of any involvement, he endured
years of suspicion. But it was no accident, and he's
now determined to prove it was murder. The prime
suspects are gathered together, and the scene is set
for past and present to collide.

"An incredible story teller!"

—Los Angeles Daily News

1-55166-445-3
AVAILABLE IN PAPERBACK
FROM NOVEMBER, 1998

We are giving away a year's supply of Silhouette® books to the five lucky winners of our latest competition. Simply match the six film stars to the films in which they appeared, complete the coupon overleaf and send this entire page to us by 31st May 1999. The first five correct entries will each win a year's subscription to the Silhouette series of their choice. What could be easier?

1

2

3

4

5

6

CABARET	___	**GONE WITH THE WIND**	___
ROCKY	___	**SMOKEY & THE BANDIT**	___
PRETTY WOMAN	___	**GHOST**	___

C8K

Please turn over for details of how to enter ➜

HOW TO ENTER

There are six famous faces and a list of six films overleaf. Each of the famous faces starred in one of the films listed and all you have to do, is match them up!

As you match each one, write the number of the actor or atress who starred in each film in the space provided. When you have matched them all, fill in the coupon below, pop this page in an envelope and post it today. Don't forget you could win a year's supply of Silhouette® books—you don't even need to pay for a stamp!

Silhouette Hollywood Heroes Competition
FREEPOST CN81, Croydon, Surrey, CR9 3WZ
EIRE readers: (please affix stamp) PO Box 4546, Dublin 24.

Please tick the series you would like to receive if you are one of the lucky winners

Desire™ ❑   Special Edition™ ❑   Sensation™ ❑   Intrigue™ ❑

Are you a Reader Service™ subscriber?   Yes ❑   No ❑

Ms/Mrs/Miss/Mr ....Initials ....
                                                    (BLOCK CAPITALS PLEASE)

Surname...

Address ....

....

....Postcode...........................

(I am over 18 years of age)   C8K

Closing date for entries is 31st May 1999. One entry per household. Competition open to residents of the UK and Ireland only. As a result of this application, you may receive further offers from Harlequin Mills & Boon and other carefully selected companies. If you would prefer not to share in this opportunity please write to The Data Manager, P.O. Box 236, Croydon, Surrey CR9 3RU.

Silhouette is a registered trademark used under license.